Adjoining Rooms

Linda L Peterson

Adjoining Rooms. Author Linda L Peterson.

First printing June 2024.

Independently published.

Printed in the United States by KDP.Amazon.com

Copyright by Linda L Peterson.

ISBN: 9798326652232

Books by Linda L Peterson

Whisky Tales: Tastings and Temptations

100 Friday Night Cocktails

Children's Books

Li's Pockets Full of Treasures

Nana's in the Attic

Nana Climbed a Tree

Lucy's Forest Adventure, Book One

Foret and Allier, Book Two

Foresta is Missing, Book Three

Kingdom of Char

Charlotte Goes to the Big City

Henry Wrestles a Dragon

Garrett Saves a Ninja

Bridget the Imagination Princess

Colson Drives an Excavator

Big Strong Katie

To Sydney, my forever love

1959

"It takes courage to grow up and become who you really are." E. E. Cummings

Chapter One

"I don't know what to do," Ginny said in frustration as she stared at Chip. With his usual air of confidence, returning her gaze with golden brown eyes, he replied, "Marry me." The two were sitting in his new car, a 1959 pale blue Chevy Bel Air, a college graduation gift from his parents. The radio was on low playing the smooth sounds of Bobby Darin's *Dream Lover*. How ironic, thought Ginny, to be listening to this song, especially the lines, "I want a girl to call my own." She shifted in the front seat so that her full body was directed at Chip.

"Chip, this is an outlandish idea. It will never work." She unbuttoned her jacket, which was his cast-off James Dean *Rebel Without a Cause* leather from high school, sighed, and ran her hand through her bobbed blonde hair-- a habit that took hold whenever she was under stress. She snapped the radio off, and before he could speak again, added, "Have you thought about this? I love you madly, but..." She let out a groan, feeling irritated, confused, and full of self-doubt as she slouched against the car seat.

Calmly, Chip held her left hand in his and with his other hand gently raised her chin so that she would look at him.

***

Virginia "Ginny" Stevens and Duncan "Chip" Foley Jr. had been friends since childhood. They grew up in the neighborhood of Readville in the southernmost section of the city of Boston, a bastion of Irish Catholic and Italian blue-collar workers intent on creating better lives for their children. Like most other kids in their parish, they attended

2

Saint Catherine School. Their mothers stayed at home and their fathers worked long hours at the Westinghouse factory, which towered over the small elementary school at the end of Readville Street. The Great Depression was slowly beginning to wane when they were born just five months apart in 1937. World War II was looming in the not-too-distant future though hardly anyone in the close-knit neighborhood was concerned with politics in European countries.

By the third grade, Ginny and Chip had found each other during recess in the school playground. Ginny didn't care much for her girl classmates' constant hopscotch and jump rope games. Chip was an only child who was small for his age and not very athletic and was pushed around and bullied by some of the bigger, rougher boys who whooped and hollered while playing stickball during recess. They both ended up sitting by the back fence in the shade of the Westinghouse main building.

Ginny boldly asked why he was called *Chip* by some people and Duncan by the nuns, the stern and cloaked Sisters of Charity. Surprised that this very smart and pretty girl would speak to him, he stammered that his dad's name was Duncan and he was named after him, but his grandmother Gigi called him Chip because they had the same bright red hair and wide mouth smile. A chip off the old block. Neither of them could understand how a little kid could look like a grownup. Not knowing what to say to that, Ginny mumbled, "Chip is a funny name." He started to get up to leave, but she put a hand on his arm and said, "It's okay, you can sit with me. Chip, I like your red hair. Can I touch it?"

"I know where you live on Norton Street," he blurted as he tilted his head so she could touch it, "I walk past your street on the way to school every day. And you draw the nicest pictures in the whole school. You always win the top prize. I cannot color at all, but my mom is trying to teach me how to play the piano. My dad said it is for girls." He shrugged his shoulders and added, "I like it."

"I like to draw, it's easy. I can show you how. I know where you live on Chesterfield Street."

Ginny could recite where every one of her classmates lived, *at least the ones on this side of the railroad tracks*, she secretly thought to herself. She elbowed him, "You can walk with me after school till we get to my street, but only on Thursday and Friday." She glanced sheepishly at him. "I've seen how the bigger boys pick on you, push you around, and call you a fairy. The only fairy that I know is in Peter Pan. Why would they call you that?" Chip shook his head. Ginny ran her hand through her hair, wrinkled her nose, and continued, "I walk with Margaret Mary McDonough the other days." And so, their unlikely friendship began.

The school years at Saint Cats, as it was known, were mostly boring and uneventful. They played with classmates enough to avoid being considered fuddy-duddys. Unfortunately, a mundane life didn't guarantee safety. There was the seventh-grade window incident as Chip later called it. The classroom was mostly empty, except for Chip and a few classmates. Some of the boys imagined hanging the quiet fairy Duncan Foley out the window by his feet would be funny. Ginny was waiting for him in the hallway with her older brother Johnny when they heard the commotion. The boys had barely hung the kicking and screaming smaller boy out the window when Johnny caught them and made them bring him inside. Ginny screamed at the boys and called them idiots but to no avail. The boys respected Johnny, though, an eighth grader, and begrudgingly apologized to Chip. He had been petrified of heights ever since.

High school separated the close friends. Chip, extremely studious and top of his elementary school class, was accepted to the prestigious to the boys-only Boston Latin School-- the school of presidents, poets, and great American thinkers. He was honored to be the only boy from his class invited to attend. Ginny, Margaret Mary, and Susan Donavan made the cutoff for Girl's Latin School, the sister school to Boys Latin. Chip was quickly welcomed onto the school debating team. Ginny excelled in her studies and art club. For Ginny, academics weren't the challenge; expectations to attend school dances with a date is what proved daunting. Margaret Mary and Susan always had a running list of boys they craved to spend time with at the school-sponsored dances. Ginny, pressured by her two friends, would only attend when Chip was her date. She stated emphatically that he was the best and smoothest dancer in all of Boston and he kept his hands off her on the dance floor, never groping like the other boys. She had long since concluded to herself that boys were not appealing and was dismayed by her girl friends' gushing excitement about them. Ginny's mother encouraged her to accept invitations from other boys, but Ginny claimed only to like Chip. His mother was grateful that he didn't "womanize" as she called it. Rumor had it that her husband, Duncan Sr., often spent the evening with lowly women at the smoke-filled bar room across from Westinghouse, neglecting his wife and son. Chip focused on his studies, determined to be at the top of his high school class, go to college, and never put a foot in Westinghouse. His aspirations to be an attorney of great acclaim drove him relentlessly forward. He hid his confusing cravings about other boys behind school books and continuous studying. His guard only came down when spending time with Ginny. She was his lifeline and his soulmate.

***

Now, sitting in Chip's car some four years after high school, Ginny was restless. One by one, her friends were getting married and she felt pressure from them and her parents to do the same. Their mothers secretly worked together to push them toward the altar. After all, in their minds, that's what young Irish Catholic couples did. But Ginny was secretly in a relationship with Beverly. Chip empathized with what she was going through. His mother was not so subtle about his proposing to her. She constantly asked about an engagement. How could he ever explain his hidden love for Richard?

"Gin-Gin, there has to be a solution to your pain, to my pain. If not marriage, then what? We *cannot* live with our parents forever. Lord knows they want us to marry, and soon."

Ginny sniffled and sighed, then rested her head on his thin shoulders. "Do you remember that time in high school when Rosemary nagged me about kissing you?" He scoffed at the recollection of the brusque Rosemary.

"I knew even then that I didn't want to kiss any boy. I was confused and had no idea what that meant."

"I still cannot believe you kissed me so passionately in front of everyone. For a while there, I was afraid you might not understand. Yeah, can you believe it took me till college to figure it out? And forever for you, slow-poke. It was such a relief for us to realize we both were, um, special. Honestly, I do not know where I would be, Ginny, if I did not have you in my life." He kissed her forehead.

"All the tears we shed, you and I, when we accepted that we were different. Even when I knew, I hid it from myself." She groaned slightly, "I felt so stupid and scared when I realized it was more than a crush on Beverly. And, I couldn't talk with Margaret Mary about it."

"Yeah, I had to push you towards Beverly. Remember?"

"Mmm, you did. I do want a life of my own," she whispered. "I want a life with Beverly. I want to be in her arms, to wake up with her in the morning." Looking up at him, she added, "Don't you want a life beyond stolen moments with Richie? Geez, maybe we should all live together disguised as one big happy family." She rested her head back on his shoulder and closed her eyes. "That's it. Let's live together, no sweat, no family pressure, happily ever after. Amen."

Sitting up straight and turning, he grabbed her shoulders and said, "Brilliant idea! Let's live together and use marriage as a cover." Ginny could see his mind racing. His eyes lit up.

"And, and buy a two-family house and, and once the door is closed no one will know the difference. It can work."

Ginny ran her hand through her hair and started to shake her head. Chip kept talking.

"It is the perfect solution. No one will suspect, and we will not have to be on guard and invisible inside our own home. I can dance with Richard and hold him close. Imagine!" He closed his eyes at the thought of holding his lover. "You will be free to love Bev, too, and have an art studio, and not have to be my constant protector." Breathless, he paused then added enthusiastically, "Damnit, I can have a piano, too."

Ginny's eyes widened as she imagined the four misfits living together. "That's crazy, Chipper. I don't mean to be a party pooper, but how could we ever make that work?" She shifted in her seat. "I'm not sure that Beverly would want to be part of a plot that is so underhanded and deceptive. You know how practical she is about everything." He started to speak, but she pressed her finger into his shoulder. "And what about Richie? He's so tied to his mother's apron strings." Ginny often called Richard 'Richie,' much to his chagrin, because of how attached he appeared to be to his mother and family, just like a little boy.

Chip was excited. The anticipation of living together as two married couples overwhelmed his common sense. "Consider this. I have been saving every penny from my summer jobs. And, I know you have been saving oodles of money from your paycheck. With your wizard-like financial skills, I am certain you will find a way to make it affordable for us to purchase a home."

Ginny smiled slightly at the compliment. He was exceptional at convincing her to accept his ideas, no matter how outlandish.

As he waited for her response, he thought about how living as married couples would erase the appearance of being unnatural; nobody would call them sick. He shivered at the memories of being taunted while walking with Richard by their favorite Boston nightclubs.

"Talk to Bev, Ginny. I will smooth it with Richard." He kissed her forehead and giggled, "I am hungry. Let's go snag some dogs and a shake at Simco's. We're going to be married." His enthusiasm had her laughing on the outside and wary on the inside. With a heavy sigh, she hungrily agreed; after all, a late-night hot dog at Simco's was the ultimate. She doodled on the drive to the take-out stand; a small sketch pad and pencil were always in her pocketbook. She found herself sketching a large house and wondering about the possibilities.

"A studio of my own, huh?"

"Absolutely. Bev would want that for you, too."

Chapter Two

"Virginia, what are you working on? Your head has been lost in those numbers since dinner. Adding numbers and erasing, adding and erasing. Is everything okay at work?" Ginny was absorbed in her notes and didn't answer. "Is Mr. Briggs making you work from home now?" She looked over Ginny's shoulder. "That certainly doesn't look like an art project."

Glancing up from her paperwork at her mother, Ginny saw quizzical eyes beyond the tired woman who was drying the last of the dinner dishes. Helen O'Malley Stevens, a small and fragile woman, and the youngest daughter of Irish immigrants, slid the frying pan on the shelf under the counter. She pushed back her rapidly greying mane of black hair, and stretched with her hand on her lower back.

"Ha, you know I'm always working on an art project. Is your back bothering you again?"

Her mother's back issues were a constant concern since the bus accident that had killed her older brother John Jr. and seriously injured her mother five years ago. Ginny missed her brother, who always praised her art, and spent hours posing for her. He called her his little Picasso.

"Mom?"

Helen stretched, straightened up, and smiled "No, I'm fine. I've been baking for the church spring bazaar tomorrow and I'm a little tired. That's all." She touched a skeptical Ginny gently on her cheek. "Now, what are you working on so intently?" She deftly steered the conversation away from her aching back.

Ginny had been crunching numbers and searching for the optimum way for them to finance a two-family house. She and Chip decided that it wasn't appropriate to have their lovers' names on the deed. That would give them away.

9

Though she had barely broached the subject with her, Ginny considered herself both in over her head and extraordinarily motivated.

"Virginia?"

"Oh, sorry, Mom, you know me. I like to make sure my monthly budget is on target, just in case I want to buy some more paints and brushes," she said, cringing inside, knowing that she was deceiving her. Then she suddenly perked up. "Is Dad playing any new music tomorrow?"

That got her mother's attention. Helen rolled her eyes. Her husband talked incessantly about his band and the new music they were always trying. She laughed, "What a silly question, he's at Harold's practicing tonight."

Ginny laughed with her mother. "You're right, a silly question."

"You and Chip are coming?" Speaking to herself, while glancing at the kitchen clock, Helen muttered, "What time is it? My word, it's nine o'clock already." She turned to Ginny, "I'm going to put my feet up and sit in the parlor and listen to *Moon River Radio* for a while."

Ginny watched as her mother untied her ancient apron and left the kitchen to listen to the weekly radio program. Her mom was her closest friend, so she felt torn. Moving out of the house would be difficult, she would miss her mother enormously, but not spending her nights with Beverly was torturous. She cringed again, as she thought of the convoluted plan that Chip was devising and that she was succumbing to. *It will work, it has to work, Mom and Dad will be thrilled to have me married to Chip.*

She had consciously been avoiding speaking to Beverly about *The Plan*, as she now called it. Bev would ask all sorts of questions and expect concrete answers. Ginny wanted to be prepared to answer each one thoughtfully and succinctly. Beverly Jean Taylor, her secret lover, was known to Ginny's parents as a friend from Westinghouse. Eyebrows were raised when Ginny first brought Beverly home for dinner after work one night over a year ago. Her parents thought that the cigarette-smoking older woman couldn't possibly be a good influence on their beloved daughter. She was English by descent, Anglican, and had an apartment on her own in Roslindale-- a good two bus rides away from Readville. She wore her long auburn hair flowing around her shoulders with a couple of simple clips to hold it back from her eyes. Her long, wavy hair had caught Ginny's attention the first day that Beverly walked into the bookkeeping pool, and the gaze of her steely blue eyes caused Ginny to swoon inside. She was inextricably drawn to her, captivated in a way she had never experienced. She couldn't comprehend why at first; that was two years ago.

It was more than a week before Ginny found the nerve to say hello to new bookkeeper. It was another week before she mustered up the courage to ask if she could sit and have lunch with her in the breakroom. Beverly, too, had been secretly watching Ginny. Beverly was gracious and charming, and Ginny felt like a twelve-year-old tripping over her words and blushing endlessly. To her, Beverly was sophisticated and patient, smoothly holding up the conversation. The rasp in her voice from years of smoking added to the appeal; she boldly smoked in the break room, shocking the other female workers. Ginny mostly babbled through her ham and cheese sandwich and couldn't keep her eyes off her.

Twirling her pencil on the stack of papers in front of her, Ginny recalled how she felt on fire after that first day of lunch together. How much older Beverly appeared, not only in years but in worldly experiences. She was thirty, independent, owned her own car, and spoke of going out for cocktails on Friday nights. In Ginny's mind, the eight-year difference in their ages shined like a spotlight on a baby's milk bottle next to her dad's double martini. Spellbound, she couldn't keep away. She sketched Beverly constantly at home in the seclusion of her bedroom. A friendship soon developed and Ginny's flame turned into a full-blown fire. She couldn't control the attraction she was experiencing toward a woman, an older woman at that, but was both drawn in and unable to pull back. For weeks she slept fitfully. *What if Beverly thought she was a deviant? What if she said the wrong thing? What if everyone else saw her attraction to her and laughed or worse at her? Could she be fired? Would she cause Beverly to be fired?*

One day, as the bookkeeping pool broke for lunch, Beverly invited Ginny for a walk and to eat lunch together outside. Ginny's heart skipped a beat and she eagerly said yes. She had noticed Ginny's growing interest in her and was confident that the innocent young girl had feelings for her that she had never acted upon. Beverly was attracted to Ginny and gambled that she was right.

Beverly found more than she expected in Ginny Stevens. She was loyal to a fault, funny and carefree, and an extremely skilled artist who put art in the background to follow her family's expectations. Yet, her innocent joy for life and wide-open heart tugged at Beverly.

The fire still burned as Ginny gathered up her house-buying papers and put them neatly in the old school bag that she used as a briefcase for work. Mostly she put her sketch pad in it along with the lunch that her mother made daily. She shook her head. "I'm still such a baby. I want to get out and make a life with Bev," she said to herself. "If I have to marry Chip, then so be it." As she got up from the table, fresh determination grew within her.

***

At 9 p.m., Beverly coolly parked in front of Ginny's house. She saw the shadow of Helen amble past the parlor window, a second light went on. Beverly shut off the car, rolled down the window, and lit a cigarette. Ginny was up to something with Chip and she wasn't sure what it was and why it had Ginny on edge the past few weeks. God, she loved Ginny, her beautiful blonde hair, her giggle, her passionate lovemaking. Bev was done with other women. Ginny was the only one for her. Ginny wasn't expecting her tonight but she couldn't keep away. The puppy had stolen her heart and she yearned to swoop her into her arms. She snubbed out the cigarette in the car ashtray, checked her hair in the rearview mirror, opened the car door, and took a deep breath. She purposely wore the dark blue slacks and blue and white striped top that Ginny selected at Jordan Marsh on a recent shopping spree. She smiled to herself. Helen would want to know why such a late visit. She liked Helen. She was a detail person, like herself.

Ginny recognized the footsteps climbing up the porch steps and hurried to the door just as the bell rang. "My goodness, who is that," called a surprised Helen.

"I have it, Mom, don't worry." A smile beamed across Ginny's face as she opened the door. "It's okay, Mom, it's Beverly from work."

"What is she doing here so late?"

Beverly expected Helen's question and called out, "There's a great new movie at the Oriental and I took a chance that Ginny might want to go. It's called *Some Like It Hot*, would you like to join us? That is if, Ginny, you want to go."

Ginny was horrified that she invited her mother. Her eyes widened and she clenched her teeth in apprehension.

Helen, getting up carefully from her chair, walked to the front door. "Heavens no, it's too late for me. But you go, Ginny, you can use a break from that pile of papers you were working on." She turned towards the parlor and called back,

"Have fun, I'm going to listen to the radio until your father comes home."

Ginny looked at Beverly, who had a knowing smirk on her face, and said, "Give me five minutes." She touched Beverly's hair and ran up the stairs to her room to freshen up.

They spent a cursory thirty minutes at the movie, and, though it was quite entertaining, passionate desire triumphed. Common sense told them that they did not have time to drive to the privacy of the apartment in Roslindale and then back to Readville so they opted for the old race track. Parked in the dark beyond the shadows of the former grandstand, they held each other closely, kissing and longing for more. Beverly pulled back first, and tilted her head as she often did when thinking, "What papers? An art project?" Ginny, still lost in the last kiss, was slow to respond.

"Huh?" Should she take a chance and bring up *The Plan*? She couldn't wait any longer. "Chip wants us to buy a house and get married so the four of us can live together without prying eyes." She leaned in for another kiss.

Beverly laughed, "Are you serious?" She paused, taking in Ginny's expression. "I can't believe it. You are serious. How in fuck's name do you two expect that to work?"

Ginny's mind went blank. Beverly rarely cursed and never the "F" word. She stammered, "Well, uh…"

"Come on, girlfriend, there is no possible way to pull something as outlandish as that off. Only Chip could contrive such a scheme. Were you even going to ask me if I wanted to live with you?" She reached for her pack of cigarettes on the dashboard and stared intently out the window.

Dejected, Ginny slid back to her side of the seat and gathered up her nerve. Quietly she said, "I thought you would want to live with me." Beverly simply took a long drag of her cigarette.

Hurrying now to convince her very skeptical girlfriend, Ginny persisted. "Please listen, Chip and I would marry, you and Richie would marry, we would build an adjoining door between the two apartments, and when we get home at night, each couple could be together." Ginny could see the shock in her eyes.

"Please, hear me out. We've not completed the final details, but financially we can afford a two-family house in Milton. Especially if both you and Richie contribute to the monthly expenses."

"You and Red are out of your minds." She crushed out her cigarette. "Do you know any homosexual couples that live together?" She noticed Ginny wince at the word homosexual.

"No, but that doesn't mean we can't try. I can't go on not living with you. And you know that sharing your small apartment will never work. My parents would never let me move out."

"What does Richard think?" Beverly interjected, her voice rising. She had never met him but from stories that Ginny told, assumed he was content living with and overly attached to his family. At twenty-seven, he showed no interest in moving out of his parents' home. His mother cooked and cleaned for him and he went to work with his father and brother every day. She was agitated by the whole juvenile idea.

"He hasn't asked him yet," Ginny admitted quietly.

"It's after eleven. I'm taking you home. This is too much, even for you." She started the car and slowly moved through the labyrinth of overgrown trees and rotted bleachers. Under her breath, she muttered, "God knows I am sick of back alleys and obscene remarks."

Ginny tentatively asked, "Please, give it some thought. I'm sure the four of us can figure this out together. I love you uncontrollably."

"I love you, too, but this is a lot to throw at me." Softening as only Ginny could make her do, she sighed, "Okay, hon, I'll think about it. God, your boyfriend has the most convoluted ideas."

***

Chip read Ginny's mood as soon as she opened the door for him. "What is it?"

He scanned the parlor and dining rooms as she walked toward the kitchen. He paused in the entranceway for a brief second, then followed her.

"What?"

She sat at the table, the site of many an afternoon of cookies and milk growing up with Ginny's brother and mother joining in with their casual banter.

"Are we here by ourselves? Your parents must already be at the dance." He pulled out the worn wooden kitchen chair and sat, leaning in towards his friend.

Ginny noticed that he had on a new light herringbone sport coat that matched his black slacks. His black plain tie and white shirt completed the outfit. He was fond of dressing in his finest for a night out. She thought her simple light orange printed dress paled in comparison.

"Last night I told Bev about our idea to buy a house and all live together. To say she is skeptical is an understatement." She brightened up ever so slightly. She did say she would think about it, though. I'm worried, Chipper, this may be way over our heads. There are too many things to consider. Could we go to jail?" Ginny frowned and pushed her hand through her newly trimmed hair.

He sat back, adjusted his tie, and stared at Ginny, undaunted by the absurdity of their moving in together. After a moment, he exhaled heavily, as she clasped her hands on the table, an unconscious holdover from eight years of parochial school, and began slowly, "We will not go to jail. We are not dirty nor sinful. I am scared to death, but I am more scared of not having a life with Richard. Let's please, please, please arrange a double date with Beverly and Richard and maybe meet at her apartment and convince them that this will work." Ginny sighed as he continued. "I'm certain that we can convince them that this is a brilliant solution." She looked down at her clasped hands and up at Chip as he continued. "Do you think Bev will let us meet at her apartment? I have to know that we are going to do this. I am suffocating. Now that we have the idea, I cannot let it go." Reading her eyes, he added, "I know you want this, too."

"Come on, tell me, honestly, have you talked with Richie about this? He's, so, I don't know, what's the word, glued, um, clingy to his large family. None of his brothers have a place of their own and his sister and new husband live across the street. Have his parents even heard of or met *any* girl that he has dated? Have you ever discussed Beverly with him?"

His scowl told Ginny the answer. Running her hand through her hair, while checking the time on the kitchen clock, she groaned and stood up. "Ugh. Come on, let's get to the dance. Everyone is expecting us. By the way, I adore your new outfit, Mr. Fashion Plate." He grinned and brushed his lapels as if to say, yes, I am.

The church hall was crowded, the band was playing a merengue, and scores of people were dancing. Ginny laughed to herself as she thought of her father playing the popular music. She gave him a wave as she passed the stage. Chip held her hand and they danced, carefree and full of happiness. They made the perfect couple together. When Chip caught sight of Richard across the room standing with his younger brother, Joe, their sister Anna, and her husband Dom, Ginny noticed and followed his gaze across the room. "Finish another dance before going to him."

He shifted his gaze back to her. "You're right. He *is* gorgeous, isn't he?" The band slowed the tempo to a waltz and the two found each other's arms and slowly swayed.

"I do adore dancing with you. You are such a gentleman, keeping your hands right where they should be."

He laughed and held her closer. "Your mother is watching from behind the refreshment table. My mother is watching from the table to your left. She is sitting with my father, who does not appear to be watching us or having a good time. Let's go say hi to them after this dance, then Richard. Shall we?"

Ginny stole a glance at his parents. Mrs. Foley wore her latest going-out dress which had an Angora collar that matched perfectly with the blue dress with its quarter-length sleeves and tight waist with a belt. Must be a *Susan Lynn* design. She knew that Mom Foley prided herself on being able to find the top bargains at Filenes Basement in downtown Boston. She tried in vain to dress up her husband for nights out. Ginny felt bad for her because Mr. Foley always loosened his tie and unbuttoned his collar and sloppily hung his jacket over a chair. He probably would drip something on his shirt before the night was over, while Mrs. Foley was still stunning to behold.

"Yes, I want to compliment your mother on how very elegant she is in that shade of blue and find out where she bought the dress."

"And here I thought you were a dungarees and sweatshirt kinda girl."

"Oh, darling, you say the sweetest things." Giggling they made their way from the dance floor.

While talking with Chip's parents, Ginny noticed Beverly entering the hall. She wore a soft green sweater with a tight-fitting dark green skirt. Ginny noted the widening eyes of Mr. Foley as he zeroed in on her lover. Beverly, unaware of the attention she sparked, paused, surveyed the room, then spotting a familiar face casually walked over to Helen.

Ginny tried to focus back on the conversation. Feigning light-heartedness, she asked, "Mr. and Mrs. Foley my dad plays a mean cha-cha, doesn't he? Don't you dance the cha-cha?"

Everyone laughed and Ginny nudged Chip and raised her eyebrows toward Beverly and her mother. He caught her cue and jumped in, "Let's go buy a slice of your mother's cake before it's gone. Mom, Dad, do you want us to get you a slice?" His parents declined. Chip held Ginny's hand and moved towards the refreshment table.

"Hi, Beverly. What a nice surprise. I didn't know you were coming," she said casually. She was confused by her appearance. "Chip, you remember Beverly from my office, you saw her a few times when you met me at Westinghouse and the office picnic last summer, I think."

"I was just telling your mother that I had to get out of the house. The man I'm dating canceled, again." She emphasized "again" and tilted her head. "Time to find someone with class, I decided, and Ginny mentioned the dance after the movie. I was already dressed, so why not make a night of it? Who knows, I just might meet Mr. Right." Turning to Chip, she said, "You must know a handsome, perfect fella for me." Helen nodded her head in agreement; after all, Chip was a bright, soon-to-be college graduate and entering law school in the fall.

Ginny recognized this as their chance to introduce her to Richard. Ginny was thinking, holy cow, I love this woman. She is clever, daring, and way ahead of me and Chip in laying out the foundation for *The Plan*.

"I'm sorry George didn't work out. He seemed promising a month ago. Come on, don't you worry," she said, as she studied the men scattered throughout the hall, "there must be someone here for you, even if only to take your mind off that slug for the evening. Hey, isn't that Rick, or Richie, oh yes, Richard Ruggiero, over there?" Chip finally caught on to the unfolding scene and nodded. "Isn't he the guy who fixed the stone wall at your house? Do you know anything about him? He is certainly handsome. Let's go introduce Beverly to him."

"Um, yes, why not."

"Bev, check out the guy with the blue jacket and white shirt standing with three others by the windows. What do you think?"

Richard was the perfect example of a young Roman god. Six feet tall, muscular with a trim waist, thick dark brown hair and matching eyes that came alive when he laughed.

Beverly grinned and winked at Ginny, "Not blonde, but definitely handsome."

Chip chuckled at that and jumped in, "Come on, let's go introduce you to him. He is a sweet guy not just bulging muscles and classic good looks. He lives at home, that is his family with him, and I see no date hanging on his arm. Come on girls." He held each of their hands and headed across the hall. Chip added quietly into Beverly's ear as they strolled across the floor. "He is almost twenty-eight, I know you like 'em young." He grinned mischievously. She didn't flinch.

Richard was in a lively conversation about the Red Sox with his brother and brother-in-law and had his back to the approaching threesome. Chip couldn't resist touching his arm to get his attention. He was startled by Chip's touch and almost let out a yelp.

Chip quickly said, "Hello, Richard, Joe, Dom, and beautiful Anna. You know my girlfriend, Ginny. And this is Bev Taylor, a friend of hers from work. Great night for the dance?"

The group was cordial, with Joe, overly gregarious compared to his bashful brother. Joe played little league baseball with Ginny's brother and had been to her house when he was younger. "Chip, you won't mind if I ask your girlfriend to dance with me? Come on, Ginny let's get out there." Before anyone could reply, he steered her by the elbow towards the dance floor.

Anna and Dom joined them, leaving Richard, Chip, and Beverly together. Sensing the awkwardness pass among them, Beverly played her emerging role to the hilt, and chimed in, "Well, he's a brat." She watched Joe as he slow-danced with Ginny. "Do you dance? Shall we leave Woody Woodpecker here twiddling his thumbs?"

Not knowing what to do, Richard's eyes sought out Chip.

"Hey! I'm no cartoon character," Chip protested, pretending to be insulted, slapped Richard on the back and added, "Go for it, kids. I will be here keeping an eye on that wise guy little brother of yours."

Richard held out his rough hand towards Beverly and in his deep voice offered, "Shall we?"

She grinned innocently, tossed back her long auburn hair, placed her hand on his hand, and looking over her shoulder said, "Don't wait up Red."

Chip raised his eyebrows and shoved his hands in his pockets. He thought of the last night that he and Richard had spent together. The motel was on Route One South. It was the kind of place that didn't ask questions. He shuffled his feet and watched them dance across the floor. The music shifted to a slow dance reminding him how Richard held him in his arms as they danced and whispered how much he loved him. If only they could dance here.

The dance was a fundraising success. Slices of Helen's cakes sold out early. The watercolor painting of the Blue Hills that Ginny donated to the silent auction sold well over the asking price. The young couples enjoyed each other's company and were invited back to Dom and Anna's home for drinks. Anna was curious to learn more about the woman who had spent the night dancing with her brother. Chip discovered that they had an old upright piano in the den. He asked if he could play it and was beside himself with excitement. He launched into a selection of upbeat tunes his mother had taught him on the old piano in the church hall. Playing the piano calmed him although he rarely talked about it. He called for the others to get up and dance. While the laughter was authentic and the conversations relaxed, internally Richard seethed. He felt thrown into the situation and had no inkling about what was going on. Chip never mentioned setting him up with Beverly. He had been vaguely aware of her, but what was she up to, and what was Chip up to?

Chapter Three

Monday morning didn't come fast enough for Ginny. She stood on the sidewalk waiting for Beverly. She was unable to call her on Sunday, and there was too much to talk about to chance being overheard in the breakroom. She saw her pull into the parking lot across the street, and waited impatiently for her to get out of the car. When Beverly finally spotted Ginny, she waved and smiled; Ginny waved and frowned, anxious to discuss the dance.

"Can we walk and talk during lunch today?" Ginny tried to maintain a calm voice.

"Sure," Beverly replied in a breezy manner. "The dance and get-together afterward at Dom and Anna's were entertaining, weren't they? Richard is a dream." She said her last contrived statement loud enough for the others on the sidewalk to overhear. *Who is Richard?* was now bound to be the topic of the day.

The morning passed by quickly. Mr. Briggs was reviewing the spring quarter numbers for the region and the bookkeeping pool was in the thick of counting, analyzing, and typing up reports. Lost in her work, Ginny barely had time to think about lunch, and was startled when the noon-time whistle in the factory blared. She noted her place in her report, closed the folder, and opened her bottom desk drawer for her lunch bag.

She met Beverly in the lobby and suggested a walk to nearby Mill Pond for lunch. "It's a beautiful day to eat outside."

Beverly agreed as she held the door for Ginny.

"How about we go to the bench near Fairview? It has the nicest view of the water," Ginny suggested. Fairview was the local cemetery on the other side of Mill Pond located on a slight hill. The bench sat just before its entrance and was a longer walk from the office. Ginny liked its privacy for serious discussions.

Beverly lit a cigarette as they walked, drawing in the nectar and exhaling with pleasure. "You really should give those up," muttered Ginny.

Beverly knew Ginny was upset, but not about her smoking. She was not in the mood to argue.

"You're right," she said lightly. She stopped and snuffed out the cigarette on the sidewalk before she crossed the street. Ginny followed.

Once at the bench, Ginny began. "Why didn't you tell me that you were coming to the dance? You caught us off guard."

Beverly opened her lunch bag and was about to respond when Ginny hurriedly continued.

"Does this mean you want to move ahead with *The Plan*? I'm a wreck. I was going nuts watching you interact so girlishly with Richie. Geez, I want nothing more than to hold you this very minute." Frustrated and anxious, she bit into her sandwich and chewed with purpose.

"I made up my mind at the last minute to go. I was, *am*, very nervous about *The Plan*, as you call it. But then the light went on for me. I figured I had to at least meet Richard to see if I could feign a romance with him that everyone would believe. God, this feels like bad pulp fiction." She shook her head but smiled.

Ginny feeling a sense of relief and a spark of desire, looked around to make sure no one was nearby and stroked Beverly's hand.

Beverly squeezed her hand back. "Oh, this is too damn maddening. Can you come to my apartment tonight? Drive home with me after work. We should talk more about the risks of our kind living together."

"But we will be married to the fellas," Ginny said naively.

Rolling her eyes, Beverly paused. "God, I forget how innocent you can be. It's not always safe for us, girlfriend.

Remind me to give you my copy of *The Children's Hour*. It's a play written by Lillian Hellman. I heard somewhere that it's going to be a movie."

"I never heard of it. What's it about?"

"It's a devastating story about secret love, hate, and," she winced at the pain of it. "Well, promise you'll read it."

Ginny, wavering as she always did when trying to be upset with Beverly, nodded, "Of course. I'll remind you and I'll read it."

"Good." She opened her thermos and poured the hot coffee into the cover that worked as a cup.

"I'll have to call home first." She paused and frowned. "I hate pretending that we're just friends." She had another bite of her sandwich and wrinkled her brow. "Oh, and Chip suggested that the four of us get together at your place to talk about *The Plan*. I think that's smart. We have to all be in it together to have any chance of it working. Is it ok?"

"Yes, soon, before I wake up and change my mind."

Ginny scowled, "Geez, what is in this sandwich? Hah, my mother tried to slip in bologna with the ham again." She put the sandwich down. "What risks? My head hurts from thinking so hard, but I'm glad we talked." She smiled, "Maybe we can do more than talk tonight?"

Beverly responded with a grin of her own. "We'll talk more tonight about the risks. Do you feel better now?" Ginny nodded as she continued, "Yes, we have to be in this crazy scam together, although I am far from convinced that we can pull it off. Let's go back to the breakroom so you can call your mother." Laughing she said, "And the gossip can spread about my losing George and gaining a new beau. You know, he is quite the good dancer." She gave Ginny a playful bump, dumped her wrappers into the trash bin, and strolled confidently toward the office.

***

25

Richard's family kept him occupied all day Sunday. After Mass, he joined his father and brothers in turning over the ground for their mother's extensive vegetable garden. Anna and Dom were coming for Sunday dinner and he was required to stay with the family for the entire afternoon. He wasn't able to speak with Chip during the day on Monday, either. He was on a construction project with his father, away from any pay phones. The lack of communication contributed to his noticeably foul mood.

"Ricardo, what are you doing? Come on, concentrate! That stone line is off-center. Damn it." His father was irritated with the slip-shod work he was doing all day. "Ricardo, those are the wrong size stones- Ricardo, that's too much water in the cement mix." Frustrated, he swatted at Richard's head a few times. He cursed under his breath, apologized to his father, and kept working.

"Anna told your mother that you met a girl at the dance on Saturday. No thinking about girls when you're working."

Later in the day, after the second or third swat to his son's head, he grumbled loudly, "About time you met a girl, I'm not going to feed you at home forever. Damn it, fix that corner."

Damn Chip, thought Richard as he loaded the truck at the end of the day. He decided to drive by Chip's house after dinner and honk the horn three times. He rarely went in Chip's house. It just felt awkward. He knew that was juvenile, so mostly they would meet in downtown Boston at the Punch Bowl night club. He was tired. Tired of his father swatting at his head, tired of sneaking around, and tired of sleeping in an empty bed. Yet, he was mostly annoyed at Chip for always being two steps ahead of him and forcing his hopes and dreams on him.

The Tuccini Playground and Glenville Avenue neighborhood where Ruggiero lived may have only been a few miles from Chip's house but their lives were markedly different. Richard had attended Hyde Park High School and had tremendous responsibilities at home. His parents demanded that he work in the family business and live at home until he was married. Confession every Saturday, Mass every Sunday with the family, and prayers at the dinner table were rituals that Chip, ironically a product of Catholic School, barely acknowledged. Before he met him, Richard thought all Irish Catholics were supposed to be quite religious, very prim and proper, and arrogant because of the Irish Cardinal heading the Boston churches.

Richard's desire for men was well hidden from years of practice. Only his God above knew of his "wretched deviance." As a young teen, he'd discovered that the hard body of a man could easily seduce him. By the time he was eighteen, he regularly cruised the clubs in Scollay Square and Park Square. Duncan Foley may have been ahead of him with his sharp intellect but *he* had manly experience. Hell, yes. He picked Chip up the first time he approached the bar at the Punch Bowl. His youthful innocence captured Richard as no other man had before. He seduced him that first night and they had been together ever since. Chip's intellect didn't just amaze him, it also frustrated him. His passion for the law and his determination to succeed impressed Richard, but mostly it was Chip's easy enthusiasm for life and the love he gave unflinchingly that held his affection. He tried to school Chip on how to be discreet in public and not draw attention to themselves after several near-violent harassments. When Chip divulged that he had been bullied as a child and still carried that fear as an adult, Richard vowed to always protect him.

He washed up and ravenously ate his dinner. Bringing his empty plate and glass to the kitchen, he kissed his Mama on the cheek and said he was taking the truck.

"Are you going to meet the girl from the dance, bambino?"

"Ah, Mama, don't start planning the wedding." He hugged his Mama, slipped the truck keys from the hook by the back door, and left.

He sat in the truck thinking while the engine idled. He was confused. *What the hell was that pushing Beverly on me Saturday night?* Frowning, he thought of how Chip had gotten much flirtier with other men this past year. Maybe he should rein him in, he didn't want to lose him. Was Chip tired of him? After almost four years of love and frustration, there was still no sign of a possible future together. What could they do? If he told his family that he loved a man, his family would disown him, he would lose his job, and it would tarnish his family's reputation. He would be banished from the tight-knit neighborhood, kicked out of his church, condemned to hell, and end up by himself, as Chip flew through law school and became a respected member of the community. Chip's education and social graces would take him far. Their affair would be long forgotten.

"Son of a bitch," he said aloud as he pulled out of the driveway.

The two men decided to head to the Blue Hills, order a milkshake at Howard Johnson's and drive to Houghton's Pond while the sun was still out. The silence was stifling during the drive. Chip wasn't quite sure how to bring up the idea of Richard's dating Beverly as part of the long-range plan. He felt the tension emanating from his lover. They sat at a picnic table at the far end of the grounds, where they would be able to talk easily. Richard practically shouted after a long swig of his drink, "What the hell was going on at the dance, and why am I always the last to know?"

"Hear me out. I have a plan. It was Ginny's passing idea, but I am convinced we can make it work. Baby, we can finally be together."

"Damn it, don't call me baby, you know I don't like it."

Chip attempted to touch him, but Richard pulled away, and demanded through gritted teeth, "Tell me what is going on."

Chip closed his eyes and started again. "I am going to marry Ginny and you are going to marry Bev and we will all share a house, a real home together." Before he could explain, Richard jumped up from the picnic table, threw his drink at the trash barrel where it splashed all over the ground, and stomped back to his truck.

Chip didn't experience Richard's temper often, but he had learned to sit quietly and let it play out. It was a good sign that he didn't start the truck; it meant he had to cool off and would come back to the table. He thought frantically about how to continue to explain his ideas without him storming off again. He recognized that he should not have led with getting married. Damn his impulsiveness, he silently berated himself. He watched the truck. Richard glared at Chip. Decisively, he got out of the truck, slammed the door, and marched back to the picnic table.

"Dammit." He sat down with a thump, shaking the bench. He yanked away Chip's drink and finished it in one long pull. "I need a real drink. Come on."

Chip slowly rose from the bench and went to the truck without speaking. *Be patient,* he kept repeating to himself.

Richard refused to look at Chip as he drove to a dive in Quincy that was dark, served beer and hard liquor, and asked no questions of the men who came in to drink their troubles away.

"Classy joint," snipped Chip, and immediately regretted what he said.

Richard called to the bartender as he pointed to a booth, "Two boilermakers."

He slid into the grimy booth facing the entrance. Chip slid in across from him and started to say that he didn't like boilermakers, but held his tongue when Richard gave him a piercing stare.

The bartender brought the drinks and waited to be paid. Richard put two bucks on the table and the bartender shuffled away. Before he was back behind the bar, Richard had downed one of the whiskies and had the other in his hand.

"Okay, wise guy, start again."

Chip slowly went over the details: the finances, the potential house location, dating Beverly, and the order of the weddings. After an hour of non-stop talking, he paused, sipped the now-warm beer, and watched as Richard finished a second beer and third whiskey.

"I gotta go." He got up to use the bathroom. His head was throbbing, his chest pounding with fear. He doubted everything he had just heard, but he wanted to trust the man he adored.

Chip checked out the bar for the first time since he sat down. It was grimier than he thought when they first walked in. Three older men in work clothes sat at the bar nursing beers; otherwise, the place was empty. There was no sign of food served. He had to get Richard to eat something after three whiskies and two beers in an hour. His mind raced, where could they walk to find something to eat? He shuddered at the seedy surroundings and was anxious to leave.

Richard returned; his eyes blurry. "I want to hear this bull crap story from Ginny and I want to know more about Beverly." He pointed a finger at Chip, "Me! Marry her, absurd. We're not done with this." With a sloppy smile, he added, "I'm hungry."

Chip was relieved that there would be no more drinking and gladly slid out of the booth.

The two men left the bar with Chip steering Richard in the direction of the coffee shop with an open sign flashing at the end of the street. Two sandwiches and several cups of black coffee later, he appeared to be sobering up.

"Shall we walk?" suggested Chip, wanting to completely sober up his lover.

"No, I'd much rather go in the truck and," he bent down slightly and whispered in his ear. Chip blushed and immediately glanced up and down the dark street to see if anyone saw them. The suggestion was much more appealing than a walk. Richard jingled his keys. Chip changed his direction back towards the truck.

Chapter Four

"Virginia, are you and Chip double dating with Richard and Beverly again tonight?" Helen noticed an extra bounce in her daughter's walk of late. "What's it been, two months since they met at the church social? I guess Beverly must be completely over that George. You know, the four of you could spend an evening here sometime. I'll make some dessert. It would be nice to get to know the new couple more. Virginia, Ginny, what do you say?"

Ginny had been busy thinking through the agenda for the night's toil on *The Plan* while waiting in the hallway for Chip and was barely listening to her mother. Toil was the perfect word. The details were proving to be more complicated than anyone realized. Now that all four had bought in, they were equally determined to make it happen, at least that was what she wished and prayed for.

"Virginia Louise Stevens are you listening to me?" her mother persisted.

"Ah huh, Mom, sure." Before she could go on any further a car tooted. "There's Chip. I gotta go." She called back as she gathered her bag and sweater, "Don't wait up, I'll be late tonight."

Helen shook her head and thought briefly about the basket of ironing in the kitchen corner. She tried to remember being young and excited about a date. Then she remembered her beloved son, John Jr. She missed him every day; and only when she was alone did she allow herself to dwell on what might have been if she had been the one killed by the bus and not him. She rubbed her back, which was aching more frequently, and relived that dreadful day once again.

It was sunny but extremely cold, a typical February Saturday morning in Massachusetts. John Jr. had joined her for a trip to Cleary Square by bus to do some shopping for his upcoming eighteenth birthday party. They usually rode the Wolcott Square bus but decided that the River Street bus would be easier to walk to. There was ice on the bridge to the Wolcott bus stop and it would be much too slippery to walk across, Johnny had said to his mother. He doted on his mother and was always happy to spend extra time with her. He thought his father was a great guy, but he was not into music. Public service was Johnny's addiction. He and his mother left early that particular morning, talking and laughing on their way to the bus stop next to JM's Market. Misty-eyed, Helen recalled how Johnny picked up some snow and threw a snowball at her; she did the same but missed him completely. Arm in arm they waited for the bus. She was gazing at him and thinking about what a handsome young man he had become. He was tall like his father, had blonde hair and blue eyes, and a smile that could charm a cat off a fish truck. He was telling her about his adventurous ideas for summer before he left for college in the fall, when he froze and then forcefully pushed her away from him. With tears trickling down her cheeks she remembered waking up in the hospital. Her first words were, "Where's Johnny? Everything hurts. I can't move. What happened?" She slipped in and out of consciousness for several days. By then John Jr. was gone. The oncoming bus had skidded on a patch of ice and rammed into them, hitting John with its full force. His pushing her out of the way saved her life but left her with a broken heart. She wiped the tears away and picked up the basket of laundry and set it next to the ironing board. "My son, my son," she sighed as sadness enveloped her. She came back to the present when she heard Ginny close the front door. She called, "Have fun, dear." Ginny was already down the steps and into the car.

"We have to pick up Richard. Gin-Gin, tonight we *will* finish *The Plan* and start living our dream." He lovingly squeezed her hand.

"Chipper, I'm all goosebumps and I don't know if it is because I am excited or scared." She squeezed his hand back. "Let's go."

Richard was standing outside his house when they arrived. He held a large paper bag and was dressed in his favorite burgundy wide-collar shirt and black slacks. His hair was slicked back and he was clean-shaven.

"He is drop-dead handsome."

"Hmm." She thought he was dressed like an Elvis Presley wannabe.

He climbed into the back seat and motioned to the bag. "I told my mother that Beverly was having a party and she insisted on sending some of her Amaretti cookies. My God, there's enough to feed an army in this bag."

Ginny leaned over the seat. "I don't know her, but I love your mother. Gimme, Elvis, quick, quick, quick."

"Hey, Irish, who you calling Elvis?" He liked Elvis and was not sure if he should be pleased or insulted. With a wrinkled brow, he passed her the bag.

After they settled in at the apartment, Chip announced that he had important news to share. "Richard, Gin-Gin, Bev," he cleared his throat and started. Beverly almost giggled at his sober face. "Yesterday I received confirmation of the gift that I have been anticipating for years. As you may or may not know, my grandparents, Gigi and PopPop, on my mother's side, owned the news and cigarette store in Cleary Square. It turns out they owned the entire building and had vast holdings across Boston. Ginny, remember how Gigi would give us a free candy bar and tell us not to let PopPop know?" She smiled. He shifted his feet. "Well, they established a trust fund for me." This caused his friends to sit up a little straighter. "The money was to be made available starting on my twenty-second birthday, which, as you know, was this past January, but not before I graduated from college. Now that I am twenty-two and *finished* my undergraduate studies and *am* entering a very prestigious law school, thank you very much, I was contacted by my grandparents' lawyer. The trust says that I am eligible for up to $4000 a year if I went to law school and it goes up to $5000 a year when I marry and purchase a home. Gigi always knew that I dreamed of becoming a successful lawyer."

Mouths dropped. Ginny was the first to comment.

"Holy moly. That's a fortune."

Beverly added, "Jesus, Red." She turned to Richard, "Did you know about this?"

Richard was jiggling his leg furiously. He tried not to explode. How could he not tell him ahead of time? He shook his head no while staring at a very proud Chip.

Chip was anxious to continue with his good news and ignored the comments.

"Here me out, I must pay for tuition with the trust first, then I can use the remainder every year for whatever I want. The trust is expected to last for years, but with careful investing, I am certain I can make it last longer." Puffing out his chest, he finished his announcement with, "I will be an established, top-notch attorney within ten years and money will be rolling in." He grinned from ear to ear.

The amount of money was staggering. He wouldn't be considered filthy rich, but he would be getting more money yearly from the trust than any of them currently earned. It was almost twice what the women each made.

"Um, say something. This money will come in handy. We will be able to afford a great house in Milton and put less of a burden on all of you. My grandparents, rest their souls, loved me to a fault."

He was excited and fully expected to hear congratulations and cheers of joy. He wanted to be the star that everyone looked up to.

Richard immediately stood up and went outside, slamming the door behind him. Chip, exasperated, rolled his eyes and followed him. When they returned some thirty minutes later, Richard was obviously still upset and Chip was frustrated.

Chip said tersely to his friends, "Let me explain, again, that the trust stipulates that the money has to pay for my education at a Catholic university, and I *must* graduate or future payments stop completely. That is why my parents worked hard to convince me to attend Newton College. They knew some of the details and intended to make sure I stayed on track. Plus, I have to volunteer at Saint Cats tutoring program at least four hours a week and give $100 a year to the YMCA in Cleary Square. Most importantly," and he eyeballed Richard, "I had no clue of the size of the trust before I met with the lawyer earlier today. My parents had no idea of the size of the entire package. The first thing I will do is give my parents $1000 to pay for my undergraduate tuition. And, remember, I am required to pay for law school with the trust. When I graduate, I will be earning my own living and not depending on it. Everything squared now? I know, this is a lot to take in all at once. It is for me, too."

Richard crossed his arms and stared out the window. It was difficult for him to accept that Chip would have this free money and only have to attend school to keep it coming. He saw his aging father struggle every day to earn an honest dollar. Between him and his father, they barely made what Chip was going to receive from his grandparents. He was jealous, angry, and confused. The money, compounded by the plan that he would marry Beverly, wreaked havoc on his nerves.

Beverly was uncomfortable with the trust fund. She couldn't quite put her finger on it. Was it jealousy or concern that she was being bought? Why hadn't Chip told Richard first instead of blindsiding him? She lit a cigarette and smiled weakly at her girlfriend.

Ginny shrugged her shoulders and was ready to move on. She was slightly envious of Chip's good fortune but also recognized that his generous use of the money would be a significant plus for the house, just like he said. In her experience, his word was heartfelt and steadfast.

"I can help you create a budget if you want."

"Thanks, Gin-Gin, but I have got it covered, lawyers and all."

With that, she got up and nudged the group to review the remaining details of *The Plan*.

By ten o'clock, their monthly action steps were printed neatly on the back of a cut-open brown shopping bag that was taped to the parlor wall. Ginny preferred to list each step so everyone could follow the process and make suggestions. The room was full of smoke from Beverly's cigarettes, and several beer cans filled the small coffee table. Ginny, the non-drinker in the bunch, stood by the list with a marker in her hand. She shifted, taking in the final schedule, and satisfied, she walked to the parlor windows and opened both of them wider.

"Good grief, your smoking is going to kill me before we even get to live together."

"Sorry, I'm nervous." as she snuffed out her cigarette. "That's it, I promise I'm quitting this instant." Even though her pack of Pall Mall was empty she made the grand gesture of crushing the package and throwing it into the wastebasket behind the end table. "Done." She tilted her head lovingly at Ginny.

Richard murmured, "Excuse us." The men disappeared into Beverly's bedroom.

"My word, those two are like rabbits. Girlfriend, add soundproofed walls to the list of building supplies for the new house." They didn't realize that Richard was still sulking and Chip was attempting to persuade him that the money was a blessing, not a curse.

Ginny laughed and eagerly jumped onto the sofa and into her girlfriend's arms. Using her most seductive voice she whispered, "Shall we?"

Beverly brushed back her rich auburn hair and in her husky voice, answered, "If we must" and kissed her blonde angel. While the women held each other closely and talked softly about creating a future together, the men were struggling behind the closed bedroom door.

"Richard, come on. The money is great. We will not have to start our life together with nothing."

Richard tried to maintain his composure. "You embarrassed me in front of the girls." He was angry. "You should have warned me ahead of time. Fuckin' hell, do you ever think of me first?"

Chip gasped. "I am always thinking about you. How could you say that?"

"Oh, mio tesoro, everything is moving so fast. The house, living together, and the god-awful marriages. I'm scared."

"Richard, talk to me. Please, why are you scared?"

"Ha! My parents, my job, my faith, the wackos who want to beat the crap out of us and destroy us. Just to name a few. I'm shaking. God, hold me. Get me through this."

Chip held him, kissed him, and stroked his face. "I love you immeasurably. We will get through this rough patch and, and have a fabulous life together. I promise."

***

The engagement was announced in the Hyde Park Tribune. The Stevens and the Foleys celebrated with an elegant lobster dinner in downtown Boston at the elegant Parker House Restaurant. It was the home of the first Boston Cream Pie and the famous Parker House rolls, and where John Stevens proposed to Miss Helen O'Malley in 1932.

The wedding was set for October, a church wedding as insisted upon by both Helen and Chip's mother, Marjorie, with a small reception back at the Stevens' home.

Margaret Mary and Susan were dazzled by the diamond engagement ring that Ginny wore on her left hand. Margaret Mary had worked for a year after high school, before attending Wellesley College, and lived at the dormitory during the academic year. She and Ginny had somewhat lost touch, but Ginny was pleased that she agreed to be her maid of honor. Susan, who was currently eight months pregnant, would be her bridesmaid. Ginny had originally begged Beverly to be her maid of honor, but she refused to be part of the wedding party. Though it was a ruse, and with tears in her eyes, she told Ginny, some things hurt too much. She said that she preferred to attend the wedding with Richard. The rejection stung Ginny and she was rattled by Beverly's tears, but she knew not to push.

Richard agreed with Beverly and he, too, adamantly refused to be part of the wedding party. Chip didn't press the issue, afraid of further upsetting his lover, as the fallout from the trust announcement still lingered. Paul, his friend from Boston Latin School, would be his best man and his younger cousin Dennis from Watertown would partner with Susan. Paul, who would have given anything for Ginny to be his, was quite surprised by the engagement. He had watched a driven Chip work non-stop to achieve his goals, and he never did believe that Ginny was Chip's priority. Best chums, yes, but not lovers. He was gracious about it; happy and sad that his friend proved him wrong.

Chapter Five

Beverly and Richard quickly realized it was their turn to demonstrate to family and friends that they were becoming a serious and loving couple. Beverly only had her father, who lived in Westerly, Rhode Island. He was older and had recently retired from the local granite quarry. Harry Taylor started as a quarry laborer and worked his way to operations supervisor. He met Beverly's mother, Sarah, late in life when she and her family summered on Westerly's shores. It was a whirlwind romance, and a sumptuous wedding. Adding to their ideal life, Beverly Jean was born in 1929. They loved and cherished their only child. Tragedy struck, though, on September 21, 1938, when a major hurricane pounded the coast. Sarah was killed when a tree crashed through the roof of the house, leaving Harry and Beverly utterly devastated. They remained close as she grew and the quarry business prospered. Harry reluctantly gave his blessing when Beverly insisted on moving to Boston to pursue a bookkeeping career. He offered to pay her double to stay on as his quarry bookkeeper, but accepted the fact that once she made up her mind there would be no persuading her to stay. He learned early on that Beverly was dauntless in her pursuit of independence and thought that acclimating successfully to life in the city would come easily for her. Nevertheless, he worried and kept in constant contact with her.

Beverly couldn't escape the small town of her youth fast enough. Once settled in the Roslindale neighborhood of Boston, she worked at Woolworth's back office in Cleary Square. A lively love life soon followed, with a series of women eager to know the stunning woman with the devilish blue eyes finding their way to her apartment. That was before working at Westinghouse and meeting the young, naïve, and striking Virginia Stevens. It was then Beverly gave up spending nights at the bars in Boston that catered to women only. She didn't miss the clubs or the stress of being exposed. She was content until talks of *The Plan* emerged. The thought of living with Ginny had her heart racing and she realized that she wanted to be with Ginny forever. The outside world be damned. Yet, she wasn't at all clear on how to tell her father about Ginny and *The Plan*. She was certainly in no rush to introduce Richard to him.

***

"You are so beautiful, no? Your eyes blue as the sky. Ricardo, why has it taken you three months to bring her home to meet your family? Beverly, come, sit, we will eat." His mother, Angela, was excited to meet the woman who had won her son's heart. She had prayed to the Virgin Mary for years for a nice Italian girl for her oldest son. Her prayers almost answered, she gathered the entire family for a celebratory Sunday dinner. Although the family ate dinner together every Sunday, today she demanded that her children dress in their Sunday church clothes. Even the patriarch, Mr. Ruggiero, was told in no uncertain terms that he had to wear a tie. Her husband knew when she meant business. She put a white linen tablecloth on the dining room table and brought out her fanciest dishes from Italy. She had spent the previous two days cooking her three-meat red gravy (*sauce* her American friends called it), ziti, lasagna, a roast chicken and roast beef, an antipasto platter, some vegetables, a cake, and two dozen cannoli.

Beverly immediately felt bowled over and somewhat underdressed. She wore a red sleeveless blouse with a white round collar and a white form-fitting skirt from *Montgomery Ward*, but it was not dressy. The Ruggieros gathered around her as soon as she arrived, all talking at once, one talking louder than the next. Richard saw her panic and shouted, "Hey, everybody, enough. Give her some room. Mama, can we eat?"

That got everyone moving to the dining room. Beverly was placed next to Mr. Ruggiero and across from Mrs. Ruggiero, who sat closest to the kitchen. The family held hands and said grace. Beverly tried to appear comfortable with the praying. Soon the homemade wine was poured and Mrs. Ruggiero went back and forth from the kitchen and overflowed the table with platters of food. The noise of familial chatter filled the room. The Ruggieros were a close, boisterous family, such a contrast to her experience as an only child. She grinned and tried to concentrate on the heaps of food Richard's mother kept piling on her plate. Mr. Ruggiero kept refilling her glass of wine as she fought back a headache from the intensity of the day. During the pause before dessert and coffee, Mrs. Ruggiero began to interrogate Beverly. Richard tried to steer questions about marriage and children toward Anna, who had announced being pregnant with her and Dom's first child the month before. Angela, though, focused on the woman her son had brought home.

"Miss Taylor, you want lots of children, yes? Me, sadly, God blessed me with only five. Don't get me wrong I love my children but nine is what I prayed for." Crossing herself, she added, "Please, Jesus, keep my children healthy and safe."

At this point, the entire table was waiting for Beverly to answer. Dom put his arm smugly around his pregnant wife. The twins, Mateo and Angelo, at nineteen, snickered like adolescents at the end of the table. Mama gave them her sternest stare then smiled sweetly at the skinny woman.

"Gosh, I believe I have to be married first." She battered her eyes innocently at Richard.

The table exploded with laughter and guffaws, and Angela again made the sign of the cross as she peered at a now self-conscious Richard. "Ricardo, you hear that?"

He knew marriage was part of *The Plan*. He coughed and heard himself squeaking, "What's for dessert?"

Angela made a *tch-tch* sound and left the table to get the dessert. She told Joe and the twins to clear the table, much to their chagrin. Her tone, though, told them to get up, clean the table and be quiet. She knew how to run a tight household.

After the dessert, the family scattered. Anna and Dom went for a walk to try to ease Anna's continuous nausea. The pregnancy was proving difficult. Mr. Ruggiero went out to the backyard to smoke his stogie.

"Beverly, come into the kitchen with me. Ricardo, go join your brothers in the parlor." She waved him away.

Richard started to object, then wisely backed out of the room without saying a word.

"I'm going to pack some food for you to take home. You're too skinny."

She started to protest but Angela put her hand up and she stopped. How she longed for a cigarette.

"Everything was delicious Mrs. Ruggiero. Do you cook this much food every Sunday?"

Angela shrugged and cut a large slice of her ricotta cake and wrapped it in waxed paper. "Beverly, are you in love with my oldest son? He is almost twenty-eight and has never brought a girl home. It's time he got married and had a place of his own. I worry that he ends up in the bar at the corner drinking beer with the old men there."

"I didn't know Richard's real name is Ricardo." Stalling as she walked around the big kitchen. She tilted her head, "We've only been dating for a few months, but I am falling for him." She stalled some more, then added, "He's a great dancer and always a gentleman." She realized that the stress

43

of publicly dating Richard had lessened, and a friendship was beginning.

"He must be a gentleman," said Angela, waving her knife in the air, "if he knows what's good for him."

Beverly, slightly tipsy from the wine, struggled to keep from giggling at the thought of Angela taking the knife to Richard's private parts. Clearing her throat, she managed, "Maybe you should ask Richard, um Ricardo, his intentions." She proceeded, "As a man, shouldn't he make his intentions clear and not string me along?" For punch, she innocently noted, "Did you hear that his friend Chip and his girlfriend, Virginia, are now engaged?"

"Mio Dio," exclaimed Angela. "I will have his father have a man-to-man talk with him tonight. She finished packing up the food, put it in a large brown paper bag, and handed it to her. "You can return the plates the next time you visit."

"Thank you, Mrs. Ruggiero, I won't forget. This has been a lovely afternoon with you and your family. Your food is absolutely scrumptious. I could never cook as well as you did today. I really should be getting home now." She smiled, "Work tomorrow."

There was some nervous, intermittent laughter between Richard and Beverly on the drive back to her apartment. Both were mostly lost in their thoughts about the difficulty of pretending and the strain the whole convoluted scam was putting on their consciences. Beverly spoke first.

"Have you noticed that Ginny and Red are sailing along with this foolishness?"

"Foolishness? I thought you fully agreed to do this?"

"I did, I do." She rubbed her face with both hands. "I'm still loopy from your father's wine and feeling sorry for myself. How are you doing, Romeo?"

"Mostly, I find myself saying 'Fuckin' hell.' Excuse my language, Miss Taylor." He offered a sheepish grin along with the apology.

"Hmm. Do you want to come up for a coffee or something? We should talk about our roles and the long to-do list that our co-conspirators gave us." Under her breath, she lamented, "Crap, are we doing this?"

"Not tonight. I'm worn out from the stress and my parents will be ready to bombard me about you when I get home." He snorted, groaned, and stopped, "Maybe I should come up and prepare for their inquest."

"Okay, lover, let's go." She got out of the car. "You know, we ought to be more like Ginny and Red, and give off a relaxed and carefree illusion."

"Sure thing, sweetheart," he leaned down and kissed her on the cheek. They both laughed as he lamely mimicked Humphry Bogart.

***

"Ricardo, this Beverly Jean Taylor is a lovely girl but she is not Italian and she is not Catholic. I am not convinced that she wants a house full of beautiful children to make her life complete as a wife and woman. And, Anna told me that she is two years older than you. Mio Dio." Angela was at the kitchen table making lunches for her men to take to work in the morning. "That's all I have to say. Go speak with your father." She dismissed him with a wave of her hand and he sulked as he walked to the parlor.

"Why couldn't he bring home a nice *younger* Italian girl? Mio Dio, what did I do wrong?" Angela muttered under her breath and made the sign of the cross.

"Ricardo, what are you doing bringing home an English girl? Your mother, she has been crying to me since you left to take her home. I like the woman. How old is she? Do you like her enough to marry her?"

Richard struggled to interrupt his father. He simply raised his arm in retreat.

"What are you going to do? Don't get her pregnant. You're careful, yes? Ricardo, what?"

Richard slumped onto the sofa that his mother kept covered in an old blanket, except when they had visitors. The old blanket reminded him of childhood and roughhousing with his three brothers whenever his mother was in the kitchen.

"Papa, Beverly is the only woman I want to be with." *This was true*, he thought, feeling his desire for Chip rising. "She's independent, smart, and willing to put up with me." Putting on his charm he said, "And she enjoyed meeting everyone today. You have to admit that we're a big loud family. She kept up with you and your wine, too. Come on, you have to talk with Mama and tell her that this might be my only chance for happiness." *A chance to live with Chip and hold him close every night.*

"Ah, son, you know how stubborn your mother is, but, yes, I will convince her to accept her. When do you think you will propose?"

"Papa, one step at a time. I don't want to scare her off too soon." His father stared at him. Richard stopped for a second to try to recollect the agreed timeline. "Not before the holidays. I know it's months away, but if dating continues to go smoothly between us, perhaps on New Year's Eve. She'll be back from visiting her father and the pressure of the holidays will be behind us. What do you think?"

"I think you should show your Mama how happy you are with this woman and how you want to build a future and a family with her. I'm going to bed. We have to pick up the crushed stone then drive out to Needham tomorrow to start the Billings job." As he left the room, he turned back to his son with a sheepish smile, "You know she expects lots of grandchildren to spoil."

"Good night, Papa." Richard huffed into the kitchen, with the sudden and disconcerting awareness that he would be expected to produce children. That was never part of *The Plan*.

His mother was bagging the sandwiches for the morning.

"Have a sandwich, bambino."

He leaned over and kissed his mother as he picked up the sandwich. "You will learn to love Beverly, Mama."

Mama was not sure she would ever love the skinny English girl.

Chapter Six

Ginny's heart was palpitating as she and Chip drove up to the old two-family house for sale on Eliot Street in Milton. It was built at the turn of the century, had five bedrooms between two apartments, and was a corner lot with a manageable size yard in the back. The house was listed as a fixer-upper and that didn't intimidate Ginny in the least. She had taken a tour of it with her mother earlier in the week. She loved it and couldn't wait for Chip to see it, and more importantly, she longed for it to be home for her and Beverly. She already decided that the second floor, which had a balcony on the front side, and attic space for a guest room and an art studio was where they would live.

Chip acted ambivalent as he scrutinized everything, upstairs and downstairs, the basement, the attic, and the outside back porches. He flushed toilets and ran water in the kitchen sinks. He opened the electrical box and walked back and forth around the outside perimeter of the property.

Ginny followed him, constantly asking, "What do you think?" They had viewed a dozen houses already, none of which excited her as much as this one and she prayed he would love it, too.

The realtor lingered impatiently in the kitchen. He was worn out from a full day of house tours. He checked his watch, realizing that the owners would return shortly. He wondered what was taking these kids so long. Finally, holding hands, they entered the kitchen. She was overly enthusiastic and somewhat pushy, and the future groom was cautious. He heard the young man say he was a law student and experience told him he would have many pointed questions and would want to negotiate. The realtor had yet to have an offer on the house and the anxious owners had given him permission to negotiate down to a certain figure.

He knew he was an excellent agent and negotiator, but still, lawyers were not his favorite people.

"We'll take it." Ginny burst out their decision. Chip rolled his eyes and pulled out the kitchen chair for his fiancé.

"Sit down, darling." He began, "We do have some questions."

The realtor dismissed her and gave his attention to the young man. They were in an intensive negotiation, getting closer to a final offer when the owners pulled up in the driveway

"The owners are here and we are obliged to leave."

Ginny pressed Chip's arm, worried that they might not get the house.

The realtor noticed her concern and said, "Don't worry. I will go outside and speak with them and let them know you want the house and your offer and the areas still open for negotiation. They will make their final decision quickly, I am certain."

As the realtor escorted the couple towards the front door he added, "I will telephone you later this afternoon, Mr. Foley. This is your parents' home number correct? Will you be there around four?"

"It's my parents' phone number. We'll be there together."

The realtor was insulted at Ginny's assertiveness. He twisted up his mouth at Chip, who winked at him and said, "Come on, darling. Let's tell your parents the good news."

As they started to drive away, Ginny gushed, "It's beautiful. Stop, there it is, our miracle home. We'll own it by Halloween, I'm sure of it."

"I cannot wait." Chip smiled while visualizing himself and Richard finally together.

"*The Plan* will stay on schedule. Oh no, darn it, we should have Beverly and Richie tour the house before we make the final offer. I can't believe that I completely forgot. They will be so, *so* angry if we even consider this without them."

Chip giggled. "I am way ahead of you. I called Richard when you said you were interested in this house. I could tell you were sold on it from the start. They toured the house this morning, long before we arrived."

Holding her breath, she squeezed his arm. "They love it, don't they? Oh, do tell me they loved it. They did, didn't they?" She was flushed and ran her hand through her hair. "Duncan Foley Jr., stop sitting there like a dummy and tell me!"

He couldn't hold back any longer. "They adored it. Of course, they agree that it has to be updated with new paint and wallpaper at least to start. Bev said she preferred the ground-floor apartment because it is smaller and cozier. Perfect."

"They adored it. I adore it. I'm so happy."

"Me, too. Richard liked the garage on the side street driveway. It is big enough to hold his truck, thankfully. That truck of his is a mess and, frankly, would be embarrassing in this neighborhood."

"You're turning into a snob. I'm telling Richie what you said. Shoot! You said Beverly wants the first floor. I want the second floor." She scratched her head as *Pretty Blue Eyes* by Steve Lawrence came on the car radio. She turned it up. "I guess I'll be on the first floor. My pretty blue eyes can have whatever she wants for putting up with me," she nudged Chip, "and you and your Mama's boy boyfriend."

"He is *not* a Mama's boy and don't you dare! He is in love with his old truck. Plus, you know he does not like it when you call him Richie. It makes him feel like you are calling him a baby."

She laughed, "Ugh! Come on, my parents are expecting us."

The anticipation was rapidly building as they drove the twenty minutes to Norton Street. Chip cut through Buckingham Street and wondered aloud, "Will you miss the old neighborhood?" He signaled to turn onto Readville

Street and then left onto Norton Street. "There is old Mr. Mullin, tarring his driveway, again." He tooted his car horn and waved. Mr. Mullin stopped and leaned on his tall rake and tried to make out who had tooted. He gave a cursory wave and went back to smoothing the warm tar. "I heard Miles Mullin joined the army and is being shipped overseas to some out-of-the-way unheard-of country. Do you believe it? Thank the Almighty, I am in law school. The men in the army may be gorgeous, but I would never survive. Do you remember how much I was harassed while at Saint Cats? I still get nightmares." He shivered.

Ginny gave a cursory "mmm" as she was blissfully caught up in the dream of living in her own house with her lover by her side. She pictured quiet dinners after work. Beverly would cook and she would wash the dishes. She would spend time on her art; perhaps painting a mural on one of the walls. On Saturday mornings they would lounge in bed and do more than lounge. Tender caresses came to mind. Her face flushed as they pulled into her parents' driveway.

"Virginia, Chip wipe your feet on the porch before you come in. I just washed the floor," called Helen from the front doorway. They did and rushed in to share their news. "Why Virginia you are flushed, you aren't going to catch a cold, are you? The wedding is in six weeks."

"No, Mom. Where's Dad? Of course, I hear him playing in the basement." She quickly gave her mother the details.

"Oh, Mom, I am so excited. We are so excited."

"Kids, this is heavenly. Let me go get John." Helen went to the kitchen and down to the basement music studio that her husband had built to keep his guitar practicing as unobtrusive as possible. Helen would tease him that it was a hideout, not a studio.

"Can I use the telephone to ring Richard? He is at Bev's apartment, I promised to call."

"Why didn't you tell me? Call them quickly before my parents come back upstairs."

He hardly had time to tell him that they put in an offer when Mr. and Mrs. Stevens came bursting into the kitchen. There were hugs and handshakes, laughter, and heartfelt congratulations. The young couple was beside themselves with anticipation.

Helen made coffee and served her homemade chocolate chip cookies. John fidgeted, anxious to return to his practice session.

The telephone rang in the hallway after what seemed like hours. Ginny jumped. Mr. Stevens picked up the receiver. Chip stood close by his side. "Yes. Hold on. He wants to speak with you." He passed the entire telephone to his future son-in-law and grinned.

"Hello, yes, Mr. Price. No, I am disappointed. Yes, yes, ah certainly, yes. That would be great. Yes, we are fully prepared. I have a lawyer. Yes. Thank you. Yes, sir, Monday, nine AM sharp." He carefully placed the receiver on the telephone cradle.

The three of them stared intently at him. "Come on, young man, spill it. Do you have the house?" barked Mr. Stevens. John Stevens had worked endless hours and fought hard to become a floor manager at Westinghouse and often barked when he should have cajoled.

"Yes, sir, the house is ours, but there is one problem." He hesitated, "The owners have to postpone the actual sale until December, late December. There is some development that the realtor didn't want to explain over the phone. If we still want it, we have to go to his office Monday. I said, yes, but, darling, what do you think? Should I call him back?"

Deflated, Ginny tried to take in what the news meant. "Delay moving into the house? The wedding. Where will we live until December?" She was thinking of the foursome, not only herself and Chip.

John, interrupted, "Larry Power at work has a short-term apartment he leases when Westinghouse officials come to town. I can call him for you."

"Could you, please?"

John immediately went to the phone. He came back grinning.

Ginny screamed, Helen placed her hand over her heart and John shook Chip's hand firmly and patted him on the back.

"Larry said the place is yours if you don't mind a furnished one-bedroom and that he and his wife live downstairs."

Chip and Ginny nodded acceptance at the same time. They were both thinking that at least they would have an apartment and not have to stay with either of their parents until the house was finalized. He could spend time with Richard there, while she could stay at Beverly's apartment whenever she wanted.

"Great accomplishment, kids. I'll see Larry at work on Monday and get the details. I want to hear about the house, but later, I have to finish rehearsing and prepare for the Knights' Autumn Dance tonight." He shook Chip's hand once again, kissed his daughter's cheek, picked up a couple of cookies, excused himself, and went back to his basement studio.

"It's ours!"

Helen gushed with joy for the young couple. Yet, try as she might, she could not convince them to stay for dinner. They had to see Chip's parents and inform them of the great news. That would be a short visit, as the two couldn't wait to meet their lovers and celebrate.

Champagne was ready to toast when they arrived at the apartment. Richard quickly switched to beer and held Chip tightly. The women kissed and hugged and hugged and kissed, while Ginny squealed with delight. When she finally calmed down, they explained the delay in the purchase

Greatly disappointed at the delay, Ginny wondered aloud if they should make adjustments to *The Plan*?

"Not tonight, girlfriend," pleaded Beverly, who was slowly unbuttoning her blouse.

"Sorry, fellas, the apartment is ours tonight. Scram."

Pleased, Beverly added, "Yes, scram you two. Go play in the truck." She practically shoved them out the door, then double-bolted the lock.

The men didn't mind leaving, a party at a downtown club was calling to them. On the drive, Richard watched a jubilant Chip sitting across from him. Smiling at his lover, he held his hand out to him. "Mio tesoro, I love you and am trying every day to be my best for you. Please, have patience with me."

"Pull the truck over. I urgently need to kiss you."

The men kissed passionately, roughly.

Panting and wanting more, Richard released himself from his lover. "You do love me."

Chip squeezed Richard's hand. "I love you. We are doing this, right? Imagine, we are going to have a home of our own." Wiggling in his seat, he added. "I am ready to party the night away. Get this truck moving."

Richard laughed. "You got it. Punch Bowl here we come."

***

Later, while lounging in bed with Ginny's arms wrapped tightly around her, Beverly's thoughts turned to the impending wedding.

"You know, this will be a legal wedding, binding and forever." She squeezed her eyes shut; her emotions were bubbling up.

"Yes, I know how real this is but my desire to be with you overpowers my fear." Moving closer she whispered, "We

54

can do this." And ran her fingers over Beverly's lips as she leaned in for a slow kiss.

Beverly felt her passion ignite and in between deep kisses, murmured, "Are you sure, completely and irrevocably sure?"

"Honey, yes. With you by my side, we can conquer anything. I love you. Let me show you how much." She pressed her body against Beverly and ran her fingers down her beautiful hips, as the night slipped away.

***

The night was theirs, but the wedding was looming. When the engagement was announced, Margaret Mary gleefully took over. She was now pushing to finalize the details, many of which Ginny and Chip were content to delegate.

Margaret Mary and Susan coordinated a bridal shower with Mrs. Stevens and Mrs. Foley. Beverly attended and was kept company by Irene O'Leary, an older single woman and office friend, and together they laughed at the stories about a younger Ginny and her constant red-headed companion. Deep inside, Beverly was full of anguish. Ginny fell into her dual role so seamlessly. At once, crushing in her love for Beverly and next totally at ease with showing the world that she was giving herself to Chip. Beverly watched her closely and smiled at all the appropriate times. When the talk of a honeymoon was broached, she excused herself to go outside and have a cigarette. Irene patted her knee and smiled while she rummaged in her bag for matches.

After a light lunch, the gifts were opened. The girlie nighties for her honeymoon received the biggest oo-la-las, causing Ginny to blush and Beverly to dream of nights together.

***

The day of the wedding was splendid with warm sunshine and a light breeze. The altar at Saint Catherine Church burst with colorful fall flowers. The bride was beautiful, the groom handsome with his wide smile and brilliant red hair brushed back in thick rich waves. Beverly and Richard held hands and squeezed them tightly when the final words 'I do' were spoken. Mrs. Stevens cried; Mrs. Foley cried.

The reception was held at the Knights of Columbus Hall instead of at the Stevens' home. Chip and Ginny gave in to hiring the hall at John's insistence that his band play for dancing. Helen had spent weeks designing the three-tier wedding cake and several days baking and decorating it. The results were breathtaking. Two tiers were chocolate with a raspberry filling, one was vanilla with a mocha cream filling, and the frosting for the entire cake was a vanilla buttercream bedazzled with miniature gold florets. A miniature blonde bride and red-headed groom were on top and surrounded by marzipan gold flowers hand-painted by Helen.

Once at the hall, guests were invited to congratulate the newlyweds and then to have a glass of champagne. Richard and Beverly lingered at the far end of the hall and waited so they would be the last in line.

"I can't take this," Richard seethed, speaking quietly to not be overheard. "I didn't know how jealous, angry, and hurt the wedding would make me." He searched Beverly's eyes for understanding.

"Me, too" She touched his arm in solidarity. "How did the two of them ever sucker us into their outrageous plan? It's too late now, isn't it?" Her eyes swelled up with tears. "We must make this work for them and us. Damn, I love her so much."

"Come outside with me, I need some fresh air before I congratulate them."

The two skulked out of the hall, which was filled with laughter and happy chatter.

Breathing in the fresh air, as if it would cleanse all his emotional turmoil away, Richard sighed, "I know. Chip has me wrapped around his little finger. I don't think either of them realizes how difficult it is for you and me." He kept his hands in his pockets, as Beverly lit a cigarette and nodded her head in agreement.

They stood in silence and smiled as a few late arriving guests passed by them.

"Shall we go back inside and put on a smile? I'm ordering a double whiskey. Want to join me?" Richard rubbed his hands over his face.

"Make mine a double, too." She snuffed out her cigarette and took his arm.

"Oh, shit," said Richard. "The receiving line is almost done. I guess we have to do this. Then whiskey!"

They were the last in line. The four put on brave faces for each other. The women hugged, perhaps a little longer than they should have and the men shook hands and didn't make eye contact.

In spite of it all, it was an enchanting wedding; the guests were elated for the young couple. Margaret Mary beamed. Susan and her husband Stan drank too much and reveled in their evening without the baby. Laughing at the absurdity of their having a baby together, Ginny and Chip joined Beverly and Richard at the bar for a quick hello before being whisked away by other guests. The newlyweds held hands throughout the evening, clearly enjoying themselves as only best friends could. They danced a slow dance together after cutting the cake. Chip whispered to his bride, "You will always be my best friend. I feel closer to you now than ever before."

She looked at him and smiled. "I guess the wedding has us all sappy." Totally caught up in the moment, she closed her eyes and pressed her cheek against his.

Chapter Seven

Christmas preparations helped ease the stress caused by the postponement of moving to the new house. Ginny spent time in her mother's kitchen preparing cookies for the church Christmas bazaar and friends and neighbors. She and her mother talked about decorating the new house and how different it was living someplace other than with her parents. Beverly, busy at work, was anxious to start her annual vacation with her father. Chip was finishing up his mid-terms and was barely seen by anyone. Law school was stretching his stamina thin, to a greater extent than he expected, on top of which he had to maintain his volunteer hours with the church after-school program. He often lingered afterward to play the old piano and decompress. Richard, on the other hand, had time to kill. Construction work had slowed to a crawl, with only calls for occasional emergency repairs or interior painting.

Finally, the week before Christmas, the four were able to set up a date to celebrate together. They spent a romantic evening walking through the Boston Common to see the lights and savored a late dinner at Dini's Tremont St. restaurant. The men planned to drop the women at Beverly's apartment after dinner before heading to the furnished apartment. At the last minute, they changed their minds and decided to go into Boston to the Punch Bowl. Beverly tilted her head as she watched them drive off. "Those two certainly like to party. Come on, girlfriend, we have our own celebrating to do."

Saddened that Beverly was going on vacation with her father and wouldn't spend Christmas with her, Ginny was determined not to let her melancholy spoil their last night together and followed her upstairs. This last night had to be special and she was going to agree with whatever her lover suggested, *Everything*, she thought impishly.

Beverly was equally disappointed about the timing of the house purchase, but she wouldn't allow it to disrupt the trip with her father. Her father was getting older and health issues were becoming more prevalent. She looked forward to vacationing with him and perhaps finding the courage to tell him about *The Plan* and the reason for it.

She didn't usually have a Christmas tree, but wanted to do something special for this last Christmas in the apartment. She bought a tiny tree and decorated it with red, white, and green construction paper chains and a box of silver tinsel that she carefully hung on the sparse green branches. "Ginny will adore you," she said to the tree while adding a red paper heart with a B loves G on it as the finishing touch on top.

The tree was a master stroke. Ginny's heart skipped a beat as she walked straight to it when she entered the apartment.

"Oh, Bev, our first tree together. It's perfect. Oh my gosh, you made decorations."

"Look closer." Thrilled, as she wrapped an arm around her.

Ginny's eyes were electric when she spotted the heart. Thinking her own heart would burst, she pulled Beverly close and whispered, "Thank you, thank you. I love you so much."

They held on tightly, savoring the moment.

The decorations reminded Ginny of her childhood and, like a child, she said it was time to exchange presents and that she *must* go first. Beverly was filled with butterflies as she took the small box in her hand. She gasped when she opened it and saw the ring.

Ginny tipped her chin up so that their eyes met. "Beverly Jean Taylor, will you marry *me* and be with me forever?" The box contained a pinky ring with a small sapphire.

Touched by the romantic sentiment, she hesitantly said, "Ah, girlfriend, you know that we can never marry or even let people know that we are lovers and besides you are a married woman," she added, attempting to be humorous.

Ginny removed the ring from the box and slipped it on Beverly's right-hand pinky finger. She swallowed hard and leaned in for a kiss. "I'm serious, Bev."

She closed her eyes, absorbed the gentleness of the kiss, and said, "Yes, you romantic fool. A million times, yes."

"Soon we we'll be in our own home living as a couple. In our hearts, we *will* be married."

Light kisses and gentle hugs led to more. The passion between them flamed and the rest of the evening was filled with a torrent of lovemaking. Satiated long after midnight, the two women fell asleep, until jerked awake by a loud, insistent ringing, Beverly groggily answered the phone next to her bed. She sat up straight while pulling the blankets to cover her naked body from the chill in the room.

"Crap. It's one-thirty. Hey, slow down. What? I can hardly hear you."

"What is it? Who is it? Is it really one thirty?"

She lifted her finger signaling for Ginny to hold on. "Oh my God, no." She covered the receiver and said, "It's Chip. Sorry, say that again. Where's Richard? You're kidding?"

Ginny was getting frantic now, "What's going on? Is Chip hurt? Where's Richard?"

"Yes, we're on our way. How much? Got it. We'll be there soon." She hung up the phone, wide-eyed. "There was a raid at the Punch Bowl. The fellas were separated in the chaos and Chip was arrested. Crap! Geez, we have to go to the police station downtown and pay his fine so there won't be any charges. He said his name is Paul Robeson and we have to bring fifty dollars. Imbeciles."

"Who is Paul Robeson?"

"Come on, hurry. Robeson is an actor, singer, and Negro activist."

Ginny paused and wondered how she knew that. She admonished herself for not keeping up. Once in the car, she asked, "Why would he use a phony name?"

Beverly let out an exasperated sigh. "Chip and I were talking recently about the clubs that he and Richard go to. That's when he mentioned that he keeps his wallet in the car or truck and uses a phony name if confronted. He thought he was quite clever using Paul Robeson."

"Why?" interrupted Ginny.

"Well, although I knew of Robeson, I didn't know that he was a lawyer when younger. Chip said he gave up being a lawyer because of constant discrimination. The hate was too much. Robeson is somehow involved with the Civil Rights Movement now. Chip admires him."

"Hmm," said Ginny as she thought about Robeson and her lack of knowledge of the world beyond her neighborhood.

"There's still so much discrimination and hate—and here we have to get Chip out of jail just for being at that night club with a man. It's a shitty world," growled Beverly.

"I guess, you're right. But right now, I am so angry at those two fools."

The women arrived at the police station within forty-five minutes. Ginny was fuming as she climbed into the back seat with Chip, who was nursing a black eye and had a torn shirt.

"Where's your jacket? You idiots." She started punching him, building up steam with every blow. "What were you thinking? We're going to pass the house papers on Monday. What if someone who knows you saw you get arrested? You and Richie are such idiots. Duncan Foley, talk to me."

"I will if you stop hitting me." Chip shrunk in the seat. He shivered because of Ginny's rage rather than the cold.

She stopped hitting him after giving him one more good hard punch in the arm. Beverly drove and didn't say a word.

He started to cry. "I do not know where Richard went. Maybe he was arrested, and maybe he is hurt. The police were hitting everyone with their Billy clubs and yelling Merry Christmas, perverts. Gin-Gin, it was awful. I was terrified."

She wouldn't let it go. "This could have been the end of all our hard work. The end of our marriage, the house, my future with Beverly, your future with *Richie*. We pass the papers on Monday. Monday, Chip! And you two had to go to the Bowl. Geez, sometimes I hate you." She fell back against the car seat and stared out the window. More than angry, Ginny was afraid of what might have happened to Chip and Richard if they had been beaten by the police.

Beverly quietly listened to Ginny's rage and waited to pull the car over when they were closer to home, and turned to Chip. "Are you hurt anywhere besides your eye?"

He whispered no.

"You can't outrun the consequences of being so damn careless forever. Crap. Do you want me to drive by Richard's house to check if his truck is there?"

"Please. I'm so sorry." He fought back the tears. Over and over in his mind he whimpered, *why does everyone hate us?*

"You did take his truck in town, not the T? It's almost three and I have to leave by seven. Ginny's right, you're idiots. I need a cigarette."

Ginny demanded to be dropped off at the furnished apartment first. She was too furious to stay in the car any longer with Chip. She would remind him in no uncertain terms when he returned from seeing Richard how he ruined her last night with Beverly.

Still wishing she had a cigarette, Beverly watched him walk Ginny to their door, then shakily stumble back to the car. He climbed into the front seat. "She said to give you this," he offered her a half-empty pack of Pall Mall.

"My good God," she said glancing back at the door where Ginny waved and held up one finger. "I love her." She held up one finger and nodded. Ginny went inside and Beverly rolled up the window, pushed the lighter in on the dashboard, lit her cigarette, and drove to Richard's house. Halfway there she realized that she had forgotten to give Ginny her Christmas present. She felt miserable and punched Chip in the arm.

He didn't say anything, just rubbed his arm and prayed that Richard was home. The truck was in the wide driveway and his light was on. Beverly tooted her horn one time, while Chip prayed it wouldn't wake up his family. Richard opened his bedroom window wide and leaned out. Chip leaned out the car window, waved, and gave a thumbs-up. Richard did the same and went back in and shut off the light.

"Idiots, as sure as hell, I'm not going through this with you two ever again. Damn it! You know how dangerous it is for us." Beverly's hands shook while she lit another cigarette. She fought back tears. "AND, you screwed up my last night with Ginny."

"I am so sorry. Sorry, truly sorry."

***

After he returned home, Richard lay awake in his bed while the adrenaline from the police raid coursed through his veins. Mercifully, his brother Joe, who shared the small room, was on his way to New York to pick up their Aunt Maria and her daughters Lena and Christina so they could spend Christmas and New Year's Eve with the family.

They had been having such a swell time dancing and celebrating with club friends, Rey and Jeff, when the bar lights started flashing signaling that a police raid was coming. It came fast and viciously. The Punch Bowl had the liveliest, swinging music and the youngest crowd in Park Square. It was their place to party. Beverly had often suggested that they go to the classier Napoleon Club down the street. But he found it stuffy and he didn't like to wear the required jacket and tie. He wanted to dance, sweat, and hold Chip tightly. Now he berated himself for not listening to her.

He rolled over feeling guilty for escaping the cops. It wasn't the first time he escaped a raid, but it was the most terrifying. His back and arms were bruised and ached from the Billy clubs that swung at him as he pushed and shoved back the police and tried to clear a path for Chip and his friends to get out the back door. When he got outside, beyond the clamor and the chaos, Chip was nowhere to be found. Others were running for their lives. He ran and hid in his truck that was parked down the street away from the bar. At the front of the bar, men were yelling and screaming and some were crying. Onlookers on the sidewalk were for the most part cheering the cops on. The cops were cursing and throwing men into their paddy wagons. Richard stayed until the last of the cops were gone. He walked around to the back of the bar again and then back to the front. The lights were out and the street was quiet. A couple of men lingered, searching for their friends. No one had seen his beloved redhead. Richard, with tears in his eyes, climbed into his truck. He pounded the steering wheel and screamed until his voice was raw.

Richard prayed. His head was pounding, his stomach in knots. Should he go to Chip and Ginny's apartment? He thought about calling Beverly but didn't know what that would accomplish. She and Ginny would be asleep. He rolled over, clenched his fists, and held back tears.

A car horn tooted. Fast as the proverbial lightning bolt he jumped out of bed, thankful that he had left his light on, and flew to the window. He lifted the squeaky window and with a heavy sigh of relief saw Chip waving to him. They gave the all's good sign and he did the same. He heard his father cursing from his bedroom and quickly waved goodbye, lowered the window, and shut off his light. Sleep did not come easily.

Chapter Eight

The paperwork went smoothly on Monday. Ginny, Chip, and his lawyer, Dennis Jenkins, a professor from Newton College Law School, met the realtor and the seller's lawyer. As part of the agreement, they would receive the keys to the house on January 1st.

"Merry Christmas, Dennis," called Ginny as she hopped in Chip's car. Chip talked with the professor for a few more minutes, shook his hand, and got in the driver's seat.

"It's ours, really ours. We did it. Want to drive by?"

"Yes! It's frustrating that we have to suffer another eleven days, count them, eleven days before we can get inside. I would have liked to have celebrated New Year's Eve there with Bev."

"She was great Saturday night. She saved me from a night in jail and who knows what else. Thanks for not still beating me up over it." He cringed thinking about the trauma of the police raid.

"I should give you a few more whacks," laughed Ginny who was in too good a mood about the house to replay the trip to the police station.

"I'll give her the $50 as soon as she returns. Or do you want to hold it for her?"

"No rush."

"Will she call you on Christmas? Oh, I forgot, she said she has a Christmas gift for you and will give it to you when she returns. I know, my fault. Sorry, Gin-Gin. Forgive me?"

This time, she did punch him on his arm for forgetting. But in the end, she always did forgive her Chipper. She didn't want to say it out loud but it appeared he was roughed up by the police more than he admitted.

"No, she can't call. She and her dad are going on a cruise somewhere. No telephones on the ocean, smart guy."

He ignored her sarcasm and continued to drive toward Milton.

"When are you going to see Richie? I'm sure he's upset about Saturday. Not to repeat myself, but you two can be beyond stupid. Why didn't you go to the Napoleon as Beverly suggested?" She pouted; her mood soured. He didn't say another word. He hated that she continued to snidely call Richard, Richie.

Chip was done reliving Saturday night and he didn't want to upset her any further. Beverly had given Richard a spare key to her apartment before she left. He wasn't sure if Ginny knew, and decided not to say a word. His only reply was, "We are going to meet later tonight. He had a whole family thing yesterday and could not get away. Just as well, I was dog-tired. Oh, my mother called while you were in the shower this morning, she wants to know when we are having a housewarming party. Geez."

"That's funny. Margaret Mary called yesterday while you slept and pestered me to set a time to talk about it. You know, you should go buy another winter coat. I'm sorry you lost your new one, even though it was your dumb fault, but this rag-tag thing you've worn since high school should go in the trash. I can't believe you had it in the closet at the apartment."

He laughed inwardly at her sudden concern about his choice of a coat. The coat was a sentimental treasure that he had worn the first night he met Richard. He hadn't mentioned to her that he was heading straight to Jordan Marsh after he dropped her off. Feeling sorry for himself, he was convinced that he deserved at least a new coat.

He bought a blue plaid, double breasted Mackinaw woolen jacket, and a tan scarf and leather gloves to go with it. A pair of black wingtip shoes somehow found their way to the check-out counter as well. Riding the T back to Forest Hills, he pursed his lips as he pondered briefly who ended up with his cashmere coat. Someone at the bar, or more than likely a fucking cop bastard, got lucky and would be warm with style this winter.

Richard was already at the apartment when Chip arrived. He had been pacing for an hour. Chip wasn't late, he just had to get out of his house before he exploded from the constant commotion made by his family, aunt, and cousins. He loved them immeasurably, but his nerves were worn thin and only holding Chip and knowing for certain that he was safe would calm him. Christmas on Thursday was fast approaching and this would be the last time that they would spend together until the end of the year. He couldn't believe it was going to be a new decade. A decade in their own home.

His thoughts flip-flopped between Chip and the tasks of *The Plan*. The agreed-upon timeline dictated that Richard was to meet Beverly on New Year's Eve, her first full day back from vacation, and to propose to her that night. An official engagement would pave the way for them to lend a hand with the Milton house repairs and to move in as soon as they were married. Richard was still not gung-ho about the bull crap proposal. His Catholic conscience ached.

Chip had barely knocked on the door when Richard flung it open, grabbed him by the back of his head, and pulled him inside while giving him a fervent and hungry kiss. Richard then fell to his knees, wrapped his arms around him, and held him, as Chip leaned back to close the door.

"I thought I'd lost you; I couldn't find you; we can't go through this again! I'm never going back to Punch Bowl. My love, my lover, mio tesoro, are you hurt?"

He slowly stood up and noticed Chip's black eye and a bruise on his chin. Wiping tears from his eyes, he held Chip's face, kissed it all over, and begged for forgiveness for not getting him out of the club safely.

Chip was taken aback by his display of affection. He had experienced Richard's anger many times but never saw fear so raw with emotion, never with tears in his eyes. He released himself slightly from Richard, touched his dark curly hair, and replied,

"Baby, I'm fine now that I'm here with you." *Damn*, he thought, *I said I would never call him baby.* Before he could speak Richard chimed in,

"You called me baby," he said. "You can call me baby anytime. Come here." He hugged his lover close, promising never to lose him again.

"I'm here now. Why don't we go sit down? I want to take off my coat and I have a Christmas present for you." Richard's tears unnerved him.

He released him and moved to the sofa. Richard wiped his face on a handkerchief from his back pocket and reached for one of the beers he had brought to toast the holidays. Chip unbuttoned his new coat, thinking this was not the time to show it off, hung it up carefully on the coat rack, and removed a small package from its pocket. Sitting next to Richard, he gladly accepted a beer, opened it, and had a swig. "To us, Richard, *my* love."

"We can talk about Saturday night later, and the fact that *we* now have our own home, but, first, your Christmas present." He passed the package, sat back, drank more of his beer, and grinned.

"I have a present for you, too. Hold on, it's in my jacket pocket." Richard walked over to the jacket that he had thrown carelessly on the floor near the small Christmas tree. "Hey, what do you know, Beverly has a Christmas tree. Huh. I didn't get her a Christmas present. I don't remember what *The Plan* said. Did it say anything about a present? You know, I like Beverly, she's very, what's the word? Caring."

He came back to the sofa and gave Chip a small box wrapped in red paper.

"Too late to worry about that now. Tonight is for us. Shall we open them at the same time?" offered Chip. "Go," he said, not waiting for an answer.

He was impressed that Richard went to the trouble of buying him a set of elite Parker Pens. He knew he didn't find them in any store in Cleary Square. He must have gone to Boston to buy them. He gushed with pride at Richard's thoughtfulness. Richard on the other hand was somewhat puzzled by the empty key rings. It was a double-ring set, he noticed, and his initials were on a miniature truck that dangled slightly.

Chip saw his confusion and rescued him. "Baby, the double rings symbolize our love together, the truck, well, that is for your truck, and the key chain as a gift will be complete when I get the keys to the house and make a copy for you. For our home."

Richard let that sink in for a moment. He smiled and replied, "Our wedding rings."

"I love you so much. Merry Christmas." He leaned in and kissed Richard. It was then he realized for the first time since he arrived how much his chin hurt. "Ow, shit," he groaned. He held on to his jaw and tried moving it around. "Damn cops. I panicked when I lost you in the crowd. Never again."

"You are hurt. My kissing must have hurt. I'm so sorry. Tell me what happened Saturday night. Did the fuckin' cops pound on you?" Fury built and his stomach twisted with the thought of it.

The two sat back holding hands and holding their gifts and discussed the horror of living through the vicious and unprovoked raid by the cursed Boston Police.

A few hours later, Richard stood up, fastened his slacks, and went to the kitchen. He stood for a moment with the refrigerator door open, smiling and glowing after their passionate lovemaking. He brought back a bag with two large submarine sandwiches from the deli near the apartment.

"I am famished. Are these roast beef with all the fixings? My love, you are amazing. Gimme." He laughed as he tore open the bag and laid it on the coffee table. Taking a huge bite from one of the sandwiches he moaned with pleasure, his aching jaw forgotten.

Richard swallowed three large bites before he was able to say a word. "This is the best sub I have ever eaten. Sorry, Mama."

Not enthusiastic about bringing up the subject, Chip nevertheless sheepishly asked, "Are you prepared to ask Bev to marry you on New Year's Eve?" He buttoned his shirt and tucked it into his corduroys.

Richard put down his sandwich, wiped his mouth with the paper napkin from inside the bag, and glanced sideways at Chip. "No. I can't do it. I am just not ready for the foolishness that will follow with my parents and brothers and sister. The girls are going to kill me. You are going to kill me, I know. I can't do it now. I'm too upset about Saturday, I don't have any work for the next two weeks, it's just too much. Plus, I don't have a ring for her. I can't give her a family ring; it wouldn't be right." His eyes pleaded with Chip to save him.

"Bev does not know then?"

"No. How could she? She's out on some yacht with her father living it up." He waved his hand in the air.

"Have you thought about what you are going to say to her or what you are going to do? Ginny will be royally pissed. Jesus H. Christ, I never gave any thought to how our emotions would be stretched and twisted. I only ever saw the end goal, us living together. Yes, spoiled and used to getting my way. Sorry." He kissed him again, tenderly.

Richard was quiet. He ate a bite of his sandwich, drank some of his beer, and mulled over a few possibilities. Finally, he stood up and paced. After his third time around the room, he stopped and with a glimmer of an idea offered, "I will ask her on Valentine's Day. That's romantic. Girls like romance. Don't you think?"

Chip stood up and hugged him, "Great thinking. I will tell Ginny and soften the blow with her before Bev comes back.

If she knows that Ginny is fine with the change, then she will be fine, too. You are a clever man. Come here, let me show you how impressed I am with you."

***

Ginny and Chip spent a quiet Christmas morning in the furnished apartment before splitting their time between their parents' homes. They sat on the floor in front of a small Christmas tree and drank hot chocolate, discussing what they would tackle first at the house and the next phase of *The Plan.*

Ginny mentioned the folder full of paint samples, furniture photos, and design concepts that she had sketched and shared with her mother earlier in the week. She longed to go over everything with Beverly. Thankfully, Beverly and Richard could officially pitch in after they announced their engagement and asked to rent the vacant apartment.

"Seven days! Almost ours, the four of us!"

Chip put down his hot chocolate and started to speak, then hesitated. He loosened his Christmas tie, as he carefully chose his words to explain Richard's state of mind and deviation from his to-do list. He tried to talk up the changing of Richard's proposal to Beverly until Valentine's Day. Ginny closed her eyes. "Richie will always be the weak link. How do I keep him on track?"

Chapter Nine

Beverly was aware of her father as he strolled to the outermost railing at the end of the deck. He was getting a tan. She tilted her head up toward the sun. She, too, felt refreshed. Time away from the oft-overwhelming *Plan* and the frantic winter holidays was divine.

Harry scanned the horizon. "What a glorious vacation," he called back to his daughter. She waved and he made his way to her. He sat on the deck chair, removed his wide-brimmed hat, held out his hand to her, and said calmly, "We have to talk, sweetie."

His tone immediately caught her attention. She had been reading *On the Road* by Jack Kerouac, an adventure beyond her sensibilities, though Mexico and its cigarettes for six cents a pack intrigued her. Did she ever refer to anyone as *cats*? Feeling old, she placed her sunglasses on her head and replied, "What is it? Something wrong?"

Harry removed his sunglasses and carefully placed them on the deck chair blanket. "Beverly Jean, are you happy?"

"Dad, yes, what a funny question. This cruise and the warm weather are incredible. What's going on?"

Harry had a habit of speaking clearly and concisely. "Oh, sweetie, there is no other way to say it. I have terminal cancer of the liver. This will be our last trip. The doctors have given me a few precious months before my body breaks down and, um, stops. I'm sorry."

Beverly hugged her father, always so robust and self-assured. She expected him to live forever. She knew he hadn't been his usual self for the past six months, but she didn't think for a minute that he had a deadly illness.

"Dad, are you sure? Have you spoken to other doctors? Is there anything I can do?" She started to cry. Questions filled her mind. Denial begged for attention. The little girl in her wished her daddy could make the bad illness go away. She couldn't lose him as well as her mother.

Harry held her close and stroked her beautiful auburn hair. "You have your mother's hair, you know." He kissed the top of her head, the same way he had when she was a child. "I'm sorry. I'm so, so sorry."

She searched his eyes for the question he seemed to be holding back. "Dad, there's more? What is it?"

"Sweetie, you know I've retired. Once I received the diagnosis, I paid off the lingering bills, and put the house in your name." She started to protest but he motioned for her to hold on. "I also opened a savings account and reassigned my stocks to you. The house you can choose to keep or sell. It's totally up to you. I only ask that I remain in our house until I die."

She burst out crying again. "Oh, Daddy, no, no, no. I can't lose you. I can't. I don't care about owning the house and having your money. I care about you. I need you."

Harry held his daughter and struggled to maintain his composure. He had purposely chosen the outside deck to tell her about his diagnosis to help him stay composed. He shifted and raised her chin with one hand, "Tell me. Tell me honestly, are you happy?"

She tried to wipe away the free-flowing tears. "Never mind about me. Daddy, isn't there anything the doctors can do?"

"Sweetie, Beverly Jean, I've had my life. It's time for you to have yours. I know that you're smart and fiercely independent. Stay away from my inflexible, self-serving family, and live your life."

With that, Harry stood up. "I'm tired. I'm going to our suite and rest. He removed a large envelope from under his blanket and passed it to her. "Here, read this while I rest. We can talk at dinner. I love you. My time is coming sooner than I expected, but..." He stopped there, kissed her on the top of her head one more time, straightened himself up to his full height, and walked away.

Beverly was too paralyzed by the devastating news to move. The large envelope sat unopened on her lap as her mind swirled. She wanted to follow him to the suite, shake him and yell for him to stop this cruel joke. Her heart sunk; tears trickled slowly down her cheeks again. With little interest, she reluctantly picked up the envelope. It was as he said, paperwork showing the transfer of the deed of the house to her, a modest bank account and stock portfolio with her name on it and the name of the law firm that would handle her father's will and be available to her throughout the process. There was a handwritten note from Harry. He said that he was honored to be her father and worried about her at the same time. She meant the world to him and deserved every bit of happiness that she could find. Lastly, were the keys and the title to his treasured Pontiac Catalina convertible. She didn't know whether to laugh or cry as she held tightly onto the car keys. She had always teased him about giving his convertible to her.

The last three days of the cruise were full of highs and lows. Both Beverly and Harry tried to be courageous and put on a good face. At times, she saw him staring off into space. At times, he saw her trying to hide her tears. After many go-rounds, Harry acquiesced to Beverly's plan to resign from her position at Westinghouse, give up her apartment and moved back home with him by February 1st. When he questioned her about companion, Ginny, she paused, thinking about *The Plan* and her list of tasks to move it forward. None of it mattered to her now. She said Ginny could visit them on the weekends. She had never told him that Ginny had married. Harry felt at ease with her explanation and was too weary to ask for any other details. It was unbearable for her not to tell him about the convoluted scheme, but why cause added stress and heartache? Staying close to him and keeping him comfortable was her only priority.

Chapter Ten

Ginny was on pins and needles in anticipation of Beverly's return. Her arms longed for her. There was so much to discuss now that the house buying was settled. The repairs, the painting, furniture shopping, and the next crucial steps to securing their future. But all that would come soon enough; their first night back together would be spent rejoicing in their love for each other.

She asked Chip to pick her up after work and drive her to Beverly's to save time by avoiding taking the bus. He easily agreed to drop her off and pick her up in the morning. On the drive there, he reminded her about explaining Richard's change of heart about the timing of the engagement.

Beverly fully expected to celebrate the New Year on a special date culminating with Richard's proposal. Perhaps with Richard's postponement, she and Beverly would be able to spend the night together instead. Ginny and Chip were supposed to be going with Margaret Mary and her new boyfriend to a New Year's Eve party at Susan and Stan's. She would gladly cancel her double date to be with Beverly. Richard's decision didn't significantly affect *The Plan*, but she wouldn't say that to Richard, even though she knew it was petty to continue to punish him for the hurt and anger from the night of the raid.

Beverly opened the door with tears in her eyes. "Oh, hon, my father is dying," she stammered. "I'm going to be an orphan." She grabbed onto a stunned Ginny.

"What, what do you mean? I've missed you so much." She tried to pull away to look at her, but Beverly held on tightly and cried achingly painful sobs. When she had cried herself out, she stepped back. Her face was red and blotchy, her nose running. Ginny searched for a handkerchief in her coat pocket for her.

"What are you talking about? Please, tell me what is going on?" She removed her damp coat, hung it on the corner coat rack, and followed Beverly to the sofa.

Between fresh tears and wiping her nose, Beverly described the afternoon on the cruise when her father broke the horrible news to her, and her safety net shattered. She clung to Ginny's hands with her own and blurted,

"I'm moving home to be with him in his last months. I am leaving Westinghouse for now and giving up my apartment. I have no choice. I have to be with him."

Ginny froze. Her future came crashing down. Her world plunged into darkness; her mind spiraled out of control. Tears of her own spilled onto her cheeks.

"Oh, Bev, no. I'm so, so sorry. Can I help? Your father's such a great guy." Then it hit her. "Are you leaving me?"

"Heavens, no. I will never leave you." She touched her face and kissed her lips. "But for now I have to be with my sick father. Please understand." She shifted her body and noticed the dying Christmas tree in the corner, Ginny's forgotten Christmas present, and her unopened suitcases from her trip.

"I keep my promises." She leaned in to kiss her. Their lips touched lightly at first. She wiped away Ginny's tears and kissed her completely. "I still have my Christmas present for you. Shall I get it?"

Numb, Ginny nodded.

Beverly wiped fallen pine needles from the top of the present and offered it. "I hope you like it. I'm afraid it's not as extravagant as my ring." She wiggled her fingers. "But come on, open it."

Ginny slowly opened the present, her mind preoccupied with the startling news. "Oh my, it's so beautiful and extravagant. Here put it on me." Beverly had given her a heart charm engraved with the words 'forever love' and dangling on a knotted gold chain.

She kissed Ginny's neck, and paused, her mind cascading back to the grim conversation. "I told my father I would move in by February first. In the meantime, I'll stay with him on the weekends. We have a month to figure this out. I know it throws off our moving in together, but I have faith in us." She inhaled deeply. "This is going to be torture, it's tearing me apart, but it is only for a few months. That's all he has." She tried to stifle her tears. "Come on, I need a drink."

Ginny was frozen in place. Her mind was swirling, her body numb. She mindlessly followed her into the kitchen.

"I'm sorry your present is so late." She kissed the top of Ginny's head. Ginny simply closed her eyes, afraid. Beverly struggled to stay strong. "I blame the two idiots for partying at the Punch Bowl. That night seems a lifetime ago. Oh hell, I'm going to have a scotch. What do you want?"

She poured a double, lit a cigarette, and passed Ginny a bottle of cola as they moved from the small kitchen back to the parlor sofa, not speaking. Each of them tried to make sense of the heartbreaking and disruptive situation and how they could stay together throughout the chaotic months ahead. Ginny tried with all her might not to start crying again. She was upset that Mr. Taylor was sick and devastated that Beverly would lose her only parent and dearest friend. She didn't know how to react. She pushed her hand through her hair and thought of her brother.

Beverly kissed her blonde hair and murmured, "Have I ever told you how endearing it is when you run your hand through your hair, your beautiful blonde hair? I love you, girlfriend, forever love." When tears filled up in Ginny's eyes again, she held her close and softly cried with her.

The two were lost in conversation when a knock on the door startled them. Chip, with Richard behind him, was grinning when the door opened.

"Happy New Year, Beverly! Welcome back."

"Come in fellas."

The men gave each other an oh-oh sideways glance, came in and shut the door. Both women's faces were red and blotchy.

Chip spoke first. "Bev, did Ginny tell you about the delay in your engagement announcement? I can explain. Well, um, Richard can explain. Not to worry, we know it will work out fine."

Beverly was puzzled by his statement.

Ginny immediately interrupted. "Fellas, Bev's father is dying. She has to move home to Rhode Island to be with him." She choked on the words and put her hand to her mouth to hold back her sobs.

The men immediately hugged Beverly. They had questions but weren't sure how to ask.

"Ginny can fill you in. It's been a long day. I'm spent and need to go to sleep. Red, would you take her home?"

Ginny absentmindedly finished her cola, while wishing she could spend the night with Beverly. She found it unsettling that Richard was giving her girlfriend another long hug.

Beverly pulled away from Richard, "Hang on a minute. No "proposal date" with you tomorrow, Romeo." She touched his chest warmly.

"I know. Don't worry about it now," said an equally relieved Richard. He stole a glance at Chip, then Ginny, begging them to not say a word.

"I can't think about visiting your parents anyway and pretending to be happy and celebrating an engagement." In her mind, she added, *the ridiculous, phony engagement*. Her agitation was at a breaking point. "I'm sorry. Go on. Go home. Please. Thank you for being here tonight, but I'm exhausted. I'll see you at the Milton house as soon as you get the key."

Ginny slowly walked to get her coat. She could see the emotional exhaustion overtaking Beverly.

"I know that this screws everything up. You understand, don't you?"

"Of course I do, I'm truly sorry that your father is so sick. I'll help you in any way that you want. You know that. Try to sleep. I love you and will see you Friday. If you need me, please, please call. I'm going straight home from work tomorrow. Darn it, Chip and I arranged to meet Margaret Mary and her new boyfriend at Susan's for her New Year's Eve party. Do you want me to cancel?"

"No. Go to the party. I have an awful lot of sorting and packing to do to get ready to move. Don't say anything at work tomorrow. I'm going to hold off until I return to the office on Monday to tell Briggs. But, will you call me before you leave for the party? Will you call me when you get back from the party, too? I need to hear your voice."

"Yes, are you sure you don't want me to stay?"

"I can't." is all she could manage to say.

Ginny gave her a loving kiss and walked out the door. Shattered.

Chip drove her back to their apartment and offered stay with her. She was grateful for the ride and once at the apartment, she wanted to be alone for a while. He promised to come home early.

The men drove silently toward the Villa Rosa Restaurant. Once seated at a booth in the back, Richard spoke first.

"Death scares me. I've seen too much of it in my family already. Shit. Don't you go dying on me."

"Oh, please. A young, handsome guy like me. I am going to live to one hundred."

"Okay, that's good. Hey, do you know what repairs you want to start on at the house?"

Chip recognized this as a sign that Richard was done talking about death and eagerly ran through his wish list of changes for the house. Their conversation was animated and their eyes were locked on each other the entire time. The reality of their own home was bringing them closer together.

New Year's Eve at Susan's was unbearable for Ginny. The party itself was lively and jam-packed with people. Margaret Mary and her date, Freddie, an undergraduate from Harvard, brought a Wellesley friend and her fiancé, Joe Albright. Margaret Mary introduced her friend as Marie from Prague but clarified that she preferred to be called by her American name, Madeline.

Susan noticed the less-than-usual liveliness emanating from the still newlyweds. She cornered Ginny at one point and asked outright what was going on. She complained about holiday fatigue. Susan didn't buy it and started to probe, but was interrupted by other guests. When midnight struck, the crowd cheered and kissed and popped cheap bottles of champagne. Ginny and Chip quietly slipped out not long after, leaving Margaret Mary with Freddie swaying cheek to cheek on the dance floor.

Richard spent New Year's Eve with his parents. His mother cooked an abundance of traditional dishes, and he overindulged in her exceptional cotechino con lenticchie. He explained to his family during dinner the dreadful news about Beverly's father and the upcoming pause in their relationship.

"Don't let her slip away, Ricardo. Do something for her to show her you love her. I'll cook tomorrow for her. You bring it to her and give her our love."

"Mama, did you say you love her?" Richard said almost teasingly.

Angela shrugged her shoulders. "If you love the skinny English girl, then I will, too. So, when are you going to propose to her? If she is engaged, she will come back as soon as she can and she won't forget about you while in Rhode Island. Ricardo, do right by her. Neither of you are kids." His father poured another glass of wine and stared intently at his oldest son.

Richard tried hard to mask his relief about postponing the engagement. Sticking to his challenging script, he answered, "I was going to propose to her tonight. Now is not the time. She's too upset to bother about romance and might think I am proposing out of pity. She wouldn't like that." He invented the last bit about pity. Continuing, he said, "My friends are getting the key to their new home tomorrow. I'm going to ask if she wants to go see it with me. It might take her mind off of her father for a few hours." He was on a roll and his nerves were building. "Maybe Chip will hire us to do some work around the house this winter, Papa."

Angela quickly responded. "What hire? Ricardo, Chip is your friend. You volunteer. He is not very tough or big. He has soft hands; you have skills. You help him as a friend. Someday, when he is a fancy lawyer, maybe he will help you. Think, Ricardo. You be there for your friends. Not ask them to pay you."

Deflated, Richard answered, "Yes, of course, Mama. I'll offer to help tomorrow." He yearned to mention that Chip had easy money from his grandparents and why shouldn't he hire Ruggiero Contracting to work on many of the overdue repairs to the old house. But his mama was right, Chip certainly didn't know how to do any type of manual labor. Richard had missed his chance to be a hero for his family. He didn't want Chip's money but, hell, his family could use the business.

Joe, who had only been half-listening, finally realized that his brother was talking about a paying job.

"Hey, do you think your friends might consider hiring me? I can help you with anything you do for him. Do they need new bathrooms? You know I do great work with tiles. And, I know some about plumbing. Will you ask?"

"Sfigato! I don't know if I should recommend my slob of a brother." He winked. "I'll ask." Joe working with him would bring in some money. He knew Chip would hire Joe in a minute. Grinning, he held up his plate, "How about another slice of ricotta cake, Mama?"

She gladly cut him another large slice. "Now go, everyone, go to your celebrations. Papa, Ricardo, put Guy Lombardo on the television. I will be in shortly."

The siblings jumped up from the table, but their father said firmly, "Stop! First, clean up so Mama can relax and watch her Guy Lombardo." The three younger men complained as usual but washed the dishes and moved as fast as they could out the door. Richard was content to stay with his Mama, it would give him something to take his mind off the changes he knew were coming in the new year.

1960

"We deserve to experience love fully, equally, without shame, and without compromise." Elliot Page

Chapter Eleven

Chip and Ginny, bundled in their warm winter coats, stood outside on the sidewalk in front of their new home, unaware of the biting cold. In their young eyes, the home was magnificent with its wide front porch and pillared balcony above it. Chip pronounced that he would call it The Eliot from now on. "A grand name for a grand house," he said grinning from ear to ear. He likened himself to being the lord of the manor. She thought he was being a tad flamboyant and the drab brown house not yet worthy of such a name, but the house was theirs. Her heart skipped a beat.

From their vantage point, they could tell that the owners had left the Venetian blinds for both apartments. *Privacy!* The conspirators snickered. The front entranceway had one double door that led to a wide vestibule. The first-floor apartment door was towards the back on the left with the stairs leading up to the second-floor apartment immediately on the right. There was a walk-in closet under the stairs. Both the upstairs and downstairs doors had stained glass on the top half and a hand ringer that turned in the middle of the door. The first-floor apartment door opened to the parlor that led to a small bedroom or study in the back of the house. The kitchen was on the other side in the back with a dining room in the middle and the bedroom on the right front of the house overlooking the wide, elegant street. The bathroom was alongside a tremendous closet that the realtor had insisted could be remodeled into a baby nursery. The upstairs apartment was similar in design but with the addition of the balcony and attic rooms.

The house was clean and empty except for odd pieces of furniture. The previous owners were told that they could leave whatever they didn't want to take, as long as it wasn't trash. The two were pleased to find on the first floor two mahogany end tables in the parlor, a sideboard in the dining room, and a beaten-up but usable kitchen table with four chairs in the corner of the kitchen. The upstairs was empty except for an old metal full-bed frame in the bedroom and an ancient refrigerator in the kitchen.

A subdued Beverly and Richard arrived fifteen minutes later. They exchanged hugs and gathered in the first-floor kitchen. Richard put the large bag of food that his mother had prepared on the table. Beverly didn't have much of an appetite and preferred sharing the food later as a first meal together. It was only ten in the morning so Chip offered to put the food in the upstairs refrigerator. Richard suggested going with him and starting a to-do list as they walked through the house. Ginny eagerly agreed and said that she and Beverly would start on the first floor. Unseen, Beverly grimaced, determined to get through the day.

"How are you doing, honey? Did you sleep at all?"

"I have to be honest with you."

Ginny sat down and held her breath. There was a loud knock on the door. Startled, she jumped up and scurried down the hallway, out the apartment door to the main entrance. Shortly, Margaret Mary and Freddie came bouncing into the near empty parlor.

"Surprise, we hoped to be the first to congratulate you and Chip on your new home. Holy moly, this house, it's the most!"

Beverly came out from the kitchen. Ginny's eyes apologized to Beverly for the intrusion. "Hello, you two, Happy New Year. The fellas just went upstairs to the other apartment. I'll go get them so Chip can say hello. Back in a jiffy." Glad to be elsewhere, Beverly went out to the split front entranceway and up the curved stairs to the second floor.

"Oh, hi. Happy New Year. Thanks." Margaret Mary barely glanced at her. She was already pulling off her winter coat and anxious for a tour of the house. Freddie stood by with his hands in his coat pockets as Margaret Mary infected Ginny with her exuberance.

Chip bounded down the stairs to greet their mutual childhood friend while Beverly stayed upstairs with Richard, filling him in about the unexpected visitors. There were no chairs on the second floor and the two stood awkwardly in the empty dining room.

"Richard, will you help me clean out my apartment? Most of the stuff is used and if you, Red, and especially Ginny, want any of it for here, you can have it. I haven't had a chance to ask her, but I will as soon as Margaret Mary leaves."

"Yeah, of course. Ah, um, I'm sorry about your father. I don't know what I would do if either of my parents were to get sick, let alone die." With downcast eyes, repeated, "I'm so sorry."

"Thanks. I'm numb from the shock of it. I'm coming back but I don't have any idea when. Do you want to continue with *The Plan*?"

Rubbing his rough hand over his face, he sighed, "We're already in it. Hard to walk away now. You know I love Chip. Did you see him earlier? He's calling the house The Eliot. He is like, I don't know, like a kid at Christmas. As tough as this is, I won't break his heart." He remembered his fear from the night of the raid and chills ran down his spine. "Oh, I never did thank you for rescuing him at the police station and paying his fine. Believe me, hand to God, we will never go to the Punch Bowl again. Did he pay you back?"

"You're welcome. Yes, we're all set. I'm not going to say I told you so, but, come on, from now on, you two have to be discreet, especially with the four of us living in this house soon."

Richard agreed and thanked her again for being such a good friend to two knuckleheads.

"I guess we should make an appearance downstairs. Hold my hand, Richard, to maintain the charade." Submitting to their fate, they walked toward the stairs, as Chip was opening the apartment door.

"We were just coming upstairs. Glad you two are decent, I was beginning to doubt if we should venture up." He chuckled uncomfortably. "Margaret Mary, Freddie, have you met Richard, Bev's boyfriend?" Introductions were made, and hands shook, as the group began to walk through the apartment.

Ginny grabbed Margaret Mary's arm, "Come out onto the balcony. This is my favorite space in the whole house. Can you imagine sitting out here in the evenings and watching the world go by? It's magnificent. I really adore the second-floor apartment."

Margaret Mary said as she shivered, "I don't want to be a wet rag, Ginny, but January is not the month to be lounging on an outside balcony."

Freddie concurred that it was a great house with lots of potential. And that it was nice seeing everyone again, but he had to get Margaret Mary home and himself to work in Cambridge. Ginny was relieved. As they were saying goodbye, Margaret Mary reminded her to call soon so they could start organizing a housewarming party; she started to go on and on until Freddie gently held her elbow and guided her out the door.

As soon as they left, Richard suggested an early lunch.

"The former owners didn't happen to leave any pans or plates and silverware, did they?" asked Beverly, always the practical one.

Chip shrugged. "Geez Louise, I have no idea how we will eat otherwise. We have to get the wedding presents here. I know there are dishes and stuff packed at Ginny's parents' house." The three of them started opening draws and cabinet doors. There were two rusted cast iron pans in the oven. That was a start. Ginny went to the dining room and searched through the sideboard.

She called out, "Scored. Come here." She had the bottom drawer open to reveal a set of dusty plates and bowls and a box of mismatched knives, forks, and spoons. "These are perfect. I'll rinse them off in the sink."

Ginny started humming as she washed the dishes, while Beverly went into the bathroom to try and scrub the cast iron pans in the sink. The pans had a thick layer of rust that her meager attempt at scrubbing didn't budge. Heavy-duty soap and a real scrubbing sponge to get them clean and then seasoning them in the oven was required. Irritated by more than rusty pans, she gave up.

"No luck getting these pans cleaned," she said as she dropped them heavily on the kitchen counter. "I'm not meant for kitchen duty."

Ginny, humming *Never Be Anyone Else but You* by Ricky Nelson, regarded the rusty pans. "Don't worry. We can turn the oven on low and put food on individual plates. The fellas went to the store around the corner to buy some drinks and stuff."

She wiped the last of the plates. "This already feels like home. In the kitchen, making a meal, and doing the dishes together. Honey, can you feel it?"

"One day, this will be real for me, for us." She saw Ginny's joy fade and hugged her. "Yes, look at you, my little housewife with the kitchen towel draped over your shoulder." She laughed, "Where's your frilly apron? Yes, girlfriend, this is our house, our future." She held her young lover, closed her eyes, and tried not to cry. "I love you, Virginia Stevens." Beverly stepped back. "Hey, you should take my radio and whatever else you want while you are here doing repairs the next couple of months." She faltered when she said months and quickly added, "Margaret Mary is tenacious about party organizing."

Ginny could sense that Beverly was struggling to hold on. "Yes, she is. Let's walk around the two apartments ourselves before the fellas come back. Which floor will you prefer to live on?" The move to Rhode Island was a looming dagger about to pierce her heart. Ginny was determined, though, to make the most of it while she had Beverly to herself for the rest of January. Holding hands they toured the house, commenting on aspects they liked and didn't like, such as the awkward back wall in the second-floor parlor. They finished touring the upstairs as the men came in the back door to the first floor.

Hearing the door shut, Ginny called out, "We'll be right down." She kissed Beverly's hand, "do you know which apartment you want?"

Beverly had overheard her tell Margaret Mary how much she loved the second-floor balcony. At the end of the day, it didn't matter to her which apartment they lived in.

"Girlfriend, the second-floor apartment with the balcony is the one for us. And, I know you were eyeing an attic room for your art, too. You deserve that."

Ginny bounced up and down, a smile as big as the Grand Canyon grew on her face, and her eyes sparkled. "Yes, this floor is perfect for us. It will be so much fun decorating together."

Chip yelled up to the girls that he and Richard were starving and to hurry up downstairs.

"Geez, he sounds like an old married man already."

Beverly rolled her eyes, "They better wise up fast if they think this is going to be fat city." The two women snickered and arm in arm made their way to the kitchen.

Ginny and Chip showed the house to their parents and other friends during the evenings the first week of January, then began what would be the long, slow task of repairing and remodeling. The goal was to have the upstairs apartment habitable for themselves as soon as possible and the rental apartment ready by late spring.

"Homeowners, us," said Ginny one evening after visiting Susan and Stan with their constantly crying daughter. "Gee, isn't our Eliot house like living a strange and magical dream?"

"Like a strange nightmare," Chip grumbled. "Sorry, I know we are following the schedule, the one I pushed for, but Richard is, um, all over the place. One minute excited, the next, um, never mind."

Ginny had been too caught up in her own drama and stress to consider what Chip and Richie were going through. She wished she could confide in her mother or Margaret Mary or Susan about Beverly. Just the day before, Irene, who had been promoted to senior clerk in the bookkeeping pool had taken her aside for unsolicited advice. "Virginia," said Irene in her wise voice, "You have been slogging into the office since Christmas. You're young and recently married and I am certain staying out late and partying with your fella. Let me tell you that Mr. Briggs has noticed. Dear, party until the cows come home if you want but always, always come in on time in the morning and do your work. That way no one can gossip about you." She patted Ginny on the arm and went back to her cluttered desk.

Ginny said thank you; ran her hand through her hair and to herself said, *Irene, you have no idea.* Irene was grandmotherly to her, even though she was only in her late fifties. She was a quiet woman who never gossiped or gave any indication of what her life was like outside of work. She was a friend but distant. Ginny wondered what it would be like to be single at Irene's age.

January passed painfully slow for Beverly and much too fast for Ginny. Chip's birthday came and went with a low-key celebration. He and Richard spent time at The Eliot, and he and Ginny had dinner and cake at his parent's house. This was at the same time Beverly was giving Mr. Briggs one week's notice that she was quitting. She was his best worker, so he offered to hold her position for two months but would have to fill it when the office started the spring numbers. She declined and didn't tell Ginny. She telephoned her father every day, even if only to say a brief hello. By the end of the month, Harry sounded weaker and he started to cough up blood. He told her that he had arranged for the housekeeper and a nurse to come in twice a week. Though she spent the weekends with him throughout January, she couldn't move there fast enough. She felt she ought to be the one taking care of him.

On the last Friday evening in January, the men moved the remainder of the furniture Beverly donated to The Eliot. While the men loaded the truck, the women filled Beverly's car with personal items she planned to bring to their second-floor apartment; boxes were labeled and carefully packed. All that remained in the empty apartment were the packed suitcases that she would bring with her to Rhode Island.

Ginny's mood vacillated between somber and despairing, temporarily lost was the excitement for The Eliot. Although she and Beverly would spend the night at the house, she inwardly mourned. She continually admonished herself to put on a brave face. She had met Mr. Taylor many times the previous summer when she spent several weekends with them at the beach. She was sad that he was dying and utterly heartbroken for Beverly. She knew it was selfish, and she never said it aloud, but she ached for Beverly to stay in Milton with her.

The men had brought Beverly's sofa upstairs but kept the two stuffed chairs and bed in the downstairs apartment. The kitchen table was cleared for the pizza, beer, and cola. Unbeknownst to them, the four gathered for what would be the last time until April.

***

Richard was coming as often as he could with his brother to strip wallpaper on the second floor and prepare the walls for painting or papering. The decision to do either was left up to the women. Joe re-tiled the bathroom with the popular shades of Regency Blue and Manhu Yellow and upgraded the fixtures. It was the only decision that the two women were able to make during the hectic month; it was Chip who pushed them to select anything except pink.

To Richard's surprise, Chip insisted that he pay him and his brother extra for any work that they did on the first floor. His excuse, which he proclaimed purposely in front of Joe, was that the apartment was going to be a rental and the rent would eventually cover the costs for their work. Joe, thrilled with the added work, promised to complete the stripping and tiling of the bathroom as soon as the second-floor bathroom was done. Richard had privately told Chip that he didn't care what color the bathroom was as long as it had some red. It was his way to acknowledge the first-floor apartment as theirs.

Over dinner, Beverly commented, "Richard, the upstairs is incredible. It's bright and airy without the heavy wallpaper and Joe's done a great renovation of the bathroom. He's quite talented, isn't he?" She knew that Richard was proud of his and his brother's work and would benefit from the ego boost.

"Thanks," he said while shoving another slice of pizza in his mouth. "Joe's going to start on this bathroom," he pointed with a beer in his hand to the room down the hallway, "next week. I'm going to paint all the walls upstairs white and paint the trim, that way when this wedding farce is over, you girls can take your time to choose what you want."

Ginny flinched at the words wedding farce. She looked at Chip and back to her left to Beverly. The two of them kept eating and paid no mind to the slur by Richie. *When is he going to be a man? Maybe I'm too sensitive.* She touched Beverly's shoulder and leaned in to kiss her on her cheek. "We'll have a lifetime to re-decorate, there's no hurry."

Beverly, overwrought with concern about her father, half-smiled and returned her kiss.

The women clung to each other when they finally made it to bed. The bedroom set had been a wedding gift from Chip's parents. The irony was not lost on Beverly as they made tender love one last time before leaving. She memorized the sweet smell of Ginny's hair, the smoothness of her back, and her deep, lingering kisses.

In the morning, the men were left sleeping downstairs in Beverly's old bed, adorned with new red sheets, and drove quietly to the Roslindale apartment. Snow was falling lightly and it was expected to be overcast and gloomy throughout the day. The weather fit the mood. It didn't take long to pack the car. The two lovers stood in the empty apartment, giving it a last forlorn glance.

"Lots of great memories here. I'll miss this place."

"I won't miss the clanging of the pipes during the winter or snoopy Mrs. Hagerty upstairs." She laughed to herself at the memory of the first time she brought Ginny to the apartment and how Mrs. Hagerty huffed as she walked by the stairs leading up to her floor, "Another manicure appointment?" Ginny glanced questioningly at the old woman and asked what she meant when they went inside the apartment. Beverly had dismissed the woman as senile; she wasn't about to tell her young girlfriend that she'd had a slew of lovers before her. Giving manicures to earn extra rent money was only the excuse she gave Mrs. Hagerty. Previous lovers were never allowed to spend the night. *How her love has changed my life*, she thought to herself.

"I have to go. Are you certain I can't drive you home?"

Ginny knew she would fall apart if she got in the car with her. She chose to take the bus and silent tears flowed as she made her way home.

Chapter Twelve

February had been cold. Chip was back in school, with classes becoming increasingly taxing with each passing day. He spent five days a week in classes and most evenings studying. He tried his best to keep Friday nights and Saturdays free for Richard and for working on The Eliot. On most Sunday mornings they would part, and he and Ginny would dine either at his parents' house or hers. Richard, who remained living at home, would attend Mass with his family and gather with them for their traditional Sunday dinners. Richard and Joe were working long hours with their father on a new contract, so their time working at The Eliot was confined to several evenings during the week. The pace was slow, but progress was being made.

During the week, Ginny trudged to work, through the snow and ice, and on sunny days the slush and mud, which annoyed her and dampened her mood. Beverly's desk remained empty. She thought she would burst and her mundane days never end. Irene, who had an inkling about her situation, made a point of sitting with her in the breakroom at lunch, to try to lift her spirits. Irene had long ago lost the only person she had ever loved and was never strong enough to proclaim her love. It was a secret she kept close to her heart.

Beverly telephoned the house late Tuesday night, March 1st, unexpectedly, and pleaded for Ginny to come to visit for the weekend. She felt utterly desolate. Ginny, elated and relieved, threw caution to the wind, said she would be there after work the next night, stay until Sunday morning and take the train back. She'd ask Chip to drive her to Westerly and she would call in sick to work on Thursday and Friday. Briggs wouldn't like her missing work, but he couldn't stop her.

Ginny thought Beverly sounded weary. Her father's health had worsened abruptly and he had taken to staying in bed. She could hear the ache and sadness in Beverly's voice but felt powerless to lift her spirits over the phone.

After telling Chip about her plans, Ginny called her mother to let her know she was going to Rhode Island for a few days. She missed her mother and after the holidays, she had noticed surprisingly uplifting changes in her mother's temperament. Helen had found her passion. On January 2, 1960, John F. Kennedy, the junior senator from Massachusetts, an Irish Catholic Democrat from Boston, announced that he was running for the office of President of the United States. Helen was overjoyed. The Kennedy family traced their roots back to County Wexford in Ireland, also home to her ancestors. She sometimes chose to dream that they were distant relatives. While presidential elections had never interested her in the past, she felt rejuvenated by the possibility of an Irish Catholic in the White House. She was inspired to sign up as a volunteer and committed to working at the Boston campaign headquarters four days a week. She could arrange her hours to be home to fix dinner for her husband, and she wouldn't have to be alone in the house during the daytime. She knew her son would have been proud of her political commitment. The pain of his loss never abated, but having an obligation would make a positive difference in her outlook. She focused on pulling in the reins of depression before it overwhelmed her.

Ginny was not expecting Richard at the door Wednesday evening. "Hi, Richie." He cringed at being called Richie. "Sorry, um, Richard. I'm heading out; Chip should be here any minute to take me to Rhode Island to spend the weekend with Bev."

"Yeah, I know, he called me from school when he couldn't reach you, he has some kind of group meeting and will be late and asked me to drive you. I don't mind, I told my parents that I'm visiting Beverly. They're worried about our," he cleared his throat, "relationship. They want us married." He picked up her suitcase while he kept talking. "Chip suggested that I take his car. My truck isn't very comfortable for long drives. Believe it or not, he had me leave it with him at school to drive home."

She put on her heavy coat and hurried to the car. Richard opened the door for her, put her suitcase in the trunk, and slid onto the driver's seat. "This car is a huge improvement over my truck. Don't tell Chip but I love driving it, and driving it fast." He playfully revved the engine. Ginny chuckled and flipped on the radio.

"You know, I think this is the first time we have ever been alone together."

She let that comment sit for a few beats, "Huh, what do you know."

"Has her father gotten worse? Is that why you're going? She hasn't been in touch with me at all." Hurriedly he added, "Not that I was expecting her to call."

"No, her father is getting worse but mostly she's lonely. We miss each other. You get that."

"Yes, I do. I hardly spend a minute with Chip when he is in full-school mode. He's another person when classes are on. I know, you hardly see him, too. I've been going out during the week with some of my club friends when I'm not working on the house."

She gave him the evil eye.

"No. I'm not meeting them at the clubs but at my friends', Rey and Jeff's apartment. Rey's a big-time psychologist in Boston. *Doctor* Reynaldo Eire Martin. He's from Cuba, but went to college here and stayed. We met years ago at the same club where I met Chip. We've been friends since the first night we shared a drink. I don't know, he's kinda like an older brother to me. Jeff's a medical technician, and, ah, let's say he's a bit of a free spirit. He doesn't take anything seriously. You'll meet them one of these days, I'm sure, now that we have The Eliot."

She had a difficult time imaging Richie being friends with a doctor. Were there gay men in Cuba?

The two made idle chit-chat for the next hour or so. The Eliot, winter, work, The Eliot again. Eventually, they ran out of common ground. The silence was awkward for both of them. Ginny shuffled through the static for radio stations but they were out of range at that point for her usual WMEX-AM. She clicked the radio off.

"Tell me about your family. I only know Joe vaguely. I remember when he and a bunch of other boys would come over after baseball games with my brother Johnny. Did you ever meet my brother? Huh, I wonder if my mother realizes that you're Joe's older brother?"

"I don't know, I never would have had a reason to meet your mother before double dating with you and Chipster. I probably saw your brother at my house, but I'm five years older than Joe. I wouldn't have paid any attention to my little brother's friends. Sorry. Do you want to tell me about him?"

She ran her hand through her blonde hair, thinking first, that she should get her hair trimmed, then, when were they going to get to Beverly's, but she answered,

"My brother was special. My parents adored him. I adored him. He was the good guy, you know? Handsome, and caring in every way. I think my mother saw him as destined for the priesthood or a senator or governor, some higher place other than Westinghouse. He was eighteen and I was almost seventeen when he died. Everything in my family has been somewhat off-kilter since. I miss him every day." She paused. "Huh, I've never said that to anyone." She flipped the radio back on and fiddled with it until she found a local Providence station.

"Did Chip ever tell you about how he took care of me back then? I don't suppose he did."

Richard shook his head and felt slightly jealous of Ginny's relationship with Chip.

"It was the beginning of February school vacation and the two of us were in my room listening to records when my father burst in. He said that Mom and Johnny were in an accident and that we had to go to the hospital. Chip never hesitated, he came with us and stayed by my side day and night. He told the nurses that he was my brother and refused to let me out of his sight. Most of that time is a blur, Johnny dying, relatives coming and going, planning a funeral, and my mother in the hospital with severe back injuries for weeks." Richard looked sympathetically at Ginny and warmly touched her shoulder as she continued.

"All through it, he stayed with me. He slept in my room, holding me all night while I constantly cried. When school was back in session, somehow, he stayed with me. I don't know if he skipped school or if his mother approved. I'm sure his father didn't. Margaret Mary would bring school assignments to me, and she and Chip guided me through them. Even after I went back to school, he came over every day to keep me company. He got me through school that year. I had stopped drawing and painting. He brought that back. He saved me when the world around me was falling apart."

"Mio Dio, I had no idea. I do know he loves you unconditionally. I'm sorry your brother died. My mother lost two baby girls born after me and before Joe. My family rarely speaks of them, but we go to the cemetery faithfully. My mother will be on cloud nine once Anna and Dom's baby is born. She's due any day now. Imagine, I'll be an uncle. Mama expects me to have tons of kids when we marry." Ginny stiffened at *kids and marriage*. Richard realized he shouldn't have said anything about having babies. He tried to make a joke about it.

"Not sure how that'll happen! Merda. I'm sorry. I guess my head is stuck in dreamland, my mother's dreamland.

Merda. Sorry. I'll shut up." He turned the radio up, which was playing *(Now and Then There's) A Fool Such as I* by Elvis Presley, and asked her to read the next line of the directions.

She looked at the hapless Richie, grabbed the directions a little too forcefully from the dashboard, and read them.

"We'll be there soon. I won't stay long; I have to get back home and give an update to my mother and get some sleep before work tomorrow."

It was almost eight o'clock when Richard pulled onto the winding driveway. The lights were on everywhere in the large Victorian house except the front second-floor window. Must be her father's room, guessed Ginny.

Beverly came running out of the house, with no coat on, and into the open arms of Ginny. She held her and cried both tears of joy and sorrow. Richard opened the trunk, removed the suitcase, and tried to ignore their embrace.

"Richard, hello, come on in you two. Brr, too cold." Beverly held Ginny's arm and directed them to the formal parlor. "My father is in bed sleeping. The nurse was here today. He is slipping away. It's horrible to watch." She sat on the sofa with Ginny while Richard stood taking in the enormous house. Pulling herself together she asked if they were hungry, knowing that Richard would not refuse food.

"What happened to Chip? I thought he was driving?" Ginny and Richard trailed after her as she headed toward the kitchen.

Richard explained the change and asked if he could have coffee to keep him alert on the way home and he wouldn't refuse an extra sandwich. Ginny wasn't hungry for anything other than her lover's arms.

After a second cup of coffee, he stopped and wrestled with Chip's instructions about the revised *Plan*. "Um, I know this is an awful time to bring up *the Plan* but Chip said I should remind you that I'm supposed to propose to you when we hopefully get together on Easter Sunday."

Beverly froze. Ginny almost spit out her cola and glared dangerously at him, which made Beverly laugh.

"Girlfriend, this is *your* doing. Ah, yes. Romeo, I'll write it down on my calendar now that we missed your Valentine's proposal. *Be lovey-dovey with Richard on Easter*; assuming we can get together. My Dad still comes first. Go home, Richard, and thank you for driving Ginny. I'll take her to the train station on Sunday."

Beverly checked on her father before she beckoned Ginny to bed. "I've missed you more than you can imagine. I want you so much. I need to touch you, to hold you, to make love to you all night. God..." Before she could finish her sentence, Ginny covered her mouth with a kiss. A kiss filled with raw need. Their hands searched each other's bodies. Their breath was ragged.

"I want you so much," was all Ginny managed to say.

Little did they know that a devastating and deadly blizzard was bearing down on them. A Nor'easter of record proportions was about to affect states from West Virginia to Maine. But on this night, when the women finally went to sleep in each other's arms, they slept sounder than either of them had in months.

The snow started during the night, softly at first, it was beautiful to see in the morning light, but its charm did not last. The winds soon became intense, the snow blinding and the ocean down the street from the large house roared, sounding angry and dangerous.

An early telephone call awakened them. The housekeeper said she would most likely not be able to come in until next week. Then the weekday nurse called to cancel her upcoming visit and to review the daily medication routine. They never considered that the snow storm could be that severe. Ginny called work to say she was sick and would not be in until Monday, never thinking the snow would last long enough to hamper the Sunday train. Briggs grumbled and intended to talk to her early on Monday morning to discuss her attitude. Ginny didn't give him or work another thought as the snow began to pile up outside. Beverly wasn't worried until the lights flickered and the house lost power and telephone service.

The kitchen was freshly stocked with food in anticipation of the weekend and there was a large fireplace in the formal parlor and in Harry's bedroom. The two women bundled up and went to the back shed to bring in as much firewood as they could manage before the storm's intensity stopped their efforts. After much arguing and cajoling, Beverly convinced her father that it made sense to have only one fireplace burning wood and that the three of them should stay in the formal parlor until the power came back on.

Ginny made a bed on the large oversized sofa, tucking clean sheets and wool blankets around the cushions to make it as comfortable as possible for Harry. They pushed the makeshift bed as close to the fireplace as they could. The drapes were closed in front of the floor-to-ceiling windows to keep the drafts to a minimum. Beverly sent Ginny to poke around in the kitchen to find storm candles and matches while she helped her father dress in warm clothes and come downstairs.

By late afternoon the three were settled in the parlor with a warm fire glowing. By Friday morning, there was no chance of digging out the car to get to the train station to try to get Ginny home sooner. All they could do was assume that everyone was fine and the roads would be passable for Ginny to get home and to work on Monday. Neither of them could imagine that it would be almost a week before the power came back on and that the roads would only be roughly plowed.

Harry was reliving the destructive hurricane that stole the life of his beautiful wife and scores of others in the region. He prayed that this storm would not rain down the same terror.

The power was out in most of New England. The wind and snow and cold were unrelenting from Thursday through Saturday. People frantically searched for loved ones stranded on the way home from work and school. John Stevens walked the ten minutes home from work on Thursday night as the blizzard strengthened. He assumed that Helen had not gone to downtown Boston to volunteer, but the house was empty when he managed to push the snow from the back door and enter the kitchen. He tried pulling the light string over the kitchen table. Nothing. He called out to Helen. No answer. After taking off his wet socks and boots, he walked in the dark towards the hallway. The lights didn't work there either. But where was Helen? He called to her again as he felt for the flashlight on the shelf in the hall closet. There was no note by the telephone, nor on the kitchen table. John sat down with a thump. His mind flashed back and forth from worst-case scenario to worst-case scenario. Didn't Helen mention over breakfast that Ginny said she was going to Rhode Island to help her friend for a few days? So, she wouldn't have any idea where her mother went. Helen wouldn't have gone into Boston, would she? Dread slowly crept up his spine and the hair stood up on his neck. His watch displayed 6:15. She was never this late if she went to Boston. Damn politics. He cursed and banged his fist on the kitchen table. The penguin salt and pepper shakers rattled and fell off their stand. He paused, took a deep breath, repositioned them, and brushed the salt off the table.

***

Chip was at the school library on Thursday afternoon with his study group. They had been meeting in preparation for a major presentation. He was going to be the lead debater; and his confidence inspired the rest of the team. None of them were aware of the severity of the storm outside. When the lights went out at about 6 p.m., the head librarian called out in the dark to the mumbling and complaining students and patrons that power was out all over campus and everyone should gather up their belongings and quickly try to get home safely. They never should have left the building.

Richard was home early on Thursday; the Franklin Park Zoo project was winding down and they had completed all that they could for the day by 2 p.m. Angela was stirring a large pot of minestrone soup when the men arrived. "It's going to snow for days, says the radio. Get cleaned up; the soup will be ready soon. Mateo and Angelo are out shoveling for Mrs. Sorrenti." She bent over and removed two large loaves of Ciabatta from the oven and put them on the rack to cool.

Richard and Joe went outside to double-check the chains and snow plows on the extra trucks. Richard assumed that Chip had left school early and was home safely at The Eliot. After the trucks were readied, the two brothers went inside for large bowls of their Mama's soup. Richard's mind kept shifting to Chip. His first stop plowing was The Eliot driveway with the hope that he had gotten home. His car wasn't there, so he drove by Chip's parents. He even plowed Ginny's former street during his search. His knuckles were white with fear as he gripped the steering wheel after not finding Chip's car anywhere. He was unsure where he would be at school and darkness along with the howling wind and snow made driving treacherous. Richard tried to swallow his panic. Slowly, he headed toward home for another thermos of hot coffee and some sandwiches. It would be a laborious three days of non-stop plowing for paying customers and worrying about Chip. Beverly never crossed his mind.

Beverly found the emergency transistor radio and batteries Friday afternoon. Sitting in total silence cut off from the outside was unnerving and worries were mounting. Harry spent most of the day and night sleeping. When he was awake, he had little appetite. The two women had brought Beverly's mattress downstairs and had it next to the coffee table, with Harry situated on the other side.

They were sitting on the mattress listening to the late-night news and were appalled at the extent of the storm, and with no end in sight. There were reports of numerous deaths, flooding, and roofs collapsing up and down the coast. People were stranded in office buildings, at schools, and on the roads. Ginny didn't regret that there would be no getting to work on Monday but was concerned about her parents, Chip and, yes, Richard. She glanced over at the sleeping Harry and prayed that he stayed stable while they were confined to the house. An ambulance would never get through. Beverly was thinking the same thing. She itched for a cigarette and had a carton in the top drawer of the dining room buffet.

"Hon, I love you. I'm so grateful that you're here. Can I ask you something?"

"Of course, silly, I love you too, ask me anything you want."

"Would you mind terribly if I had a cigarette? I'm frantic for one."

Ginny was more amused than annoyed. "The world is ending and you want a cigarette." Beverly sheepishly smiled.

"But I don't think you should smoke near your father."

"Of course not. I'll be back in a few minutes."

"Hey, is there any of the chocolate cake that you bought for me left? Any hidden stash of cola anywhere? I finished the last of the six-pack."

Beverly stopped at the door, not sure about the cake and cola.

"My goodness, go have your cigarette. I don't mind."

Beverly blew her a kiss, grabbed the flashlight, and bolted from the room.

With difficulty, Harry leaned up on his elbow. "Her mother smoked. I've tried to get Beverly Jean to quit, but some things are out of our control. I'm glad she has you." He was too weak to continue and lay back down and closed his eyes. She was speechless.

Beverly was gone a good fifteen minutes, which had Ginny thinking she was smoking an entire pack of Pall Mall.

"Hey, open the door, quick, this is heavy."

She opened the parlor door to find Beverly holding a dusty case of soda and an entire frozen sheet cake in her arms. She lifted the cake off the soda and moved aside so Beverly could place the case on the floor by the doorway.

"While I was smoking, I remembered how I used to hide in the cellar to smoke when I was a teenager. Then I remembered that my father kept a storm pantry there. It's cool and dry and he has a freezer loaded with food. It's all still completely frozen, with meat, bread, and at least three cakes. He always had room for cake." Ginny's eyes widened at the sound of more cake. "There are candles and stuff, too. He was prepared for any disaster. Lucky us."

She sneaked a peek at Harry to make sure he was sleeping. "He started the storm pantry after my mother died, I think. He had his housekeeper keep it stocked and gave her the older items whenever she refreshed the pantry. I'd forgotten about it."

"I'm glad for once that you are addicted to cigarettes or we never would have found all this. I'm going to put the cake near the fire to defrost it. Yum."

She glanced at Harry and back at Beverly. "He told me that he was glad you have me. Does he know?"

Harry, with his eyes closed, smiled weakly. "Yes, I know. I've known since last summer, that weekend on the beach. Sweetie, anyone who knows you can see how much you love Ginny. I've been watching and listening to you both for the last few days. It's so obvious that you are in love. Please be careful, the world is full of hate. No matter what anyone thinks of your love, I know that you are worth it."

Beverly choked back tears and kissed her father. He outstretched his hand to Ginny and drifted back to sleep. The two women sat quietly for a long time. Being accepted for who they were by Harry took their breath away. Their hearts sang and for a short time, they forgot about the raging storm outside.

***

Chip trudged slowly to his car. He realized immediately that he wasn't going to be able to move it. His eyes hurt from the wind and snow. It was dark. Other students and staff were scrambling to find a way out of the parking lot without their cars. Someone suggested that they walk to the closest dormitory up on the hill. Several students and library staff huddled together and made their way up the hill. An older man, a professor, Chip assumed, slipped several times. He and another student held on to him the last one hundred feet as they neared the dormitories.   He reminded Chip of Richard's friend Reynaldo. *Did Richard say he met him recently for drinks?* The old doctor was a little dull and prone to over-analyzing everything.

The group banged loudly on the doors until a residence director opened them and allowed them to enter. Students were wearing their hats, coats, and gloves, and sat close together with their blankets and pillows along the first floor. Several candles were burning and gave off an eerie light. The residence director and a couple of the students had flashlights. Someone placed a transistor radio on a table and the announcer was telling people to stay inside and to seek shelter because the blizzard was expected to last for several days. Chip was hungry and he bet that he wasn't the only one. The small snack room in the dormitory was closed and by midnight, the cold and hungry students hounded the residence director to let them raid the storage room. There wasn't much beyond cereal, apples, bread, crackers, and peanut butter and jelly to eat. The residence director ordered calm and had the students line up. He also unlocked the vending machines and allowed the students to take one drink each. By 1 a.m. everyone had something to eat and drink, meager as it was. Chip had a peanut butter and jelly sandwich and dreamt of falling asleep in bed at The Eliot with Richard. Richard was probably out plowing with his brother and father and Chip wished he would plow to the dorm and rescue him.

Later that night, Chip had to use the bathroom. He didn't have a flashlight and fumbled his way to the men's room he had noticed beyond the snack room. He thought he heard a commotion as he opened the door. The sound wasn't normal. There was a flicker of light from a candle perched on the sink counter. At the far end, a big man was pinning a young male student against the wall. "Hey," gasped Chip as he stepped forward. The man banged the young student's head against the wall, pushed him to the floor, and turned, knocking the candle into the sink as he charged Chip. He caught him with a double blow to his jaw and ran past him out the door. Chip fell back, hit his head and blacked out. The young student groggily stood up, with tears flowing down his face, he fixed his clothes, and ran out of the bathroom. Chip was left bleeding on the cold floor.

***

Helen paced back and forth at the Kennedy Headquarters and watched the storm through the oversized glass window.

Two thoughts ran through her head: *John will be home in less than an hour and not be pleased that I'm not there to greet him and prepare his dinner. Should I attempt to take the Orange Line to Forest Hills and hope that the Hyde Park bus will still be running?* She never considered that he might be worried about her safety. Going against the advice of the other volunteers, she put on her heavy coat and left.

Richard plowed Eliot Street and their driveway in front of the garage several times in despair and prayed that Chip's car would show up. He had a premonition that something was wrong and he didn't know what to do.

***

Before day break Chip was discovered unconscious on the bathroom floor. Blood had congealed at the back of his head; his jaw was swollen. The residence director assumed that he slipped in the darkness. The hospital was nearby and somehow in the midst of the storm, a school plow truck managed to bring him to the hospital. He was admitted with a severe concussion and a fractured jaw.

John had spent the better part of two hours shoveling the driveway and the sidewalk. He tried calling the Kennedy Headquarters, but the phone was dead. As a last resort, he got in his car and drove towards Cleary Square. He prayed that he would find her safely waiting for the bus inside Liggett's Drug Store or Lodgen's Market. The chances were slim, but he had to try. His car slipped and swerved and got stuck several times before he made it to the Square a mere mile and a half away. He stopped his car in the middle of the mostly deserted snow-filled street and started calling her name at the top of his voice. "Helen, are you here? Has anyone seen Helen Stevens?" There was a murmur in the small shivering crowd under the eaves of the closed corner market.

"John, is that you? I'm here," called Helen.

John sobbed as he ran to her, and they hugged like young lovers.

"Quick, get in the car so you can warm up." John beckoned to the others, "I'm going to Readville, Norton Street. I'm happy to fit in as many people as I can in my car. After six people, crammed into his Chevrolet, he called out to the remaining people. "You should go down the street to the police station to keep warm. The radio said the MBTA is not running any more buses tonight. Please, go now." Again, the remaining near-freezing people murmured and then started walking in the blinding, wind-driven snow toward the safety of the police station.

It was almost 10 p.m. by the time John and Helen arrived home. He escorted her inside and wrapped a blanket around her shoulders. The house was getting cold fast and Helen shook uncontrollably. John piled extra blankets on the bed and put Helen's warm dress coat and his heavy woolen work socks on her.

"I was afraid I was going to lose you, too." He kissed her. "You're home now. Let's try to sleep."

***

On Sunday morning, the sun came out.

Chapter Thirteen

Chip could barely move his mouth and cried when he spoke briefly with his mother. His jaw was wired shut and his head pounded ferociously. He asked the nurse to call Richard but the Ruggiero telephone was still down and Ginny was unreachable in Rhode Island.

Richard telephoned Ginny and Beverly late Tuesday night after he found Chip in Saint Elizabeth's Hospital. He told her that once his parents' telephone service was restored, he had spent the entire afternoon calling every hospital in the area. Beverly informed him that her telephone service was sporadic, but the electricity was on. Ginny was beside herself after Richard described Chip's accident and painful condition. She had only just learned about her mother's ordeal and wanted to get home, but the trains were still inoperable. She cried when Richard said he would come to her rescue on Wednesday evening; one week to the day from when he dropped her off. Maybe Richard wasn't so hapless after all.

Both women were worn out by the intensity of the week. The excitement of the first night was a vague memory. There was a constant chill in the room regardless of the number of logs feeding the fire. Nerves were frayed and Harry was sleeping and coughing and groaning in pain regularly. Beverly called his nurse as soon as the telephone came back online and much to her relief, the nurse said she was hoping to come to the house by the end of the week.

Regardless, leaving was a difficult decision for Ginny. She was worried that Beverly would collapse from exhaustion. She wasn't eating as much as she should and she was smoking non-stop either in the kitchen or standing outside the back door.

When Richard arrived in his father's plow truck, he cleared the driveway and shoveled off the front steps. When he finally came in, he was bearing another of his mother's now infamous bags of prepared meals. She had an old stove that could be stoked with wood for cooking and it had been a Godsend during the blizzard and afterward. The exhausted women gave him a warm hug, grateful to see a familiar face and another human being. He felt the chill in the house and immediately offered to check the furnace and attempt to get it working. He said it should have kicked in when the power came on. Harry was asleep so the women went with Richard to the basement, eager to hear any news about how people back home were doing. An hour later and up to his elbows in soot, Richard told Beverly to flip on the switch and to keep her fingers crossed. After a fit of sputtering and clanging, the furnace came on. The three cheered and made their way upstairs. Beverly patted Richard on the back and said, "I'm glad I'm marrying you, my super handy, snow plowing, Romeo."

"Um, excuse me, you are already taken."

Beverly winked at Richard and kissed Ginny, amused by the hint of jealousy in Ginny's tone.

Richard never tired of Beverly stroking his ego; it made him feel like a powerful man.

He was directed to the bathroom so he could wash up while the bag of food was opened and some soup warmed. Harry had heard the commotion and called out. Cheerfully, she told him that the heat was on and there would be warm, delicious homemade Italian chicken soup to eat. She introduced Richard. Harry, with all the dignity that he could muster, made a gallant effort to stand up and shake his hand. He couldn't manage standing but he sat up as straight as possible and used both hands to shake hands with the young man with a deep voice and slicked dark brown hair.

He motioned for his daughter to pass him his wallet because Richard should be paid for coming and spending time plowing and fixing the furnace when he could have been visiting the two beautiful women in the room. Richard vehemently tried to decline Harry's offer.

Harry, through the intense pain, conjured up his best 'I am in charge voice.' "Richard, I am dying, you cannot say no to a dying man. Now take this and be quiet." He folded some bills and put them in the top pocket of Richard's shirt. Only later did Richard realize that he had given him an exorbitant $200.

Harry weakly hugged Ginny goodbye. "Please, take care of my daughter, she loves you. Don't break her heart. Promise," he whispered into her ear.

Beverly had tears in her eyes. Not knowing when she would hold Ginny again was stinging. She knew she wouldn't have survived the blizzard without her. She walked with Ginny and Richard to the front door. Richard went to warm up the truck while the they said good-bye. The women kissed as if they would never see each other again. They kissed and pulled back and kissed again.

"I'll come back as soon as I can. I love you. Call me often, and take care of yourself."

"Let me know how your mother and Red are both doing. You know I'd be there if I could. Call me every day, if you can. I need you desperately."

Ginny struggled to break away, it was getting late and the drive would take hours. She wondered if she still had a job; she was not looking forward to approaching Mr. Briggs.

The truck started slowly down the driveway. At the last minute, Beverly ran after the truck. Richard stopped and Ginny rolled down her window.

Out of breath, she held Ginny's face, kissed her, and said, "I love you. Forever love." Peering across to Richard, she added, "I can't promise, but I'll try to see you Easter weekend, Romeo." She backed away from the truck, ran inside from the cold and watched them leave from the doorway. When she walked into the parlor, Harry was gone.

At first, she thought he had fallen back to sleep after the excitement of company. She walked over to adjust the blanket, and she knew. Holding him, she screamed a guttural sound that echoed throughout the house.

***

Richard didn't know anything about Ginny's mother's situation but had lots to tell her about the blizzard damage in Boston and their neighborhoods. "People died, dozens of people. *And*, Chip almost died." He choked on the last words. Appalled, she touched his shoulder and asked him to describe again how her Chipper ended up in the hospital.

"I don't know really. I stopped by the Foleys earlier today, once I found him on my own yesterday. Mr. Foley wasn't home, he was working, I imagine. Mrs. Foley let me in and apologized for not calling me or his other friends when the hospital first called. She didn't have my telephone number and your mother hadn't answered the phone." That worried Ginny.

"As I said, I visited Chip late last night. The nurse let me stay a few minutes." Unsteady, he wiped tears from his eyes. "You must think I'm a crybaby." She shook her head. "As soon I saw him, I lost it. His head was bandaged, his beautiful red hair shaved, and his jaw's wired shut. Wired shut; God damn it. His entire face is black and blue and he can barely talk through the wires. He tried to say something to me but he was in obvious pain. God, he has to keep a pair of scissors next to him in case he gags or throws up and the wires have to be cut off. I held his hand and he slipped back to sleep." Richard banged his fist against the steering wheel.

Stunned, she placed his fisted hand in hers. "What happened?"

"He stayed with others who were stranded at a dorm on Thursday night. Someone found him on the floor in the men's bathroom early Friday morning. They assumed that he fell in the darkness. He was unconscious for the first two days and when I saw him, I thought I would die. Merda, why do these things happen to him? First, the police raid, now this. He's not a tough guy."

There was nothing else to say. Richard lifted the rosary beads that he kept draped on the rearview mirror and held them in his left hand. She watched as this big, muscular man prayed for the one he loved. She closed her eyes and they rode in silence.

It was quite late when he dropped Ginny off at her parents' house. The front porch light and the parlor lights were on. At the sound of the truck doors closing, John Stevens put down his music catalog and walked to the front door. Richard placed her suitcase inside the hallway, said hello to Mr. Stevens, and declined an offer to come in to warm up. Ginny kissed her father on his cheek and eased off her coat and gloves.

Her first words were, "Is she any better?"

John stole a glance up the stairs and led her into the parlor. He sat in his easy chair and motioned her to sit close to him on the sofa. "She has barely gotten out of bed since I brought her home on Thursday night. She won't eat hardly anything beyond tea and toast. Doctor Kavidka was here earlier. He says her vital signs are good; her toes are slightly frostbitten but should heal fine. He says she is in shock from her experience. He renewed her depression prescription, Dexamyl, and insisted that she follow it to the letter. I've gone back to work, and I am afraid to leave her alone during the day. This is what she was like when your brother died. Do you remember?"

"I remember. I am so sorry I wasn't here."

"It's not your fault or anyone's fault. The damn blizzard is to blame. I hate to ask this, but can you take some time off

116

from work? I'll talk to Briggs and the personnel office. It's a lot to ask with your being just married and paying for the new house. I don't know what else to do. Your mother will never allow a stranger to come in. She insists that she just wants to rest. I'm worried about her slipping away more."

She was taken back by his request. He never asked about Chip, if he would mind. Didn't he know about the accident? She enjoyed work, if not her boss, most of the time, and didn't really want to jeopardize her job. *The Plan*'s path to happiness seemed like such a distant dream, fading in the harsh misery that surrounded her.

"How can I say no, Mom comes first." She swallowed hard. "Should I go up and see her? Do you think she's awake?"

"Wait until morning. Also, why don't you come with me to work tomorrow and we can speak to the powers that be together? You can be back here by nine to sit with your mother."

"Maybe. I think I'll go to bed. It's been a hectic week and my old bed will feel good."

"Oh, um. Do you think Chip will mind? How's your friend's father? I'm tired, too, you can fill me in on your week in the morning."

With a hint of sarcasm that John did not notice, she said, "*My husband* is in the hospital, Dad. I thought his parents called you. He fell during the blizzard, broke his jaw, and has a concussion. I called the hospital before I left Rhode Island; they said he'll be there another week. I have to go see him tomorrow morning. I'll come to Westinghouse afterward. I can only give you a week at the most to care for Mom, I'm sorry. I think I have that much sick leave saved. Also, Bev's father is dying, as you know. I'm no judge but I thought he appeared to be much weaker when I left." She wanted to cry out in anguish over having to leave Beverly, but she only said, "She's struggling to keep up."

"I didn't realize how serious Chip's injuries were. I'm sorry. He's young, he'll be okay. Please, if you can stay at least until he gets home. Damn this storm. Yeah, that's too bad about your friend's father."

She winced at his use of the word friend.

"What a week. Good night, Virginia, I'm relieved that you're here. I'll see you in the morning."

He kissed her cheek and shut off the porch light on his way upstairs.

She called after him, "Good night." To herself she added, *Chip's in the hospital, my lover is on her own with her dying father, my mother is depressed, and you want me to take a leave from my job. Life is just A-OK, Dad.* For the first time in her twenty-two-plus years, she said aloud, *"Fuckin' hell."*

Chapter Fourteen

The unprecedented number of deaths related to the blizzard was overwhelming for the local undertakers. Beverly had to endure three unbearable weeks for a reservation for the funeral service for her father. Ginny, confined first to caring for her mother, then Chip, was only able to visit one Saturday. She developed a new appreciation for Richard's generosity and his father's reliable truck.

It was just as well that she was unable to visit, as the Taylor relatives converged on the house. Rarely seen aunts and uncles conspired to walk away with family heirlooms and financial gains. The late Harry had prepared for their onslaught. His lawyer met with the family at the Taylor home to read the terms of Harry's will and to highlight the ramifications if there was any balking at the generous gifts. Beverly, knowing the terms, sat in the back of the room while the will was being read. She smoked a cigarette and sat with her cousin, Pamela, a trim and fit true suburbanite, and snickered at the huffing and puffing exhibited by their mutual Aunt Trudy as her gift was announced. Pamela was married with three young children, who were home with the live-in maid. Married to a stockbroker who was married to his career in New York City, Pamela had become bored and jaded. They lived in Connecticut where she spent time tending her garden and her social activities. She saw her older cousin only about once a year during the holidays since the children were born. Beverly didn't mind; their close childhood relationship had been altered as they grew and developed different views of the place of women in the world.

Pamela put her arm around her older cousin. "Are you doing okay, Bevie? Do you have someone you can count on?" She had an idea of her cousin's predilection for women, but it was a subject generally avoided. What was not appropriate to discuss was not apt to get in the way of family togetherness and her social standing. Upscale social interactions were critical to her husband, and she dared not disappoint. In a judgmental way, she cared for Beverly.

Beverly snuffed out her cigarette and stared at her. "I'm fine, Pammy. *She* will be at the wake and funeral. Along with several close friends."

Pamela patted her shoulder before she removed her arm. The lawyer concluded his reading of the will and was answering some lingering questions. Beverly left the room and went to her old bedroom and closed the door.

The ground was still too frozen for a complete burial but the graveside service was held regardless. Afterward, family and guests were invited to the Taylor home for an afternoon of remembrance and lunch. Mr. and Mrs. Ruggiero and three sons quietly paid their respects. Angela hugged her and cried tears of sorrow for her loss. Mr. Ruggiero also hugged her and reminded his son to take care of her during her difficult time. Richard's parents growing love of Beverly both touched and troubled him. He hated deceiving his family. Beverly was grateful for their presence and their heartfelt kindness had an impact that she would always remember.

After being introduced to Pamela, and receiving a very cold shoulder from her, Ginny hovered with Chip in the background. He kept his bag of straws and emergency scissors close by his side. She and Richard had both tried to dissuade Chip from coming. Headaches tortured him continuously. He was frail and distraught at having to miss the remainder of the school semester but refused to be left behind. Ginny sat with him in the formal parlor by the fireplace so he would rest and could carefully drink a fortified chocolate milkshake prepared by the caterer. Her eyes never left her lover, who was pale and drawn. Beverly, wearing a long sleeve black dress and her mother's turquoise beaded necklace that highlighted her blue eyes, occasionally noticed and raised her eyebrows in acknowledgment. Ginny's longing for her intensified during the course of the day and she was frustrated by having to be there as only a friend. She yearned for the normalcy of their lives.

Slowly, the crowd of mourners gave their final condolences. The remaining relatives retrieved the heirlooms that had been wrapped and packed for them and bid goodbye. Pamela and her husband were the last to leave.

"Bevie, be careful of the life you live with this woman. That tall, handsome man appears to care for you. Be smart, return *his* love," Pamela warned.

"Goodbye, Pammy. Thank you for being here." She stiffly hugged her and walked away. Pamela closed the door, never to contact her cousin again.

Ginny ran to Beverly as she re-entered the parlor. Exhausted from the day, and the finality of Harry's death, they crumbled into each other's arms. Chip gingerly shifted in his chair and motioned Richard to follow him out of the room to give them some privacy. They didn't hear the men leave. Ginny touched Beverly gently on her cheek and led her to the loveseat at the far end of the room. She soothed her with soft words and gentle touch. Her mind was racing. She tried to think about what people said to her at her brother's funeral. When she ran out of words to say, she pulled her closer and Beverly fell asleep in her arms. Neither moved for an hour. Richard peeked in at one point and Ginny simply shook her head at him. She could hear the caterer cleaning in the dining room. Richard wisely stood guard next to the closed parlor door and kept the caterers away from the room. When Beverly finally woke, she put her arm around her lover's waist and nuzzled close to her neck. A knock on the door interrupted the moment.

Richard apologized for intruding. "The caterer wants the last of his dishes and chairs, and to finish cleaning, can he come in now? It's getting late and he's getting impatient."

When they were done, Ginny noticed that Chip was asleep across the hall on the sofa in the casual parlor, as she had started calling it. He had a painful expression on his face and Richard had placed a crocheted throw over his legs.

Easter was in less than three weeks, with signs of spring struggling to burst through the last of the snow. Aware of the impending marriage proposal from Richard, a weary and fragile Beverly stated that she had a lot to consider before moving back to Massachusetts. Ginny wanted her back as soon as possible but didn't want to push. Still checking on her mother almost daily after work and mindful of Chip's constant state of duress, she now understood the gravity of what Beverly had been going through since the holiday cruise.

Once the four were alone, Richard said he had something to say. His tie had been loosened and his shirt sleeves rolled up, exposing his muscular arms. Richard cleared his throat, "Um, I learned something these past few months. You three are everything to me, and, um, our lives can turn to crapola when we least expect it. Damn it. What I'm trying to say is, we belong together, we're a family. The Eliot really home. That's it, that's all I have to say." He silently prayed that he had the strength to stay committed for a lifetime.

The room was quiet, Richard sat down next to Chip and put his arm around him. Chip lifted his drink and spoke as loudly as he could through his wired jaw, "To *The Plan*."

Beverly added, "My turn. I want to thank you for being here today." Her voice cracked. "I've come to depend on you two idiots as much as I depend on Ginny." Regaining her composure, she turned, "Romeo, I want her to pick out the engagement ring. Keep it very simple. This is the real one." She held out her hand with the ring that Ginny had given her. "Deal? Okay. I'm beat and as much as I want you all to stay," again, staring lovingly at Ginny, "I need to be alone here for a little while longer. I promise to be home soon."

Chapter Fifteen

Easter weekend was upon them in a flash. Richard was apprehensive about announcing the engagement to his family. He wanted reassurance from Chip, and drove to The Eliot first thing on Saturday morning, hours before the planned lunch with the girls.

Chip was downstairs when Richard arrived. He could read the concern on Richard's face.

"You are here early. What is the matter?" he stretched up to give Richard a quick hello kiss.

Richard pulled him close. "I needed to see you. I'm nervous about tomorrow. Can we talk alone?"

"We are alone. Ginny took my car to pick up some last-minute things at the store. Come on, let's sit in the kitchen."

"How are you feeling? Your jaw hurting?"

"It is still uncomfortable." He shrugged and pulled out a kitchen chair to sit on. "Tell me what's going on."

Richard sighed, "I just want to be with you a while, alone and quiet before the madness begins tomorrow." He took Chip's hand and sighed.

***

Beverly was on her way back from Rhode Island, missing her father and wondering what he would think about the upcoming phony engagement. She rubbed the pinky ring and sighed. For the past few weeks, she had been too busy with her father's lawyers and financial advisors to give it much thought. She decided to sell the house and invest some of the money. The rest she would put into a trust for Ginny, in case anything ever happened to her. Ginny might be legally married to Chip, but in Beverly's heart, Ginny was her responsibility.

***

The Ruggieros leaped from the dining room table, everyone shouting at once with happiness over the engagement. Angela came and kissed her on both her cheeks and Mr. Ruggiero did the same. Richard's brothers patted him on the back, punched his arm, and hugged him ferociously. Beverly was lifted from her chair and surrounded with hugs and love from her new family. She was speechless.

Angela was the first to ask when the wedding would take place. Beverly readily said early June. Richard jumped in to add that a June wedding would improve their chances of securing the rental apartment in Chip and Ginny's house. And that he could work on the apartment specifically for themselves. Joe listened but was suspicious. He had recently finished what he could in the house and something felt off. He sat back and watched and couldn't dismiss the peculiar sense of casualness emanating from the couple. He peered into his brother's eyes; passion was missing.

Beverly spoke as the noise died down. "I don't have any family left in my hometown of Westerly. Without my father to walk me down the aisle, I want a simple justice of the peace ceremony, no church, no large party."

The room went silent. Richard cringed, anticipating the explosion from his parents.

"My son, no get married in the church?" Angela made the sign of the cross. "How can that be? Ricardo, God will never forgive you." Her eyes begged her husband to intervene. Her children held their breath.

"One minute, can we talk about this? Your mother has dreamed of you walking down the aisle at Most Precious Blood Church for years, since you were a small altar boy. The priest, Father Doherty, he is a friend of the family. Irish, I know, but a friend. Don't do this. Don't break your mother's heart, Ricardo?"

Richard inhaled, held his fiancé's hand, and claimed, "I have spoken to Father Doherty. He knows that she is not Catholic and he can't conduct the wedding in the church because of that. But, hear me out, Father Doherty said that he is willing to come to the house to give us a blessing and to pray with us. Mama, Papa, this is our decision. Come on, this is my engagement day, be happy for us."

His siblings jumped in to support him. Joe laughing said, "I'll finally have my own room. Can you get married this week?"

The usually quiet Anna passed Dominic Jr. to Dom and went next to her mother. "Mama, they are adults. Beverly has been living on her own for a long time and making her own decisions. We want her to be part of the family. Come on, we must do this for them." She turned to the couple, "We can have the wedding and a family party here at the house, can't we? The backyard is beautiful in June. Mama, she has no family. You can do this for her."

Disappointed, Angela, shrugged her shoulders neither disagreeing nor agreeing. Mr. Ruggiero opened the dining room cabinet and pulled out his bottle of Sambuca. "Everybody, here, toast to the beautiful couple." He poured a small glass for each one in the entire family. Holding up his glass he toasted, "To my oldest son and his soon-to-be bride. May they be happy together and be blessed with many healthy children."

The *healthy children* comment had Beverly almost choking on her drink. Richard put his arm around her waist and kissed the top of her head as he silently prayed to God, begging not to have his soul damned for all eternity. The deception moved forward, hiding his secret, illicit love of Chip Foley.

Chapter Sixteen

Chip surprised Richard with an overnight in Boston to take his mind off the engagement. The wires on his jaw had recently been removed and he wanted to celebrate. The women were invited, and he booked adjoining rooms at the Copley Square Hotel to keep the illusion of two couples intact. After an early dinner and a movie, the four went back to the hotel bar for drinks and snacks. Chip was drinking water after the second cocktail, as his headache throbbed. He tried to hide his pain, but the others could read his face. He excused himself and headed towards the men's room. He had a strange sensation that someone was watching him. It was not the first time since the blizzard that he felt it, or was it since the raid at the Punch Bowl? He certainly didn't want to mention it to Richard and ruin the weekend. Dismissing the notion of either, he opened the men's room door, where a man in a suit was washing his hands. Chip nodded. The man snickered, "Pansy" and gave him a slight shove with his shoulder as he left. Chip ignored him. When he entered a stall, he heard someone come into the bathroom. A man with a ghastly voice snarled, "fucking pervert" while banging on the stall door. He froze and became light-headed and had to brace himself from falling. The voice brought fear into his chest as the door slammed. "Richard, I'm scared, baby, please come find me," he whimpered. When Chip didn't immediately return, Richard decided to see what was taking him so long. His headaches sometimes overpowered him and because of the workload from being behind in his classes, he hadn't rested much lately.

He was shocked to find Chip trembling on the floor. He lifted him up and insisted to know what was wrong.,

"Take me out of here."

Richard opened the door; Ginny saw them out of the corner of her eye and recognized that Chip was in trouble. She motioned to Beverly as she jumped off the bar stool and went to him. Beverly hailed the bartender and had him bill the Ruggiero room for the tab, then joined her friends, who were walking towards the elevator.

"What's going on?"

"I think the drinks got to him. Let's get him to the room. Come on, buddy, we're almost there."

Once in the room, Chip lay on the bed and curled into a fetal position. Richard didn't know what to make of it. Ginny offered to get him a glass of water and some aspirin, assuming it was one of his headaches. Richard peered helplessly at the two women, then knelt next to the bed and stroked Chip's head.

"Are you sick? Is your head hurting? Look at me. Talk to me," implored Richard.

Chip relaxed as Richard stroked his head and arms. After passing the water and aspirin to him, the women stood apprehensively at the foot of the bed.

Chip wiped his eyes with his shirt sleeve and sat up. "I walked into the men's room, shut the stall door, and heard a very grotesque voice whisper 'fucking pervert' and he banged on the door. I have heard that voice before. I do not know where but I have heard it, and it frightened me like, like death was coming." He put his arms around Richard who held him tenderly.

No one knew what to think. The message was horrifying even though the men had heard that slur and worse thrown at them in the past when near the clubs in Boston. Beverly had suffered similar harassment in her club days.

Beverly pressed, "Have you two been to the clubs again? Maybe it was someone who saw you there."

"No, I swear we have not been near any club since the raid. We don't dare. We've been focusing on Chip getting healthy and fixing the house. Merda, you know that,"

Richard's voice was strained, his eyes irate. "How can you accuse us?"

Beverly didn't acknowledge him but instead looked at a pale and shaken Chip.

"Red, you're going to be fine. You're safe with us. Maybe you heard wrong. It was probably just some drunk jerk. Forget about it."

Chip tried to straighten up and relax as the three hovered around him.

Ginny hugged him. "You've been under a great deal of stress between your accident, the house, and catching up with school. Didn't you tell us that the cops at the Punch Bowl kept calling you perverts? Maybe it was that bad memory."

She stood up as he wiped his eyes with both his hands. "You and Richard should stay in the room; we don't need to go out anymore tonight. We'll leave. Do you want any room service before we call it a night?"

Both shook their heads. Ginny bent over and gave Chip a light kiss on his cheek and trying to break the tension said, "Good night hubby. Don't let the bed bugs bite." This elicited a slight hmm from him.

"Good night, wifey-poo."

"Meet here at nine, we can order breakfast. Check-out is at eleven. I'll take care of him tonight," assured Richard.

"What the hell do you think that was about?" asked Beverly. She was more fearful of a hateful physical attack than she would admit. She could still envision the attacks by the police last Christmas and knew how vulnerable they all were.

"I don't know. I suspect that he's not as recovered from his accident as we would like to believe. Don't worry, Richard will take good care of him tonight. Now, how would you like to take good care of me?" She purred in her most seductive voice.

129

She didn't waste any time coming to Ginny. "I'm at your service, girlfriend."

Ginny giggled as she happily pulled her top over her head. "Let's wear this bed out."

Beverly smiled lustfully as she turned off the bright overhead light.

In the adjoining room, Richard took off his shoes and climbed onto the bed. Chip rested his head on his shoulder as Richard put his arms around him.

"Mio tesoro, do you want to talk about this, about what happened?"

"No. I feel like a fool collapsing in front of everyone. Am I crazy?"

"No, of course not. Maybe you had too much to drink. Did you take any pain pills earlier? Maybe they messed up your head."

"Yeah, maybe. I am tired. Will you hold me?"

"Always. You sleep. I'm right here."

***

Chip was too relaxed and breezy over breakfast; acting as if nothing happened. When the women inquired, he brushed off the incident from the night before as too much to drink mixed with his medication. Inwardly the bullied little boy in him cowered, but years of hiding his fears enabled him to cover his anguish and he forced himself to act carefree.

The four checked out, stored their suitcases at the front desk, and enjoyed a stroll through the Boston Common and the Public Gardens. On a lark, they joined some tourists riding on the Swan Boats and threw popcorn to the ducks. Beverly treated everyone to lunch in Chinatown and they browsed the Chinese gift shops for dragon and phoenix souvenirs for The Eliot to keep away evil spirits.

Richard had driven Chip's car in town and on the drive home drove straight down Blue Hill Avenue towards Milton. Ginny asked him to stop for some hot dogs and subs at Simco's on the ride by. There was a spacious new refrigerator from Sears and Roebuck in the upstairs apartment. And even though her mother and mother-in-law often cooked for the young couple, what she hankered for was a large ham and cheese sub to cut up for lunch at work. She missed having her mother pack her lunch every day.

With a large sandwich and bag of wrapped hot dogs in hand, she tapped Richard's shoulder and said to Beverly sitting next to her in the back seat, "You know, this is where Chip and I came after he convinced me to marry him and *The Plan* was hatched. Wow! Chipper, remember how excited you were to be graduating from college and driving your spanking new car? That was only early April last year. Geez, I feel so much older and how our lives have changed. Now, we have The Eliot."

"We're home," said Richard.

Chapter Seventeen

The remainder of spring progressed smoothly at The Eliot. Beverly had found a part-time bookkeeper position as an independent contractor in Mattapan a short drive from the house and on her days off worked on the finishing touches for her and Ginny's apartment. She splurged and used some of the money from the sale of the Westerly house to purchase an outdoor teak table and chair set for the front balcony. The Ruggieros were told she was staying in and fixing up the first-floor rental apartment for her and Richard ahead of their June wedding. Somehow the foursome hadn't quite thought through how to completely disguise the living arrangements--it was complicated, but they rarely worried.

Ginny went to work every day with a physically-recovered Chip dropping her off at Westinghouse on his way to school. He didn't tell anyone that he often thought that someone was watching him. It gave him the creeps and reminded him of the night at the hotel in Boston. He chastised himself, thinking that it was probably his headaches that were behind his uneasiness. Maybe it was his thick red hair that attracted gawkers. He tried to convince himself that it was anything except the man with the haunting voice.

Richard was working non-stop. It was the busiest time for him and he could barely stay awake on the weeknights that he came to The Eliot. He spent time on the landscaping that had been neglected and made a list of the repairs needed on the outside of the house before painting. At the same time, he and Beverly finalized the details for their June wedding. It was to be family only with Joe as his best man and Ginny as the maid of honor.

Anna organized a small bridal shower for Beverly. Angela invited her sister and two nieces, a few cousins, and her closest friend Mrs. Sorrenti. The homemade wine started flowing early and continued throughout the shower. Beverly had reluctantly taken the first drink but then found the afternoon moving along nicely as the wine kept finding its way into her glass. Ginny and Irene, who had become a good friend, were the only two not drinking and they thoroughly enjoyed themselves, especially while eating large slices of Angela's ricotta cake. Espresso was served with the cake and it lifted up the party to a higher level of laughter, which eventually led to the playing of Frank Sinatra songs on the stereo. Angela and her sister sang at the top of their lungs until their daughters told them that Beverly was leaving. Angela kissed her and had Anna wrap some cake and a bottle of wine for her to take back to the apartment.

Angela cried, "Why can't you be a nice Italian girl, a good Catholic girl?"

"Mama," shouted an embarrassed Anna. "Ricardo loves Beverly. You love her, too. Tell her you're sorry, Mama."

Angela shrugged. "Mia figlia, don't listen to the tears of an old lady. I've had too much of Papa's wine. I love you. You are too skinny, but I love you." She gave Beverly a big, sloppy hug then walked to the chair across the room and promptly fell asleep.

Ginny picked up the box full of presents, Beverly carried the cake and wine, and Irene carried an extra slice of ricotta cake to take home. The three left the family waving to them at the door and drove to Milton, giggling all the way and trying to sing Frank Sinatra songs. Irene was invited to stop by The Eliot but she said she was tired and asked to be dropped off at her home.

The rain poured the day of the wedding, requiring everyone to squeeze into the Ruggiero home. The three younger brothers brought in the baskets of flowers and Anna had them placed in the parlor by the window. It was a mad scramble for a while, but the results were charming and cozy. Beverly wore a simple but elegant cream knee-length dress from Jordan Marsh. Her auburn hair was up and held in place with clips that had belonged to her mother. The outfit was completed with a pair of light blue earrings and a matching necklace that her father had given her on her twenty-first birthday. Richard, looking handsome in a new suit, traditional navy in color, with a white shirt and a new red printed tie, stood stiffly during the brief ceremony and blessing. Although Joe eagerly embraced being his older brother's best man, wearing a suit and tie made him itchy and uncomfortable. Ginny wasn't the least bit uncomfortable being the maid of honor. Beverly had helped her select the green and white dress she wore. She looked quite stunning next to Joe and winked at Chip, at the start of the ceremony while he stood with the rest of the Ruggiero family.

The rain did not dampen the day. Mr. Ruggiero's wine once again filled everyone's glasses, the dining room table was bursting with food, and the stereo played cheerfully. Unforeseen by bride and groom, neighbors came and went throughout the afternoon, offering congratulations and shaking the hands of the bride and groom, and having a slice of cake before departing. Angela had found a way to have a lively neighborhood celebration for her son.

Ginny and Chip left fairly early. They finally comprehended firsthand how Richard and Beverly felt at their wedding charade. It was like a hole in the pit of their stomach. They brooded back at The Eliot and waited for them to come home. Both were asleep on the upstairs sofa with the television blaring when the downstairs door slammed and the two very drunk newlyweds entered; trying unsuccessfully to be quiet. Joe had dropped them off because Angela wisely wouldn't allow her Ricardo to drive.

"Oh, Chipster, I'm home," slurred Richard.

"Oh, Gin-Gin, I'm home," slurred Beverly, mimicking Richard. The two of them hooted and stumbled their way upstairs.

"Honey-poo, there you are," said the new bride. "Honey-poo, I'm married two times. Shhh! Don't tell anybody. How did that happen? I don't want to go to jail, Gin-Gin. I need a cigarette." She sat heavily on the side chair, pulled off her dress shoes, and smiled lovingly.

Richard stood by the doorway and tried whispering to Chip. "Chipster, I'm home. Come downstairs and come to bed with me. I have a big surprise in my pocket for you."

"That's it," replied Ginny and she smacked Chip on the shoulder and said, "Take this drunken sailor downstairs before he embarrasses himself further. And missy, time to get you in bed."

"Are we going to have a honeymoon tonight, honey? Hey, that's funny, honeymoon, honey."

Ginny rolled her eyes as she helped Beverly up.

Chip led Richard downstairs and called over his shoulder. "Check in with me in the morning, late morning."

Chip thought he saw a shadow across the street as he closed the Venetian blinds to the bedroom. He started to peek through them when Richard came up behind him and pulled him towards the bed. Richard was a sloppy drunk but a smooth and considerate lover. He melted Chip with his deft touch and sumptuous lips. The shadow was soon forgotten.

***

Routine fell into place during the weeks and summer months that followed. The Eliot repairs were rapidly finished by Richard and the outside was being painted by a contractor.

Feeling bored from all the focus on house repairs, Ginny suggested that they take a break from repairs and school work and head to Provincetown for the weekend before the cold weather set in. Although not completely necessary in the liberal seaside town, they enjoyed their adjoining rooms scenario. Chip said he'd find a hotel and set it up. Beverly, who was loving her father's white convertible, offered to drive. She had always imagined driving proudly down Commercial Street in a convertible with the top down and a beautiful woman at her side.

The weekend was a rousing success. They caroused with the drag queens late at night on Commercial Street. They sunbathed and tipped their toes in the ocean during the afternoons. Ginny was impressed with the number of art galleries and envisioned her paintings on display one day. A gallery owner explained as the two women toured her gallery, that artists had been coming to Provincetown since the turn of the century. And, that writers such as Tennessee Williams and Eugene O'Neill, "known homosexuals," the owner whispered, helped create a welcoming atmosphere for artists of all types. "In fact," she proudly continued, "I met Patricia Highsmith several times when she visited. You know, she is the author of *The Price of Salt*, Claire Morgan was her pseudonym." They were astonished to learn that entertainment by and for homosexuals had largely emerged in the past ten years or so, despite regulations banning drag shows and same sex gathering places by the town selectmen.

By coincidence, Rey and Jeff were in town and met them Saturday night at the foursome's adjoining rooms for drinks and introductions to the wives.

When the drinks were running low, Richard, Chip, and Jeff decided to walk to the liquor store in the center of town before it closed. Rey relished the opportunity to get to know the women in his young friends' lives and more about the unusual arrangement. He was bewildered that the reserved Catholic Richard would marry a woman under false pretenses. Yet, he found Beverly engaging and quite in tune with the stresses and difficulties of being a homosexual with the desire for a lifelong commitment to a partner. She was head over heels for the younger and seemingly innocent blonde. Ginny was worth probing more.

"Rich tells me that you have known Chip since childhood and that you were always expected to marry him." Rey's Cuban accent surfaced when he was drinking too much.

Ginny laughed and said, "And here we are. An old married couple." She was puzzled about his deep tan and increasingly strong accent as the night wore on. He seemed so out of place in her world, and made a note to ask Chip about this Cuban doctor.

Rey was amused and slightly concerned about her casualness. "You know, neither Jeff nor I have any family nearby and we're simply roommates to neighbors." He shrugged. "Do you believe you can pull this off for the long term?" He noticed that Beverly, who was refreshing her drink, paused to hear her lover's answer.

"I don't see why not. The fellas are comfortable downstairs and the two of us are upstairs. And no one is going to walk in unannounced. We are ALL committed to this." She pushed her hand through her hair and turned. "Right, honey?"

"Indeed, girlfriend."

"I hope so. By the way, how's Chip doing? That was one hell of a head injury, going by the way Rich described it." Rich was beginning to sound more like *Reach* as Rey finished off another drink.

Ginny's expression changed. She winced slightly at the sound of *Reach*, then quite seriously confirmed, "That whole month of March was horrific. He still doesn't remember falling in the dorm bathroom. We can only guess that the floor was wet from snow being dragged in and he slipped, hit his jaw on the sink before falling and cracking his head on the floor."

"I've tried discussing it with him, but he continues to evade and ignore me. *Reach* believes it's in the past and they've moved on. What do you think, Beverly?"

137

"I go back and forth. I sometimes wonder if he was more traumatized by the accident than he lets on."

"Oh, come on," interrupted Ginny. "He's fine now."

"Hmm," responded Rey. He wished that his young friend would confide in him more. He knew that Chip thought of him as square. Something was off with Rich as well. Before he could add more, the three men returned with their arms full of snacks and booze.

Chapter Eighteen

The carefree days of summer passed quickly and autumn was soon upon The Eliot. The leaves had fallen off the trees and the four were in the backyard raking and cleaning before winter set in. Beverly was pruning the rose bushes that she and Chip planted in June after the wedding and explaining to a not-so-interested Ginny how to properly care for them. Chip moved to the front of the house to start trimming the forsythia bushes that lined the sidewalk. He stopped in his tracks as a car slowed to a crawl and a man rolled down his window and pointed menacingly at him, then sped off down the street. The color drained from his face and his knees buckled. He managed to get himself to the front steps without collapsing just as Richard walked to the front yard with an empty barrel.

"Buddy, don't you want a barrel to put the branches in?" He dropped the barrel and rushed to Chip's side when he saw him with his head in his hands on the porch.

Richard had started calling Chip buddy right from the beginning of their relationship. Richard feared reprisals if someone in public heard him calling Chip, mio tesoro, my treasure. Chip accepted the term buddy once he understood it's true meaning, though he swooned over being called *my treasure*.

"What's the matter? Worn out already?" As he got closer, he saw the fear on Chip's face.

"What's wrong? Is your head hurting?"

"There was a man in a car and he rolled down his window and pointed at me, then he sped down the street toward Blue Hill Ave."

Richard paused and scanned both ways down the now-empty street. "Maybe he liked the new house color. Maybe he thought he knew you. Hmm, why would he scare you?"

Feeling stupid, he shakily stood up. "I am fine, hunky-dory; my imagination flared up. Yes, acting like a scaredy-cat. You going to work with me on the front bushes?"

Richard hesitated. "Nah, you got this, buddy." And patted him on the back. "Here's your empty barrel. I'll be out back loading the truck for the dump." He didn't give it another thought; Chip thought of nothing else.

Helen was volunteering non-stop as the neighborhood coordinator for the Kennedy campaign; a position awarded to her during the spring. Local coordinators in key precincts stretched the range of the campaign. Senator Kennedy had won the primary and was in a too-close-to-call race with Vice-President Richard Nixon. The last of four televised debates were over. Helen explained in her best campaign voice to anyone who would listen why it was important to understand the issues and to vote for the pre-eminent candidate for the presidency. Her candidate.

It was a week until the election and Helen had assigned her volunteers to tasks that would carry them through election night. As her strength and self-assurance grew, Helen confidently went to Campaign Headquarters regularly for meetings, updates, and supplies. She felt blessed to be alive and nothing was going to stop her again. Her renewed fortitude astounded John. He even pitched in on occasion during the evenings with mailings and drove her around the neighborhood to deliver signs requested by Democrats to place in their front yards. Otherwise, John practiced with the band whenever he could, in preparation of the onslaught of requests to perform at holiday parties. His mood was lightened by the return of a familiar routine.

On November 8, 1960, the young, junior senator from Massachusetts, John Fitzgerald Kennedy, won a close battle for the presidency. Helen was beyond elated. The first Catholic ever to be elected! Thinking ahead to Thanksgiving she hoped to show her gratitude to her neighborhood team and to her family for encouraging and supporting her work on the campaign. She baked a dozen pies and dozens of cookies to give as thank-you gifts to her team. It was going to be the start of a joyous Christmas season.

Chip paid little attention to Helen's commitment to the upcoming election and studied at school as much as possible to catch up on the classes he had missed last spring. He had somewhat caught up over the summer, but this year's requirements demanded studying at a punishing pace. He was carrying a double load and it put a strain on his relationship with Richard. Whenever Richard questioned his studying so hard, he repeated that law degree requirements were incredibly stringent, and he was adamant about graduating on schedule. He was often tempted to say, *Richard, you just do not appreciate my commitment to excel.* His headaches were subsiding slightly with the aid of the pain medication, and he kept pushing at a breakneck pace. He requested and received the unique dispensation of private tutoring for one of his required courses. The course was taught by his house-buying lawyer, Professor Dennis Jenkins, who was fast becoming a friend. Dennis recognized Chip's potential and encouraged him to be assertive in classes and vocal during study groups. The most engaging course of the fall semester was an elective that focused on civil rights, the direction of practice Chip told Dennis that he was leaning towards.

"You have the skills to be a successful attorney, whichever area you choose. Challenge yourself and you will be top in your class and be highly sought after. I know it."

He took Dennis's words to heart and searched within for the strength to follow his emerging convictions and pursue a career as a civil rights attorney, a champion for the ignored and excluded. A civil rights attorney wouldn't be the money maker that corporate work produced, but it would allow him to work with victims of discrimination, voting rights for Negroes, women's rights, and homosexuals. The area of need was broad and he felt the pull toward making a difference. He hadn't discussed this shift in focus with Richard, who supported his drive to be a lawyer but didn't quite comprehend the many pathways he could specialize in. Nor had he discussed it with Ginny, his usual touchstone for major decisions. He was determined to make up his mind on his own.

Most notably, Chip had become increasingly aware of the rumble of activism by other gay men. Reynaldo had stated at the party in Provincetown that the FBI was investigating men and women who worked for the Federal government and were suspected homosexuals, and as provided by an Executive Order by President Eisenhower in 1953, were being categorically fired. He doggedly investigated Reynaldo's accusations. The reality that this was boldly taking place daily across the country shocked him to the core. Helen was spot on; Kennedy was the better-qualified man and not Eisenhower's Vice President Nixon, he thought. On his own, he started reading the *Mattachine Review*, and learning about the emerging role of Franklin Kameny, a gay astronomer who was fired and subsequently became a vocal activist, speaking out about the horrors experienced by others who had been fired. One case in particular, the suicide of a man who was fired for being a homosexual after having served in active military duty and working for the Foreign Service, irritated, frightened, and saddened him to no end.

By December, his energy level was depleted, and he was counting the days until the end of the semester. He could close his books for a few weeks and celebrate the upcoming New Year without thinking about being followed and the trauma being suffered by others like him. He craved quiet time with Richard; his mind screamed for rest.

The first Christmas in their home together would be festive. The couples planned to host family and friends and have an open house both upstairs and downstairs to kick off the holidays. The major work on The Eliot was completed; the final colors for the apartments were neutral, and no one would assume one apartment was for the women and the other for the men.

Richard had asked Anna and Dom to sell him their old piano. They readily agreed, thinking that the den could be a nursery. Richard, Dom, and Joe moved the piano and surprised Chip on the day he finished his final exams. The piano drew the guests together and Christmas songs filled the air. Richard kept the piano on the first floor and told his brothers that they could move it upstairs after the holidays. Chip and one of his friends from the school music department took turns entertaining the crowd.

After the last of the guests had departed, the two couples gathered in the upstairs parlor. Richard was staring at the back wall and casually mentioned that someone at the party thought the wall was an add-on. The other three glimpsed at the wall and had no idea what he meant. Richard got up, took down Ginny's acrylic painting of the ocean, inspired after their trip to Provincetown, and started pounding the wall with the palm of his hand.

"What on earth are you doing?" asked Ginny.

"Can one of you get me a hammer? I think whoever it was might be right and this wall is hiding something."

Reluctantly, Beverly went into the kitchen and got out the toolbox that was under the sink. "Here you go big guy, knock yourself out. But you're fixing any holes that you make and repainting the wall."

He felt around the wall with his hands, then with an "a ha" picked up the hammer from the toolbox and swung with all his might.

"Jesus H. Christ," stammered a suddenly alert Chip. "You actually made a hole in the wall."

Richard put his hand through the hole and pulled back a large section of plasterboard. He grabbed the flashlight in the toolbox and shone it through the hole.

"Look at this. There appears to be a stairway behind the wall. Come on, help me pull this section of the wall down."

"You three do it. I have to bring my latest paintings to the Holiday Art Show early in the morning. Clean up your mess when you're done." Ginny, stretched and left the room. She heard banging and whooping it up for the next hour until Beverly came into the bedroom.

"Hon, are you awake? You have to come see this." Ginny put the pillow over her head, but Beverly persisted and dragged her out of the bed.

The floor was a disaster, but there as clear as day was a staircase leading up to the attic and down toward the first floor.

"Huh, well I'll be a monkey's uncle."

Richard was covered in plaster dust. Chip was sweeping, trying in vain to contain the mess.

"What's next? Why do we need an old staircase?"

Richard said he would work on it during the week and figure out if it was safe and how it opened up downstairs and to the attic. He promised to clean up the remaining mess in the morning.

"Wonderful. Now go to bed. Bev, you're with me. Good night fellas. Great party."

The demolition work took half of the week to carefully open the exits to the attic and the first floor of the staircase. Richard had everyone's blessing to open the walls to expose the stairs and he delighted in the challenge. Beverly was curious about the origin of the staircase and why it was hidden. She drove to the Milton Town Hall to ask the town clerk how to find the original house drawings. The clerk lived at the far end of the street and had been in the house as a child. He remembered the old staircase. He explained that in the past the home had the back staircase for the maid. With a smile, he directed her to the Registry of Deeds to search for blueprints.

Beverly found what appeared to be the original house blueprints and shared them with the others. Before the blocking of the back stairs, the upstairs parlor had originally been divided into two rooms and the second-floor kitchen was a bedroom. She was intrigued by the reconfigurations of the old house and labored with Richard on the days she wasn't working. He was easy to work with and they joked often. Richard found that he worked harder when she was with him. She encouraged him and never swatted his head. On the last day of the demolition when the final bags of trash were carried out to his truck, the two decided to celebrate by going out to lunch. They washed and changed after the dump run and drove to Villa Rosa in Quincy.

"My mother will skin me alive if she finds out that I went to an Italian restaurant. But this place makes a dynamite roast beef sandwich," said Richard who didn't bother to pick up the menu.

"Pushing thirty and you're still afraid of your mother?" she said kiddingly. "I don't blame her. Your Mama cooks the pants off anyone I know. I'll have the roast beef, too, and a beer." She opened her purse and found a pack of Pall Mall. "You don't mind, do you?"

Richard shrugged his shoulders and signaled to the waitress that they were ready to order.

"The back stairs will make it easy to run up and down. I want to add a window in your parlor and build a door with shelves in front of the staircase. In the downstairs kitchen, I'll build a similar door with shelves on the front. They'll be real secret doorways. I'll do that first and refinish the steps over time. You want to continue to be my apprentice?" Richard sat back in the booth. He was gratified with the work they had accomplished and looked forward to her pitching in with the remainder of the project.

The day, despite the back-breaking work, was one of the best times that they had experienced together.

1961

"Not everything that is faced can be changed, but nothing can be changed until it is faced." James Baldwin

Chapter Nineteen

Helen spent days trying to entice John to come with her and the team from the Kennedy Campaign Headquarters to the Inauguration and the Presidential Parade. The bus was leaving on Thursday. They would view the outside Inauguration on Friday, attend some of the celebration parties, and return home late on Sunday. Hotel reservations had already been made. John couldn't take the time off from work and definitely couldn't envision Helen riding on a bus to Washington D.C. She nagged and pleaded, he was firm, and she pleaded again. He staunchly opposed her going without him. Helen said John was treating her like a child and she was going with or without him. He was worried about her mental health and didn't know how to say it without damaging her newfound self-esteem. The anniversary of John Jr.'s death and what would have been his twenty-fifth birthday were a mere three weeks away. February continued to be the month he dreaded not only because the loss of his son but for the depression that captured Helen for days on end every year. He was anxious that after the Inauguration and the end of her busy volunteering, Helen would completely collapse. He could no longer demand that his daughter stay with her mother. He had already quietly confirmed the yearly memorial Mass on February 19th with Pastor Riley at Saint Catherine Church. Marjorie Foley had committed to lending a hand with the desserts afterward as she had every year. John watched Helen pack for the trip, thinking that she was the most obstinate woman. He walked to the kitchen, made a martini, went to his studio, and played his guitar as his frustration saturated the room.

Helen's trip to Washington, D.C. was a tremendous success. She watched the Inauguration Parade on

Pennsylvania Avenue and met the President's sister, Eunice Kennedy, at one of the Volunteer Thank You parties. John Stevens stayed home and stressed. Helen was exuberant about the possibilities for change that would improve health initiatives, create a Peace Corps, and significantly address civil rights. She was determined to stay working for the Democratic Party in Massachusetts.

After the trip, the Boston Campaign Volunteer Director promised to write a recommendation for her for a part-time position with her local representative, Arthur Walsh, a staunch Democratic representative in Washington, D.C. Helen's aspirations were soaring.

The prospect of a potential part-time position was a relief to her husband John. Although he knew cold dinners at home would be in his future, Helen's foray into politics kept her busy and away from disconsolate thoughts. He prayed that she would get through the month of February without incident.

***

Almost eleven months after the blizzard, Chip still intentionally avoided the dormitory on the hill. The building gave him the chills and try as he might, he couldn't remember falling in the men's room. Falling and hitting his head and breaking his jaw didn't make any sense to the usually agile young man. Instead, he walked the long way around to the busy public way to get to the bookstore to buy supplemental readings for his Civil Procedure class. While standing in line to pay and daydreaming about being the star of the class, a sensation made him turn. There at the end of the line was a big man. He appeared too old to be a student and he didn't have that professorial edge about him. Maybe he worked for the FBI. The man stared at him. He turned away and gave his books to the cashier, paid, and left in a sweaty panic. Once out of the building he ran as fast as he could to his car on the other side of campus. Hurrying inside, he locked the doors, put his arms over his head, and leaned against the steering wheel.

He yelled to no one, "Who is that man?" Groaning to himself, he thought, *why am I afraid of him?* Shaking, he hungered to go home. He admonished his reflection in the rearview mirror, "This is absurd. There are lots of people on campus. People that I do not know and encounter every day. What is it about him?" His head started to pound. He opened his satchel and swallowed two pain pills. He checked his watch, only ten minutes until his next class began. He forced himself to get out of the car and ran to class.

His fear grew during the tedious class; he was anxious to leave for the safety of his home. His mind was tormented. The droning of the professor was a blur. He stopped taking notes from the lecture and started writing questions: *Who was the man at the bookstore? Who was the man who drove by the house in the fall? Are they the same person? Why do I always think someone is watching me? Could it be the FBI and do they want to get me kicked out of school? Am I going crazy? I am twenty-four, why am I acting like a scared kid? Why? Why do I avoid talking about how I feel with Richard or Ginny or anyone? Should I call Reynaldo?* He closed the notebook, closed his eyes, and tried to convince himself to tell someone.

He practically flew out of the lecture hall at the end of class and drove home like his red hair was on fire; his head was exploding, his heart racing. He knew he was being followed, again. The Eliot was his only refuge.

The same evening, Beverly met Ginny in the visitor parking lot at Westinghouse. They were going to Mattapan for a casual dinner and a movie at the Oriental. Beverly, a fan of Shirley MacLaine, thought they would enjoy her latest movie *Can-Can* with Frank Sinatra. Girls' night out away from the husbands, Ginny told Irene over lunch.

Beverly eased out of the parking lot and held Ginny's hand. "By the way, Shirley MacLaine is going to be in the movie version of *The Children's Hour*. I can't wait until it comes out. She's so talented."

"That book scared me. The meanness, calling us sick. I wish I hadn't read it."

"Sorry, girlfriend, it's frightening and horrifying, but a strong dose of reality now and again is good for us." She recalled how her father, in his roundabout way, had cautioned her about the hate in the world. She was intent on raising Ginny's awareness of homophobia. They needed to be financially independent to be prepared for any backlash from society. The idea to start her own accounting business began to stir in the back of Beverly's mind.

"Hey," she raised Ginny's hand to her lips and kissed it gently. "Let's have fun tonight and forget about the world."

***

Richard's truck wasn't parked on the side driveway. Chip wondered where he was; Richard always got home before him. Out of his rearview mirror, he saw a car slowly coming in his direction. He parked in front of the house, grabbed his satchel, and made his way toward the front door, never taking his eyes off the approaching vehicle. The vehicle slowed as he inserted his key in the entranceway door. Richard was putting his work boots in the hall closet. Chip let out a startled gasp when he saw him. He dropped his satchel and squealed,

"There is a car following me outside. I know it is the same one. Why is a car following me?"

Richard was out the door and down the steps before Chip could react. A neighbor was backing out of his driveway making it impossible for the mysterious car to speed off. Richard wrenched open the driver's side door and pulled the large man from the seat and out onto the street. The man didn't have a chance to put his car in park and it rolled slightly and hit the curb. Richard was screaming incoherently, the man was screaming and fighting off Richard. The neighbor was headed in the other direction and never noticed the commotion.

"Why the hell are you following Chip? Who are you? What do you want? I ought to bash your brains in."

The man appeared petrified. "Who the fuck is Chip and what the hell are you doing? Get off me, asshole." He threw a punch at Richard, who stumbled against the curb. Chip came out of the house and ran towards Richard as the man got back in his car and pulled away. But before he did, he glared maniacally at Chip.

Richard pushed Chip away and got up by himself. "Fuckin' hell, he said he doesn't know you!"

He didn't notice that Chip had paled. Chip slowly backed away from Richard and in a strained voice said, "That, that man was the same one I saw in the fall, remember when we were raking and cleaning the yard. It has to be the same person. Has to."

"What? What are you saying? Maybe he lives on this street. Merda, my feet are freezing. I don't have any shoes on. Come on, let's get in the house before the whole neighborhood sees us out here looking like a couple of fools."

Chip walked to the kitchen, opened two bottles of beer, and sat down. He watched Richard dry off his feet and put on warm socks.

"Where is your truck? That man would not have slowed down if your truck was here."

Richard put on his last sock and threw the wet towel on the floor. "One of the gears was sticking so Joe dropped me off. He's going to work on it at Dom's garage tonight. Talk to me. What's going on?"

"That man, I am sure of it, is the one following me at school. There is something about him that reminds me of my accident in the dorm. And, and, Jesus, he scares me." He leaned in closer to Richard and softly whispered, "He might be with the FBI." He gulped down his beer. "Do you have any of that god-awful whiskey in the cabinet? Anything stronger than beer? Look at my hands, they are still shaking."

Without saying a word, Richard got up and walked to the shelf over the refrigerator, and grasped his bottle of cheap whiskey. He opened the cabinet next to the sink and removed two juice glasses and poured whiskey into both. He drank one down, then refilled the glass.

He handed a drink to a still pale Chip. "Fuckin' hell?" Richard tried to be calm. He was puzzled and thought to himself, as he drank his second glass slower. *This is insane. Is he losing it or is he just weak and afraid of everyone these days?*

Chip heard his father's demanding and brutal voice even though it was his beloved Richard speaking. He immediately shut down. Years of hearing his father yelling at him to be a man and to fight back when being bullied were seared into his mind and he retreated.

"Talk to me. What's going on with you?" Richard was frustrated. He finished another whiskey and watched as Chip stared blankly at him, rose from the table, and left the room.

"Fuckin' hell," was all Richard could say to himself.

***

Helen was watching out the window, itching for John to come home from work. The office of Arthur Walsh had called and made an appointment for her to come in for an interview on Friday. She had spent the previous two hours going through her clothes, trying on different combinations of tops and skirts, dresses and sweaters, dresses and no sweaters, different shoes, boots, and even jewelry. She settled on her black woolen skirt and a white cashmere sweater and pearls, black pumps if the weather held out, and her black ankle boots if there was any snow on Friday. Of course, John was late. She was losing her patience. She marched back to the kitchen and stirred the simmering pot of beef stew, adjusted the heat to low, and put a towel over the rolls to keep them warm. Where was he?

***

Chip didn't say another word. He was convinced that being followed was not a figment of his imagination. He went to bed early leaving Richard alone and worried. Richard wished the women had chosen another night to be out. Rey was in Miami again and he urgently needed someone to talk to about Chip's behavior. He wasn't getting any better; the headaches lingered and the incident outside on the street was a nightmare. That poor guy in the car might never ride down Eliot Street again. They were lucky he didn't call the cops. Agitated, he downed another double shot of whiskey.

The women arrived home late and had barely reached the upstairs back door when Richard came barreling up the outside steps. He tripped on the last step and steadied himself on the porch railing.

"It's about time you two came home. I have to talk to you."

The women were tired and not in the mood to listen to him.

"It's late. You're drunk. Go back downstairs and go to bed. We can talk tomorrow. I'll be home all day."

"He's driving me crazy. He's..., I don't know, what's the word, I don't know. He's..., he's off his rocker!"

The two women eyed each other. Ginny finished unlocking the door, opened it, and switched on the light. Richard followed her in.

Resigned, Beverly said sarcastically, "Okay, I guess you're coming in."

He went straight to the refrigerator while the women removed their coats.

"Don't you have any beer in this fridge?"

Ginny came over and closed the refrigerator door. "No. I'll make you a coffee if you want. Go sit down and tell us what you mean."

Richard told them about incidents that he could trace back to last summer, in which Chip insisted that someone was either following him at school or driving by the house, or watching him from across the street. He reminded them of the night at the downtown hotel. He couldn't quite remember but he thought that was the first time he showed signs of being paranoid. When he gave the details of the car right in front of the house the women gasped. Ginny was worried that the neighbors might have watched. What if they began to question what was going on behind closed doors at The Eliot? Beverly noticed her reaction and, unperceived by Richard, shook her head and touched Ginny's hand to calm her rising concern.

"I thought he was weirdly paranoid because of the raid and getting arrested. But tonight, he added something different. He said that the man in the car triggered a memory of the accident during the blizzard and that he could be with the FBI. I asked him to explain, but he couldn't. He drank two whiskies and a beer. He hates whiskey. I don't know.

Merda, what the hell! And, naturally, Rey is nowhere to be found. He refuses to discuss anything with Rey and when I suggested he make an appointment with his regular doctor, what's his name? Doctor Hannan, no, Doctor Harris, he said he'd resolve it himself."

Ginny heard the kettle whistle. She made a cup of instant coffee and put it in front of Richard. Unconsciously, he picked it up and drank.

The women stared at him, dumbfounded. Had they been so preoccupied that they hadn't noticed any odd behavior? Would someone follow Chip for months? It couldn't be the FBI, that was absurd. Were his headaches the cause?

"Hon, hasn't he confided in you?" probed Beverly. She was beginning to worry that a local troublemaker might be purposely targeting him, harassing him whenever he was away from Richard.

Ginny racked her brain. "He spends so much time at school. He's there constantly. On days when he drives me to work, we're both usually comatose and barely say a word. I assume he's going to drive me tomorrow. Do you want me to prod him about this, Richard?" She ran her hand through her hair, yawned, and looked at the clock.

"I guess he's going in tomorrow as usual. Yeah, definitely. I'm stuck and don't know what else to do. I'm going to talk with Rey when he gets back later this week."

Beverly placed her hand on Richard's shoulder. "It's almost midnight. We're tired. Go downstairs and go to bed. We will figure this out and take care of him together."

Richard went to the parlor and used the secret door. *Gotta put the finishing touches on this*, he said to himself.

Ginny stared at the parlor long after Richard left. "Do you think he's crazy? Why would anyone follow him?"

"Back when I was going to clubs, there were always troublemakers around. Guys who got their kicks from harassing us. Some were dangerous, most were not. This is exactly what we were talking about before the movie tonight.

We're getting increasingly visible and the creeps are finding it easier to target us with their taunting and violence. They're convinced we're perverts, deviants, and abominations heading straight to hell. C'mon, it's late, let's get some sleep and talk about this tomorrow. Okay?"

Ginny was tired and confused. She didn't know what to think and was determined to get some answers from Chip during their ride in the morning.

***

John arrived home thirty minutes late from work. He was hardly ever late and Helen was beside herself when he came through the kitchen door. He immediately noticed her agitation, or was it jubilation? He gave her the usual kiss on the cheek, hung his jacket on the hook by the door, and kept moving. "Hi, hon, sorry I'm late. I helped a guy change a flat in the parking lot. Let me wash up. I'm starving. Is that beef stew I smell?"

As he walked to the bathroom, Helen called out, "Representative Walsh's office called and I have an interview this Friday."

"That's wonderful, dear. Where's the interview?" John hadn't realized the implications of the date on Friday. As he dried off his hands and hung up the towel, it hit him. Friday was the anniversary of John Jr.'s death. He stood and looked in the bathroom mirror and questioned whether he should remind Helen or let it go. The remembrance wasn't until Sunday. She was in such a good place and he didn't want to ruin her mood. Plus, he was hungry.

***

Chip let Ginny know that he was running behind, but would still get her to work on time. His hangover pounded, he had forgotten to set the alarm, and Richard was already gone. Richard had left a note on the kitchen table that Joe had called late and said the truck needed a new part, which wouldn't be available for a couple of days. And that he would ride with him until then. He dropped the note back on the table and sighed heavily. He made a couple of peanut butter and jelly sandwiches to take to school while scarfing down the last slice of Angela's homemade pizza. Ginny was leaning on the car when he came outside. The air was crisp and the wind blew slightly. She was bundled up in her heavy coat, hat, and mittens. Her usual thermos of hot chocolate was in her hand. She didn't look at her watch, but he could tell that she was anxious to get going.

He only grunted when she said good morning. He hadn't had a hangover in months and was feeling miserable. He threw his satchel in the back seat and jumped into the front seat and started the car, hoping that the heat would come up quickly.

"Richard told us about the man in the car yesterday. Why haven't you said anything about being followed?"

He didn't respond. He maneuvered out of his parking spot and headed up the street before speaking.

"What do you think about increasing the size of the driveway on the side of the house? I do not like parking in the front. There is space along the side of the garage and we could make it wide enough to hold two cars at least. Richard and his father could do the work. What do you think?"

"Yeah, sure, why not. About yesterday?"

"Darling, I am way too hungover to have this conversation. Plus, it is probably just my overactive imagination, as you call it." She ignored him and persisted.

"Richard is worried about you. He bolted upstairs after we came home last night and told us that there has been more than one incident and that you remembered something about your accident in the dorm." He gave her a sideway glance and tried not to frown. "We should get this out in the open. C'mon don't freeze up on me. Oh, and remember, we're going to the Copley tomorrow after work."

"Give me a break. I do not want to talk about it. Period. I want to relax this weekend and not stress about school, or Richard, or the psycho who is hounding me."

"Okay, done. Bev is going to meet me at my parent's house after work. My mother called early this morning. She has an interview tomorrow with an Arthur Walsh. I guess he's our representative. I was hurrying to get ready for work myself and cut her off. I can tell her that you are at school late on Thursdays. They'll miss seeing you."

"I will be at school late tonight now that I know you have a ride. It is easier to study in the library than at home with Richard hovering over me. Say hi to your parents."

He pulled up to the drop-off and gave her a peck on the cheek. "I will be fine. Do not worry about me. Richard is just overprotective." She didn't believe him. He knew she didn't. He was trying to be a man. He drove toward school and attempted to focus on the day's classes ahead. She watched him drive away and worried about the slip he made: *What psycho was hounding him? Did he know him? Was there a psycho?* She waved at Irene, who had just gotten off the bus with a group of workers, and walked with her to the office.

***

Helen had pork chops frying and insisted the two women stay for dinner.

"Call your father. Everything's ready. Beverly, dear, would you carry the dishes to the dining room? Tonight, we're going to celebrate my good fortune."

Dinner was delicious and the conversation around the table was carefree. John was disappointed that his son-in-law was at school. He continued to think of Beverly as much too old and world-wise for his daughter; and why was she here and not home with her husband? He was pondering just that when he heard Helen gushing once again about the opportunity to work for Representative Walsh and how her months of volunteering had paid off.

"1961 is going to be a banner year for Democrats and I have a role to play in making that a reality." Her morale was soaring. Her small family was delighted for her. "Why don't you three go to the parlor and I'll bring the dessert. Girls, you can help me with the dishes afterward."

When they entered the parlor, John put on the nighttime news with Walter Cronkite, to cover up their voices.

"Virginia, don't you remember what tomorrow is?" He whispered and glanced towards the kitchen where he could hear Helen getting plates down from the cupboard.

She was caught off guard, then gasped. "Oh no, I completely forgot. It's Johnny's anniversary. Mom hasn't said a word about it to me. Is the Mass arranged for Sunday night? Is she going to cook Johnny's dinner? Gosh, Dad, the four of us are going to Boston for the weekend. Should we cancel? I'll cancel."

Beverly was about to speak, but John quickly replied.

"No, go ahead and have your weekend. The arrangements are set. Just be here for dinner and the Mass. And, no, she hasn't mentioned a thing about cooking and I'm afraid to bring it up because she's over the moon about the interview. I guess it's just a formality. I don't know. Should I remind her or stall until after the interview? I don't want her to slide back into her usual February depression."

John was stymied. He half-expected Ginny to resolve his dilemma. He was saddened that she had forgotten and was going to be away on Friday and Saturday. She had found a way to move on.

Beverly didn't say a word. The anniversary of her father's death was barely a month away. She was devastated by his loss and could only imagine how dreadful it must be for Helen and John to relive Johnny's death every year. She craved a cigarette.

Helen bounced into the room with a tray of freshly made chocolate cake, plates, a pot of coffee, and a cola for her daughter. The silence in the room was deafening as John got up to turn off the television.

"What?" She said as she placed the tray on the coffee table.

Beverly interceded. "Is this what I think it is? I've missed your chocolate cake. Richard's mother is a good cook but she doesn't bake chocolate cakes. No one can bake like you, Mrs. Stevens. That's no lie."

John joined in. "Make my slice a large end, Helen. I'll pour the coffee. You girls want a cup?"

The cake, as usual, was divine. Helen offered to wrap a slice for Chip to have when he came home from school.

The doorbell rang.

"I'll get it," said John putting his plate on the coffee table. "We were just talking about you."

Chip was immediately worried that Ginny had retold their morning conversation.

"Helen made chocolate cake and wrapped a slice for you to have later."

"I'll take a slice home, and gladly have a slice and coffee now."

Comfortable in his surroundings, he walked into the parlor, shrugged off his coat, and said to Helen, "I finished my readings early and thought I would join you. Do not tell Ginny, but I have been drooling for some of your home cooking." He sat on the sofa and purposely kissed his wife. From across the room, Beverly wished that she was the one playing out the cozy scene.

"I have a couple of thick pork chops left; would you like me to warm up a plate before you have a piece of cake?" Helen knew Ginny wasn't fond of cooking every night and her poor husband probably suffered because of it.

"I love you, Mom. Yes, please." He preferred to call Helen, Mom. It reminded him of his childhood and simpler times.

Ginny groaned and called out to her mother in the kitchen, "Stop spoiling him, Mom!"

While eating his dinner, he commented that the four of them were heading into Boston for the weekend for a late Valentine's celebration. Beverly added that Richard had bought a special red tie with tiny hearts to wear at dinner. She joked about how red was his favorite color and that he would wear a red suit if he could get away with it. Everyone laughed at the idea of a red suit on big muscular Richard.

"Except maybe at Christmas, then he could play Santa Claus," added a relaxed John.

The levity of the evening overshadowed all thoughts of John Jr.

Chapter Twenty

The Eliot foursome headed into Boston as planned, giving each other the impression that they were without a care in the world. The truth be known, Ginny was worried about her mother and regretted going away on John Jr.'s anniversary. Beverly was reminiscing about the last month of her father's life. Chip was thinking he'd drink away his fears while Richard fantasized that the weekend would wash away his and Chip's problems. As the other three chatted while he drove, Richard thought to himself. *I'm fed up with playing straight. Screw The Plan. How does Rey manage to live with Jeff seemingly without any consequences?"*

Sitting together at a table in the hotel bar, Chip explained what he was learning about the subversive efforts by the federal government to discredit, expose and fire homosexuals across the country. "Remember when we met Reynaldo and Jeff in Provincetown? Reynaldo told me about it and I have since started my own research."

He looked cautiously around the room.

"There are cases," he said as he firmly tapped his finger on the table. He tried not to raise his voice and shifted forward in his chair, "Right here in Boston a man was fired because of this. Kicked out like he was garbage. It must stop."

The others listened, noting Chip's growing vehemence.

He added that they had to pay attention and stand up and be activists. Beverly and Richard had experienced the vitriol first-hand from homophobes in the community but didn't know anyone who had been fired. Yet being activists was not how they wanted to present themselves to the world.

Something inside Chip had him worrying that it might be the government following him. Reynaldo's conversation about the insidious Federal 'witch-hunt' played over and over in his head. *Was the FBI in the car? Or was he going crazy? Should he say something to his friends, after all Ginny pushed him to talk.* Before he built up the nerve, Ginny said she simply couldn't imagine the government doing that or anyone being fired for no valid reason. He envied her naiveté and finished his drink. Out of the blue, he decided to mention his interest in becoming a civil rights attorney for the disenfranchised.

"I have been thinking," he began. "I might change some classes so my focus shifts to working on Civil Rights discrimination cases." He waited for a response.

Beverly noticed his usual yearning for approval. "Great, Red, but is this about the Feds?"

Richard waited for a beat then touched Chip's shoulder, aware of being in public. "Buddy, you be any kind of lawyer you want." Ginny nodded in agreement as she played with the ice in her drink.

"No, Bev, it is more than that. You know, women are discriminated against. And the Negroes, look at what is going on in the South." When Richard and Ginny stared somewhat blankly, he sighed and persisted, "Voting rights are continuously being squashed, Negroes cannot mix and mingle with white people, even bus riding is segregated and restricted. The more I pay attention to what is going on, the more I am convinced that I have to somehow be part of the solution."

"Will you be able to help as a, what did you call it, a Civil Rights discrimination lawyer?" Ginny asked. She remembered Beverly telling her about Paul Robeson. "I'm proud of you. We should learn more about this. Right, honey?" Beverly nodded.

Energized now and feeling confident he added, "Yes, in fact, I have been hearing something around school about groups riding to the South in buses this May to protest the segregation. I am thinking I should do this during my school break. Maybe we can go together." He leaned back, pleased with himself.

Richard was not so pleased. "Ah, you're going away? When were you going to tell me?"

"It is nothing definite, I, um, um, am just thinking out loud. But I do believe we have to be more proactive in fighting discrimination on all fronts." He gave Richard his best smile. Richard returned the smile with a shake of his head.

Chip quickly proposed ordering another round of drinks. After which Richard suggested taking a cab to Playland. When Beverly hesitated about going to a club, he reminded her that Playland drew a mixed crowd and had never been raided by the police.

What started as carefree drinks and a late-night snack in the hotel bar, devolved into a raw need to throw caution to the wind. They were depleted from playing traditional roles with their families and living on the outskirts of society. They thirsted to drink, to dance, to scream away their pent-up frustrations. Already slightly drunk and feeling sorry for themselves, they eagerly grabbed their coats. The music at Playland was loud, the drinks cheap and the clientele ready to party. Sweat and sex permeated the air. The four soaked it in as they entered the club. Their inhibitions dissolved.

They stumbled to their adjoining rooms sometime after 2 a.m. and once asleep, didn't stir until almost noon. The *Do Not Disturb* signs on their doors kept hotel housekeeping away, but not the hangovers.

The open drapes welcomed the brilliant sunshine in as it rounded the south side of the hotel. Ginny, usually the non-drinker in the group, drank the least, but it was no consolation to her aching head and rumbling insides when she was struck in the face by the sun. Grumbling, she rolled over and hugged her sound asleep and naked lover. A soft moan emerged with the memory of the lovemaking that possessed them in the wee hours of the morning. Ginny thought about getting up and was shocked when she saw the time. She slipped her arm away from her lover, got out of bed, and headed into the bathroom to shower. Her mouth tasted like dirt scuffed off the bottom of an old shoe. Her tummy rumbled. She was still in the shower when she heard Beverly cursing at the sunlight. "I'm in here, come join me," she called.

Next door, the men snored their way through the morning hours and into the early afternoon. Ginny slipped a note under their door to let them know that they were up, going to eat, and then off to shop. She said to be ready for their 7 p.m. dinner reservation.

That evening, they dressed in their finest and, arm in arm as married couples entered the Copley Plaza dining room. The room was decorated with red roses, candles on the tables, and soft music playing in the background. No one said a word about the wild night at Playland. This night was for veiled romance and love, dammit. The maître d' escorted them to their table and presented the two ladies each with a single red rose. Complimentary champagne was delivered in an ice bucket and a glass was poured for the couples. As they settled in with the appetizers, the women described their afternoon of shopping and purchases for their apartment. The men grunted their acknowledgment and nursed their hangovers gingerly with the champagne.

The hotel had a small orchestra set up in the ballroom for after-dinner dancing. Egged on by Beverly, the group ventured in. Richard instantly swung her out to the dance floor. Chip and Ginny quickly followed.

"Has Ginny spoken with Chip? He keeps saying, not now." Richard twirled her around. They danced seamlessly together. If only he could twirl his man on this same dance floor.

"She tried to get him to say something, anything, on the way to work the other day, but he clammed up. I almost thought he was going to say something during drinks at the bar last night. Now that we're aware of it, we'll keep our eyes and ears open. I don't know which is worse, that there *is* someone following him, or that he is getting paranoid."

"Thanks, you're first-rate. Another twirl, then back to the table?"

"Sure thing, Romeo."

Chip 's eyes lit up when Richard sat next to him. "I do love you in that red tie," he crooned.

Richard leaned over. "Maybe I'll wear it later tonight." He sat back in his chair and winked. Chip blushed at the thought of Richard wearing the red tie and not another stitch.

Morning came too quickly once again, and they had to check out by 11 a.m. With the reverie behind them, the sleepy group packed their bags, said goodbye to the adjoining rooms, and headed back out to the cold reality of being adults on their own in 1961.

On the drive back, Ginny reminded Chip that after getting home they should change quickly and go straight to her parent's house. She was concerned about her mother. She couldn't believe that she had completely forgotten. Dismayed, she began to feel guilty about the weekend.

"Hey, come on, don't beat yourself up. You deserve to live your life," Beverly consoled her. "You'll be there for dinner and the Mass. Come on, it's okay. Richard, we should attend the service with them." He looked at her in the rearview mirror but didn't say anything.

After they arrived home, Beverly went downstairs to ask Richard again to go to the church with her. He had planned on going to the afternoon Mass at his family's church. When he hesitated, she added that they didn't have to go to the Stevens' house, just to the church service. Richard preferred his own Parish church and decided to attend both services. Maybe God would notice his efforts and help allay his internal pain.

Chapter Twenty-one

Helen sailed through the Friday morning interview and was invited to join the small staff for lunch. Helen was ecstatic, a bit nervous, but ready to embrace her newfound life. The conversations throughout lunch were stimulating. Everyone was buzzing about the new president. His inaugural speech infused a sense of optimism lacking under the former president and the rabid Congress. Life was about to get richer for every American. Helen exuberantly concurred.

She arrived home late in the afternoon and changed into her casual house clothes; a simple housedress with pockets on the sides and flat shoes for her tired feet. She couldn't wait for John to come home so she could share her day with him. As she was walking into the kitchen, the phone rang. Her older sister, Martha, who lived in Ohio was on the other end. Helen told her about the job interview and how happy and grateful she was to the state Democratic Party.

Martha was concerned and paused.

"Oh, Helen, that's wonderful news for you." Hesitating, she said, "And to be able to move on from your sadness over Johnny..." Before she could utter another word, Helen grasped that it was February 17th. She dropped the telephone and slid onto the telephone chair.

"No," she wailed and began to sob, shocked that she had forgotten her son.

Martha frantically called out to Helen from the other end of the telephone.

Helen picked up the phone and said, "I have to go, Martha, thank you for calling." She hung up the phone, lifted herself off the chair, and went to bed.

That is where John found her when he came home from work. As he walked up the driveway, he saw that the lights were out. He stopped short, held his breath, and slowly walked to the back door and into the dark kitchen.

"I'm home. Helen?" He hung up his coat, removed his shoes wet from the melting snow and turned on the kitchen light, calling again for his wife. He knew. He lost his appetite and switched off the light. His heart broke, as it had every year on this date. His boy was gone and his Helen had most likely slipped once again into a crushing depression.

He walked through the dark house and found the light switch for the upstairs hallway. He paused as he prepared for the worst, then climbed the stairs to their bedroom. Helen was asleep. The light from the hallway reflected on the framed photo on her bureau of John Jr. taken with the family on New Year's Eve only a month before he was killed. John shut off the hallway light, placed the picture on the nightstand next to him, climbed into bed with Helen, and silently cried.

On Sunday, Ginny and Chip were at her parents' house by early afternoon. Bracing for gloom, they parked in the driveway and went to the back door. Helen waved to them from the kitchen sink. That was a good sign.

Helen opened the back door and kissed them both. Her eyes were red and her face blotchy from a weekend of tears but she was up out of bed and cooking dinner. John was in his studio practicing a hymn that he would play on his guitar during the Mass. His eyes were red as well.

"Dear, you're finally putting on the weight you lost. Let me look at you. Yes, you're such a dashing young redhead." She passed him a plate of shrimp rolled in bacon. "How's school?" Before he could answer, she continued, "I know I just saw you Thursday night, but still, you don't come by often enough." He had no time to explain—she was off on another tangent. "Virginia, go get your father. He's been practicing that hymn over and over. If he doesn't know it by now, he never will." Chip knew that when Helen was nervous or worried, she talked nonstop like this.   "Dear, sit down, try these appetizers," she extolled him, continuing to gab. At least, he thought while enjoying the shrimp, she is not in bed, depressed, and refusing to see anyone.

Helen's early dinner was ready by 4 p.m. They ate Salisbury steaks with mushroom gravy, mashed potatoes, and baby peas, John Jr.'s favorite, on the afternoon of his anniversary Mass every year. Dessert would be served after the Mass when family members and a few friends and neighbors would join them at the house.   Helen was determined to keep her son's memory alive, this year more than ever. The Mass and gathering would not be a blur experienced through the eyes of depression, but a celebration of the eighteen precious years John Jr. lived. She firmly believed he watched over her and was instrumental in her calling to support fellow American Irishman, John Fitzgerald Kennedy. She would not let him down.

After the Mass, Richard and Beverly were talked into coming to the gathering at the house by Helen. She was impossible to refuse. Her sweet smile was usually backed up by her stern motherly tone. Richard was quiet and stayed in the background. He didn't know anyone, until, to his surprise, his brother Joe came through the front door with several of his friends. He watched as they went up to Mr. Stevens and shook his hand. Joe walked over to Helen and hugged her. She seemed pleased to see him, hooked her arm in his, and walked with him to the dining room. He and his friends emerged with large slices of cake. It was then Joe noticed his big brother.

He left his friends and came over. "It never crossed my mind that you would be here. Is your beautiful wife here somewhere?" he said looking around.

"Hey, Sfigato. Ya, she went upstairs. Girl stuff." He pointed to the stairs while taking another bite of cake. "I didn't expect you and your friends here either." Joe sat down on the arm of the couch; his mouth full of his oversized slice of cake. Before he could swallow and speak, Richard remembered the connection. "Oh, right, you played baseball with Ginny's brother. Chip's in the kitchen with his mother." His subconscious was screeching, *damn, I hate this bullshit.* Chip was not simply his friend while they pretended to be happily married to Ginny and Beverly. The bitterness choked his throat.

Mr. Stevens saw the two speaking and realized that they were brothers. It had never occurred to him that Chip's friend was from the same family. He called Helen over to come to say hello while the two brothers were together.

"I wondered why you always were vaguely familiar, you're much older," said Helen. "Readville is a small town, I shouldn't be surprised. Excuse me. John, we should thank Pastor Riley for coming by."

Joe finished his slice of cake. "Gotta run. The guys and I only stopped by to pay our respects. Hey, Mama was complaining to Pops that she's heard no word about a bambino coming." He lightly punched Richard on the arm and winked. "Get to it stud."

Richard rubbed his arm and cursed. "Bye, Sfigato." Unable to pretend for another moment, he put down his empty plate and walked out the front door as soon as Joe left.

Chip helped his mother wash the used cake plates and coffee cups. She inquired about school. He asked about the VFW Ladies Auxiliary that she avidly supported. He wanted to tell her about the man he believed was following him. He was trying to figure out a way to broach the subject when she mentioned John Jr.

"Johnny was an incredible young man. To think all these years after his death so many people continue to attend his memorial Mass and come by the house to pay their respects."

He thought of Johnny's charisma and mettle. How he stood tall in the world. No one would dare harass him, he sighed to himself. His mother was asking a question.

"Sorry. What did you say?" He picked up a stack of plates and moved them to the cabinet. After a lifetime of being in the Stevens' kitchen, he knew where every plate, pot, and pan was stored.

"I was saying that I remember how Johnny used to watch over you while you were at St. Catherine's. Helen told me, sometime after he died, that once when he was in the ninth grade, Johnny came home with bruises on his knuckles and his cheekbone. He tried to toss it off as nothing, but he couldn't hide anything from his mother. He said that she had to promise not to say a word about it, but that he was in a fight with a couple of boys who were giving you a hard time. He was walking home from the bus stop and behind them. You were almost running to get away from them. He called out to the boys and challenged them to a fight with the deal that if he won, they would never bother you again. He won. Such a brave boy. I guess he was your secret big brother." Chip grimaced at the memory of being constantly chased and bullied. He wondered why, if his parents knew, they didn't do anything to help him. He started to speak but pulled back as she continued. "So sad. Huh, I thought you had finally stood up for yourself because, by the end of the eighth grade, you didn't run to your room and cry after school anymore." She glanced at her son, knowing the difficulties he had as a young boy. Her husband had demanded that she not interfere; his son had to become a man. Her eyes apologized; he glanced away, not willing to go any further.

"Here you are now, married to Johnny's sister. You two are such a perfect match."

He half-heartedly acknowledged his mother while he racked his brain trying to figure out who Johnny fought with. If Johnny was in the ninth grade, then, yes, he was in the eighth grade. Someone was always following him and giving him a hard time. Ah, eighth grade, Frankie Lombardi and Martin McKenna, the doomsday duo as he used to call them behind their backs. They had stopped chasing him before winter that year. He assumed they got bored. If only he wasn't the weak little brother.

Mrs. Foley dried her hands and kissed her son's cheek as she went by him to check the desserts on the dining room table and to see how many people remained. It was getting late and time for the numbers to dwindle.

Chip stayed in the kitchen. The repressed memories of bigger kids following and bullying him swarmed through his mind, tampering with any manly strength that tried to surface. He had been followed his whole life by bullies. He couldn't take it anymore.

His father-in-law came in just as Marjorie left. "Oh, hi." He moved to the bottom cabinet next to the pantry door and pulled out a bottle of gin and a smaller bottle of vermouth. "I'm making a martini. Ah, would you care to join me?" He had never known Chip to have a martini but made the offer anyway.

"Yes. That would be great. Make it a double."

"You got it, kid. Two doubles coming up." John fixed the drinks and sat down next to his weary-looking son-in-law.

"The girls are still upstairs gossiping, I guess. You know, John's friends show up every year without fail. A number of them have moved away, but the local kids still show. Damned good of them. Hey, here's to Johnny and you and Ginny. Maybe you two will have a Duncan the third one of these days."

"Here's to Johnny and my favorite in-laws." The drink was harsh and burned but was the perfect salve for his wounded spirit.

Mrs. Foley started cleaning up in the parlor and dining rooms to signal to the remaining guests that it was time to leave. Ginny, Beverly, and Margaret Mary came downstairs for another slice of cake. They had been going through the remainder of Ginny's things that she had left behind. Margaret Mary excitedly claimed some of the school souvenirs. Beverly was way past wanting any reminders of her teen years.

Chip heard the girls from the kitchen, finished his second double martini, and excused himself. John chuckled to himself as Chip swayed a bit when he stood up.

"Gin-Gin, my darling," he slightly slurred. "Time to go home. Monday tomorrow, back to the grind." He searched the room, but couldn't locate Richard.

Beverly went out to the front porch and saw that Richard's truck was gone. There was no excuse for his disappearance and her anger swelled. She was bored out of her mind and anxious to go home after spending an hour in Ginny's old room with Margaret Mary and listening to the two of them giggle about high school dramas.

"Damn it," she sighed. She went back inside. "I'll drive. Give me the keys, Red." She found her coat and said her farewell to Mr. and Mrs. Stevens while Ginny retrieved several slices of cake wrapped by Mrs. Foley to bring home.

Once in the car, Beverly aimed her anger directly at Chip. "What the hell is going on? Why'd Richard take off without telling me? Did he tell you? Crap, Red, I'm doing everything I can here. Sorry, girlfriend. He knew this was a special night for your family, and he left. God damn it."

Chip wasn't listening. He had fallen asleep in the back seat.

Ginny attempted to touch Beverly's leg to soothe her, but she shoved her hand away. She put her hand in her pocket and yanked out a pack of Pall Mall. Ginny ran her hand through her hair thinking *Richard was the idiot who left, why is Bev mad at me?*

Chip stirred as the car pulled up to the house. He ran his hands over his face and through his hair and climbed out without saying a word. Beverly got out and slammed the door. Ginny followed them to the front porch. Beverly unlocked the outside door and marched straight to the first-floor apartment door and banged on it as loud as she could.

"Open the damn door, Richard."

Chip grabbed the keys from her and fumbled for the door key as Richard opened it. He didn't acknowledge any of them.

Ginny's gaze went from one to the other. "I'm going to bed." The weekend of partying and the stress of another memorial for Johnny had her exhausted with a massive headache. She stomped up the stairs, unlocked the door, and went straight to the bedroom. She wasn't so infuriated as to re-lock the door, but she did close it.

***

Just as a tense week followed at The Eliot, a tense week followed at the Stevens household. Walsh's office had not called Helen with a start date. She was beginning to worry. John was beginning to worry. They danced around the subject, talking about the nice turnout for the memorial, inconsequential news, the weather, people at Westinghouse, anything except the JOB. By Friday, Helen couldn't take it anymore. John's tiptoeing around made her jittery on top of her already frayed nerves. After he left for work, she sat by the telephone until 9 a.m. Shaking, she called the Representative's office and asked to speak to Bob Crosby. She was told the director was out of the office with the flu and asked if she would like to speak with anyone else. Helen explained that she had been the one in for the interview a week earlier and was told to expect a call the past Monday. The receptionist placed her on hold. Helen tapped her foot, stood up, sat down, and prayed for John Jr. to intercede. It felt like hours before the receptionist came back on the phone.

"Mrs. Stevens, I do apologize for taking so long. I called Mr. Crosby at home on your behalf. He said that he had fully intended to call you himself on Monday, but the flu knocked him out over the weekend and he forgot. He said he was sorry." She paused.

Helen froze, swallowed, and meekly asked, "What do you mean?"

"He's sorry about not calling, but, yes, come in on Monday for your orientation and to set up your hours. Congratulations, Mrs. Stevens. Welcome to the team."

Helen was overjoyed. "Thank you. Thank you. I will be there at nine sharp on Monday morning. Have a nice weekend and thank Mr. Crosby for me."

Helen calmly put the receiver down, hugged herself, and called out, "Thank you, Johnny, my angel." Bolstered by the belief that he was watching out for her, she sighed, "You've saved my life again."

***

Friday did not go as favorably at The Eliot. Richard was still pouting, although he wasn't sure why, at that point. Chip spent as much time as possible at school, worrying about his class work, but mostly worrying about the psycho. "The St. Cat bullies were real, this psycho is, too. Yeah, psycho is the perfect name for you, shit bag, even if you are FBI," he said aloud to his image in the mirror while he shaved.

He had a passing thought that perhaps he should mention the FBI on campus to Dennis. He hadn't told Richard that Dennis was tutoring him twice weekly this semester, one evening with a group and one evening one-on-one. Richard's insecurity and more frequent outbursts worried him. He was not about to add fuel to the flame. School agitated Richard enough as it was and he couldn't comprehend why. Dennis offered to tutor him with his Civil Procedure course and invited him to join the group sessions. Chip had gladly accepted. Dennis was patient and had a wealth of knowledge. At six foot two, with wavy brown hair, green eyes, and an easy smile as wide as the Mississippi, it was obvious why his students gravitated towards him. A graduate of Harvard Law School and a Rhodes Scholar, he brought to the study of law startling new concepts that Chip found intriguing. There was nothing other than academics to the relationship; at least that was what he told himself. Although Dennis had suggested going out for coffee or drinks, Chips concentrated on the tutoring.

Ginny rode with Chip to work every morning and Beverly picked her up. Since the episode after the drive home from her parent's house, it was a toss-up as to which ride was more torturous. Chip because he was preoccupied with school, or so she thought. Or Beverly, who was colder than the weather outside. Something had to give. Ginny was at her wit's end and tempted to take the slow crosstown bus to avoid riding with either of them.

Helen called Friday night, eager to talk about her starting date at the Representative's office and to invite her and Chip to a weekend dinner. Ginny bowed out of dinner. For fear of appearing to have marriage troubles, she said that they had already had plans. She promised to call her Monday night to hear how her first day went. Beverly overheard the conversation. Ginny rarely refused an opportunity to spend time with her mother and Beverly blamed herself. What she wouldn't give to be able to have dinner with her mother and father again. As Ginny hung up the phone, Beverly came up behind her and wrapped her arms around her.

"I'm sorry. I've been an ass all week. Between Richard bailing on us at your folks' house and missing my father..., please forgive me, my love. I'm sorry. Especially after we had such a delicious time at the Copley."

"Can we go downstairs and confront the idiots? You know, I have no idea what you three did Sunday night and why everyone is acting like, yes, idiots."

"We drank and argued. I smoked too many god-awful cigarettes and we drank Richard's cheap whiskey. You were out cold when I came upstairs."

Chip heard the secret door open and Beverly calling out. Richard was having a beer and sitting on the sofa in the parlor. He got up when they came in.

"Wanna beer? Mrs. Foley, you want a cola?"

"Ok, I'll have a cola."

Beverly said no to the offer of a beer.

"What's going on girls, juicy assignments from *The Plan*?" Richard was as sarcastic as he could be. He sat down heavily at the end of the sofa. Chip sat in the middle and nursed his beer.

"My mother starts her political *career* on Monday. She calls it a career and says she's going to save the world."

"Can she save me?" mumbled Chip.

Everyone's eyes shot to him. The conversation about the tense week was quickly forgotten.

"What do you mean?" asked Beverly caringly. She wanted to follow through on Richard's request to pay attention to him and his delusions about being followed. *Could someone be following him? Was the school incident intentional and not a fall?*

He didn't answer, just drank his beer. Richard gestured to Beverly the go-ahead.

"Is there someone harassing you? What's going on?"

Ginny added, "Please Chip. It's more than a difficult semester at school."

"Mio tesoro, you can count on the three of us. Who's bothering you? I would beat the shit out of anyone who bothers you. You do so much between school full time, extra study groups, and managing The Eliot. Something's gotta give. Let us help."

"Yeah, I am weak. I know. Everyone has to save poor, weak Duncan Foley."

Ginny ran her hand through her blonde hair. She was growing it out some and it was annoying her. "Chipper, what the heck are you talking about? Spill. We're your family here. Tell us about this psycho." His eyes shot up at her. "Yeah, you called him that in the car last week."

He finished his beer. Holding in his fears was grueling. He closed his eyes.

"I am so tired." Inhaling and leaning on Richard, he began. By the time he was through describing the times when the psycho had followed him or spoken to him, the others were frankly sickened.

Beverly, though startled by his revelations, could imagine the harassment. If she was revolted by the idea, then Chip must be petrified. No wonder he seemed to Richard to be losing his mind. Why hadn't they paid closer attention? Was he that good at disguising his true emotions? Why did he take so long to confide in us?

"You should go to the police."

"What will they do? I can hear them, 'The pansy wants us to protect him from the big, bad, scary man.' No. I had enough of the cops at the Punch Bowl, and besides, he might be with the cops or the FBI. Just like Reynaldo said. Gay men and, yes, lesbians are being targeted. I am targeted."

The thought scared them. Could this man be dangerous? Was he a psycho or simply an asshole getting his thrills by stalking Chip? He couldn't be with the FBI, that was simply ludicrous, but was it? The room was quiet.

Ginny scoffed at the idea that anyone could follow Chip around *for a year* without any of them noticing. It had to be something else. Exhaustion, his headaches, coincidence. Something.

"Is it possible that this man was in the dorm men's room? Richard said you remembered something from that night," asked a reticent Beverly, aware of the potential implications. It was enormously troubling. She squeezed Ginny's hand, her fear growing.

It had been taken for granted that his concussion and broken jaw were the results of a fall in the dark bathroom. Chip insisted he couldn't remember any specific details. What else may have occurred in that room? What could have provoked a man to viciously attack him? Suddenly, all three wondered if he may have propositioned a straight man, a vengeful, psychotic man.

Richard started fuming. *Chip would never flirt with a stranger, never a straight man, and during a blizzard no less. Would he? The man must have been crazy, must still be crazy. Had he been following him before the blizzard?* Frustrated, he got up, left the room, and went to the kitchen and let out a loud scream, picked up the old kitchen chair, and almost smashed it against the refrigerator. At the last second, he held his temper in check and came back to the parlor red in the face, and stared down Chip, daring him to admit to the unthinkable. Chip scrambled off the sofa suddenly aware of what had crossed Richard's mind and precipitated the scream. He walked to Richard and stopped directly in front of him.

Softly but adamantly, he said, "Richard, I do NOT know this man. Trust me. You have always been and will always be the only one." Through gritted teeth, he added "I cannot remember what occurred in that men's room. But whatever it was, it was not because I flirted with anyone."

Richard unclenched his fists and hugged the man he adored. "God, I can't take all of this drama. It's got to end. What do you want us to do?"

"I want to get through this semester. I have a summer internship that I am applying for in Boston. I have been under a lot of stress, and my classes are incredibly challenging, but I can handle this. If you want, I will give old Reynaldo a call for some stress-relieving tips." He closed his weary eyes and dug deep to pull up the strength to continue. Confiding in Reynaldo would soothe Richard. He had to keep moving toward his dream.

"What you said makes sense, no one would follow me around for a year. It must just be stress grabbing wildly at my imagination. I love you three." Though his stomach turned and his head ached from the tension in the room, he smiled. Then dismissed the conversation by giving Richard a passionate kiss.

Richard slowly pulled away from him, "Sorry for my reaction, girls. Mio tesoro, I think Rey can help. Call him soon, please."

Acknowledging the change in mood, Ginny got up. She was ready to move on. Though she wouldn't admit it, intense emotions and conflict were difficult for her to handle since the loss of her older brother. She feared becoming like her mother and hiding away when life became too demanding.

"Richard, I'll forgive you if you promise never to ditch me again like you did at the Stevens'. Idiot." Beverly said with a smirk, which broke the tension in the room slightly. "I almost pounded down your door several times this week."

"Oh, about that. Um, sorry? The pressure caught up with me, and I bolted. And, my mother is starting to ask about a baby." Now it was Richard's turn to smirk.

The spacious room filled up with groaning and laughter, and ended up once again with pillows from the sofa being thrown at each other.

Chapter Twenty-two

Beverly didn't want a memorial service for the anniversary of her father's death. She preferred to travel to Westerly and visit his grave at the family plot. Together the four friends cleared lingering snow off his headstone and that of her mother's and laid a wreath of flowers on both. Instead of driving by her former home, they drove to her favorite childhood beach. In the cold, they walked along its shores. The wind at times took their breath away. Beverly walked until she could go no further, sat on the sand, and let the tears break loose. Ginny sat down on the near frozen sand and held her. The men joined and hugged their girls.

The Ruggieros couldn't fathom why there wasn't a church service for Beverly's father and insisted that Ricardo and Beverly bring their friends come to dinner at their house on Sunday. Angela offered a remembrance prayer before the meal. She yearned to ask about a baby but listened to her husband and held her question in check.

The remainder of March shifted daily between being the proverbial lion and the lamb. Some days it roared until the sun pressed through the clouds and took the chill from the air. Chip begrudgingly called Reynaldo and he and Richard met with him together and separately.

"I'm very proud of both of you for seeking my support. I may not be out to society, but my commitment to professionally support fellow gay men is a large part of my practice. As a friend, I'm always here for you both." Chip moved restlessly in his seat, while Richard acknowledged Rey's assistance in helping them through this rough patch.

"Chip, you've had quite an intense year. Marriage, new home with Richard, school, and the accident." The doctor recognized that he had to tread lightly with him. He was concerned and had some trepidation about Chip's wellness.

He worried that Chip would refuse counseling if he or Richard pressed and he had to maintain the line between their friendship and his professionalism.

"I guess that is significant." He squeezed Richard's hand. "We have both had quite a lot to adjust in our lives."

"Anxiety and stress build to a breaking point and sometimes we're not aware of it until too late. Did you know that I seek the counsel of a colleague when I sense my stress rising? It can be easy to become confused with all that I experience in my practice. But enough about me." He opened his calendar book and the three set aside several additional dates for in-person appointments and phone calls.

They discussed coping strategies for anxiety and stress. Rey suggested that Chip inform his regular doctor if his headaches interfered with his daily routine. He reiterated that the FBI was *only* investigating people who worked for the federal government and that they wouldn't be following a student. Over the course of several sessions, the doctor accepted, though, that it was possible that Chip was being stalked and recommended that the Milton Police and the Newton College Police be contacted immediately the next time the man appeared.

***

Easter was coming early in April. Ginny's, Chip's, and Richard's parents were trying to entice their respective children to come to their home for church and dinner. Chip insisted that he'd have nothing to do with church beyond the tutoring of the high schoolers studying for their college entrance exams. God had abandoned him and he was wounded. Beverly, never a churchgoer, preferred the idea of celebrating Easter together with an egg hunt in the two apartments, eating jelly beans, and being silly. She fancied being a child again, if only for a day. She lobbied hard for playtime at The Eliot as a family.

The decision was made to stay at The Eliot and visit their respective families in the evening for dessert. They bought Easter decorations and dozens of eggs to paint on Saturday night. Beverly secretly bought everyone a child-size Easter basket and filled them with candy, including a set of acrylic paints for Ginny, a comical red-headed Woody the Woodpecker miniature figurine for Chip, and a garish red tie for Richard. She hid the baskets in the guest room in the attic. The weather was beautiful the day she brought the baskets up. She opened the door to the small porch and let the fresh air in. She was struck by the view of the Blue Hills; their bedroom window faced the street. The attic art studio had several large windows and a skylight but trees obscured the view of the hills. She contemplated if Ginny would like to move their bedroom to the attic floor. It certainly would be very private and the view lovely.

Ginny, Beverly, and Richard were working on the Thursday before Easter. It was the start of Easter break, but Chip was going to the campus early in the morning to review his application for the summer internship in Boston with Dennis.

Chip looked forward to the festivities of Easter, getting dressed up, a special dinner, and the baskets stuffed with candy from the Easter Bunny. He, too, had bought everyone chocolate bunnies, a couple of Easter surprises for Richard, and fancy Easter bonnets for the girls to wear during the egg hunt. The purchases were in the trunk of the car and Thursday would be the first time he would be home alone and could slip them into the house unnoticed. He was relieved that the driveway extension was going to start later in the month. He was anxious to get his car off the street and safely onto his own property. He would be able to go to the back door and get in the house easier. He'd feel safer. He brought the bundles in and left for school. His anxiety began building during the drive to school. His head ached and he was exhausted from lack of sleep.

The morning did not go as planned. Dennis decided to visit friends for Easter and cut the session short. Chip was back home early, irritated and jumpy. The house was cold and empty. He had taken to keeping all the blinds closed in case the psycho was lurking. It gave him comfort. Prying eyes and taunting shadows wouldn't paralyze him. He liked that Richard thought it was for intimate privacy. Little had been said about his fears since the others confronted him in February. After the sessions with the Reynaldo, Chip was committed to completely dropping the notion of the FBI or some weirdo following him. He focused on returning to his former self and easing Richard's concerns. His haunting memories of being bullied as a child were easing. He acknowledged that the sessions were helping him to understand his fears better. At least that was what he tried to convince himself, and to the others he appeared self-assured again. Reynaldo recommended that the formal sessions continue and he volunteered to speak with him informally whenever his fear and anxiety increased. Chip was working hard at emulating John Jr.; be brave, he heard John Jr. whisper in his ear, confident and strong. But, alone in the house he weakened. He tried to focus on Reynaldo's strategies for coping. His head was pounding. Shaking, he took a double dose of his pain reliever.

***

Thursday evening Beverly drove her car straight from work to meet Ginny at Westinghouse. They stopped on the way home to pick up submarine sandwiches and french fries that Beverly ordered from her office. When they rounded the corner to Eliot Street, lights were flashing from an ambulance. Neighbors were standing in clusters on the sidewalk. Beverly slowed the car and they realized at the same time that the activity was at their house. She pulled the car over to the curb in front of the house behind the ambulance, and they ran, alarmed, toward their door. The door was open and Chip, unconscious, was being wheeled out on a stretcher. Richard was close behind the stretcher, pale and his eyes feral. When Beverly called out to him, he searched for her but kept following the stretcher. They met on the steps.

"My God, Richard, what happened!" screamed Ginny. She tried to get close to Chip but the ambulance medic pulled her away. Richard said sternly to the medic, "I am going with him and this is his wife."

"Look, pal, no one rides in my ambulance. We're going to Milton Hospital. Meet us in the emergency room." The medics put Chip in the ambulance and one medic stayed with him and shut the door, while the other climbed in the front to drive. They left with the sirens wailing and lights flashing.

Completely stunned, Ginny and Beverly tried to catch up to Richard who was running back to the house.

"Richard, stop. What's going on?" Beverly stammered, out of breath.

Chip's family physician, Dr. Harris, was talking on the telephone in the parlor and Richard was coming out of the kitchen with his truck keys. He had forgotten about the doctor and paced impatiently for him to finish his call. The women tried to speak with him but he held up his hand for them to hold off for the doctor.

The doctor observed the two women as he hung up the phone. "Are one of you ladies his wife?"

"I am. Doctor, what's going on? What happened?"

"Oh, yes, I remember you. You're John Stevens' girl. What I was telling this young man earlier, after I examined Chip, was that he should be sent to Milton Hospital for tests and observation. I'm inclined to say he has had some sort of mental breakdown, but it's too soon to say that's the final prognosis. I suggest you go to the hospital and complete the admission forms and visit your husband. I'm going there shortly myself."

Ginny nodded speechlessly.

"I'll let myself out. Mr. Ruggiero, it was the smart thing to do, calling me." The doctor held out his hand to shake Richard's and left the apartment.

"Richard, my car is out front. Come on, I'll drive, and you can tell us what happened," said Beverly.

On the drive to the hospital, Richard explained how the night before, Chip had come home from school late, tired, hungry, and agitated about some berating by a professor. After he ate and took a few of his headache pills, he started going from window to window, peeking out and mumbling about the psycho watching him.

"I tried looking out from a different room and saw nothing, absolutely nothing. When I told him there was nothing there, he started pacing and holding his head, and muttering that I never believe him and that it was real and he couldn't stand the doubts. I said that I would go outside and walk around the house, but he wouldn't let me leave him. I called Rey and he said to try to distract him, calm him down, to tell him that I believed him and would keep him safe. And, to be prepared to call his family doctor if he appeared out of control. I tried all that, and he still got worse. I think maybe he is taking too many pills." Ginny started to interrupt but was stopped by Beverly.

"Finally, after he drank a couple of whiskies, I convinced him to go to bed. He hid under the blankets and clung to me all night. This morning he said he was going to school just for the morning and would be back by lunch. I asked if he was feeling well enough to go to school and if he'd like me to take the day off and go with him. He said he was perfectly fine, that his mid-terms had worn him out. His reaction was way off, but I was afraid to say too much and have him, I don't know, have him act crazy. I came home from work early to check on him. What time is it now?"

Ginny glanced at Richard in the back seat. "It's five-thirty."

"I guess I was home around three-thirty or so. I called him when I came in the back door. His car was out front. I called to say I was home. He didn't answer so I checked the apartment. When I didn't find him, I thought he might have gone upstairs for something. When I opened the door to the back stairway, I found him huddled on the steps in the dark. He had his coat on and was hugging his school bag and murmuring to himself. I couldn't quite make out what he was saying. Jesus, this is a nightmare. Girls, fuckin' hell?" He paused and ran his hands over his face.

"We're almost at the hospital. What did you do when you found him?" asked Ginny.

"It took a while but he finally agreed to come into the kitchen. I got his coat off and offered him something to eat or drink, but he said he couldn't stay in the kitchen because a shadow was outside the window. We went to the parlor and he made sure the blinds and curtains were closed and sat as far from the window as he could. I didn't know what to do, so I called Rey. We just met with him last week. He seemed fine, well, better anyway. When he saw me go to the phone he went berserk, yelling and screaming that we couldn't call anyone, the psycho would be listening and the FBI had tapped the phone. It fell apart from there. He started ranting and crying and hovering in the corner. He was shaking and holding his head. He ran to push a chair against the front door. He began muttering to himself again and finally, he didn't recognize me. *Me*. He didn't recognize me. He put his hands over his head and sat on the floor shaking. That's when I called Rey. Jeff said he was in Miami helping children escaping from Cuba. I don't know what that means. I hung up and called Doctor Harris."

Beverly pulled up to the emergency room entrance. She spoke before Richard could get out of the car. "Richard, I'm sorry, but remember Ginny is his wife, they'll only speak with her. Don't worry, we'll stay with her the entire time, okay? Also, someone has to call his parents. You didn't call them, did you?"

He fought off the frustration of being delegated to the role of a concerned friend. "No, of course, I haven't, let's go. I get it. Beverly, stay with me, please."

They made their way to the emergency room and located the check-in desk. Chip was being examined and the nurse said his wife would be called as soon as there was any update.

Within the hour, Ginny's parents and Mrs. Foley had joined them. Mrs. Foley had left a note for her husband and kept repeating that he would arrive soon. Richard excused himself and went to the Chapel to pray and to escape the tension created by the parents' presence. Helen held her friend's hand while John went to buy everyone a cup of coffee and something to eat. The dinner in the back of the car was long forgotten.

Well after visiting hours ended, Dr. Harris announced that Chip would be admitted overnight. He had come out of his stupor but was quite confused and incoherent. He was given a sedative and would be examined by the psychiatric team and observed for at least three days and possibly up to several weeks. The doctor said that nothing else could be done and he was going home; he recommended that they do the same, and left the small group in shock.

Chip's parents went in first to say goodnight. Ginny's parents kissed her and said they would come by the house in the morning. After the Foleys and the Stevens left, Ginny quietly ushered Richard and Beverly into the room. Chip was asleep and pale. The nurse who was checking his IV nodded and whispered, "I'm sorry, you have to leave, we're about to bring him upstairs."

Chapter Twenty-three

Helen gazed out the window at the heavy morning rain and thought of the words by Irish poet William Butler Yeats that her mother used to recite during a storm:

Bolt and bar the shutter,
For the foul winds blow;
Our minds are at their best this night,
And I seem to know
That everything outside us is
Mad as the mist and snow.

Helen never understood the meaning of the poem; it scared her as a child. She had visions of ghosts and goblins attacking their small cottage in Ireland. Her brothers teased her, which made her fears worse. Helen's mother suffered from depression. "Haunted," the family called it all those many years ago, and it had found its way to Helen. She was afraid now that it had found its way to her son-in-law.

"For the foul winds blow," she said to the rain outside. The blackness in her mind was spreading. First, she lost her only son and now Virginia's husband was suffering from what appeared to be a nervous breakdown. She closed her eyes, willing herself to fight back.

John walked into the bedroom. Dressed and ready to drive to Milton, he noted Helen by the window. "Hon, are you ready? It's almost nine-thirty. We should get going; we promised to help. Helen?"

When she acknowledged him, he could see the shroud of depression enveloping her. He walked to his wife and hugged her. "We have to go. Please, get your things."

Helen had risen and baked in the very early morning hours. Baking, her escape from the perils of the day when

John Jr. died. She walked downstairs to the hall closet and put on her raincoat, stood up straight and tall, then picked up the two cake holders and stoically walked in the rain to the car. "Bolt and bar the shutter, for the foul winds blow," she repeated over and over in her head.

***

After a sleepless night for everyone, Friday shifted into a whirlwind of activity at The Eliot. Margaret Mary and Susan came over as soon as they heard. The Foleys arrived shortly before 10 a.m. Paul came about noon, clearly shaken, found a chair in the parlor to sit and wait for the medical update. Ginny had called the hospital as soon as she awoke but was told to call back after 1 p.m. when the doctors completed their first round of tests.

Richard was struggling to stay upstairs with so many people coming by or telephoning. The hospital refused to give him an update; he was worried beyond belief and yet he had to stay in the background. He gripped the arm of the sofa until his knuckles were white. He should have been the one receiving updates, not the Foleys and not Ginny. As soon as the Foleys went to the kitchen to have a cup of coffee with Helen, he approached Ginny. Beverly followed him, concerned about what he would do. As far as she could tell, *The Plan* was not disrupted. *Crap*, she thought, *why am I even thinking about The Plan? How are we ever going to handle this?*

"Will you come downstairs with me?" Richard pleaded quietly.

She was thankful for the break. The three went down the stairs to the apartment and locked the door. Beverly gathered Ginny into her arms as Richard paced in the parlor.

191

He burst out, "I can't take this madness. Chip's in the hospital and may be sent off to some loony bin and I have no control over any medical decisions or even visiting him. I can't let anyone know that I'm the one in love with him. I'm losing my mind." He fought back the tears as he played with the key chain with the little truck.

"What do you want to do? Tell the world that you're gay, queer, a homo. That Ginny and I are a couple, that we're all deviants? What would that serve?" It hadn't been twenty-four hours since Chip was admitted to the hospital and Beverly's usually steely nerves were already beginning to fray from worrying about him and trying to console Ginny and now Richard. Her father's decline and death played over and over in her mind. Why was she always consigned to the role of level-headed practicality?

Ginny was surprised at Beverly's outburst. "None of us want his life ruined. I can't think, Richard. What happened to our Chipster? How'd he get so sick and we missed it?" She leaned into him as her emotions overwhelmed her.

He hugged her and guided her towards the sofa, "I don't know. I don't know. All I know is that I, we, have to make sure he returns to normal. Beverly, I hear what you are saying. I promise I'll handle this. I have to. I just needed a moment with the two of you."

Beverly closed her eyes, sat on the sofa with them, and tried to replay Chip's recent actions. After the sessions with Dr. Martin, he was visibly more relaxed. On Tuesday night he came upstairs and gushed about his new Brooks Brothers suit for Easter and was excited about painting Easter eggs. The outside door opened followed by footsteps of several people making their way upstairs.

"Sounds like Margaret Mary and Susan have come back with lunch. Are you ready to come upstairs? Do you want me to come with you?" Beverly turned to Richard. "What are you going to do?"

"I'm staying here. I think I'll see if Rey is back; he doesn't know about Chip; maybe he can call the hospital. I don't know. Thank God I have the day off."

"Bev, come with me. Richard, I'll come back down as soon as I hear from the hospital. Geez, it's going to be a long day. Do you mind if I go wash my face first?"

He pointed to the bathroom. "Can I talk with you for a minute before you go?"

When Ginny came back from the bathroom, Beverly gave her a quick kiss and said she would be up shortly and motioned to Richard.

"What is it?" she asked tenderly.

"I just want to sit with you and go over the chaos from yesterday. Merda, when will I be able to go to him? Please sit with me?"

She sat next to him on the sofa and held his hand.

"Thanks." He rested his head on her shoulder.

She whispered, "My Romeo."

Chapter Twenty-four

The call from the hospital was not encouraging. The initial evaluation convinced the doctors to transfer Chip to the psychiatric ward where he would receive care that might bring him back, if not completely to a functioning state. Treatment might potentially include electric shock treatment and high-dose drugs. The transfer to an institution full-time was not expected as of yet, but the family should be aware of all options. Due to his fragile condition, visitors had to be limited to immediate family until he showed signs of improvement and stability.

Ginny hung up the telephone and told everyone in the room the details. She thanked their friends for coming and said she would stay in touch.

Mr. Foley was furious. "My son is NOT crazy. How could they lock him away? What the hell do they mean by a 'functioning state'?" He wouldn't have it.

Mrs. Foley sat quietly, trying to absorb the information.

Ginny looked from Beverly to her mother and back to Beverly.

Helen, wishing her husband had been able stay longer, jumped in, "I'll go with you to the hospital as often as you want." Ginny nodded enthusiastically as Helen spoke in a calming tone to her dear friends. "Duncan, Margie, this hospital has a solid reputation when it comes to treating people with mental breakdowns. I should know, I was treated by doctors there for months after John Jr. died. You remember, Margie."

Duncan huffed while Margie held her hand out to Helen and whispered, "Yes."

Helen continued, "Your son is certainly not me, and everyone's nightmares are unique. Dear, call Dr. Harris. He might be willing to meet with you since he's known Chip his whole life." As an acknowledgment of his parents, she added, "I think he should include you two, also."

"Damn right," said a frustrated Duncan.

"Would you like that?"

Ginny didn't know what she should do but had faith in her mother.

After much back and forth, Duncan acknowledged that Ginny, as the wife, was legally the one to make the final decisions about his son, though he insisted on input and knowing the measures undertaken each step of the way.

Once the apartment cleared, the women headed downstairs to Richard. They braced themselves for his outburst once he found out that he wouldn't be allowed to visit Chip in the foreseeable future.

Much to their relief, Jeff was with Richard when they came in through the secret stairs. They shared the update from the hospital and the recommended course of action for the next few weeks. Jeff worked at Boston City Hospital and was able to clarify some of the complexities of hospital procedures. The legal spouse was always the first to be contacted, and medical teams and the presiding physician controlled every aspect of treatment. And, he emphasized, Ginny needed to be very engaged each step of the way to ensure Chip didn't fall through the cracks. Everyone looked at her. Her eyes were wide with trepidation.

Jeff emphasized that most importantly, now was not the time to mention Chip's being a homosexual. Richard steadied himself at the prospect of not being allowed to visit him and said he'd drive to the hospital that night. He'd sit in the waiting room with Beverly. Richard prayed that he might be able to slip in to visit him if only to briefly see Chip's face.

Friday's visit was short, Chip slept and the nurse encouraged everyone to go home early. It seemed that nothing would be done over the holiday weekend except to keep the patient comfortable.

Richard went to an early Easter Mass with his family and came home afterward to pick up Beverly so they could go together to his parent's house for the afternoon. The noise was raucous as usual and the food was abundant. Relatives came and went. It wasn't easy for Richard and Beverly to disguise their torment amongst the large gathering.

Beverly helped clear the table after the dessert. An excuse to get away from the laughter and commotion. She was worried about Ginny, who was with her parents. In the kitchen, Angela asked how she was doing and if their friend was improving. She promised that she and Mr. Ruggiero would pray for his recovery.

"Ricardo, he is not himself. I can see it. He is a big man, but a sensitive boy. Hospitals have frightened him since his sisters were sick when he was very young. May they rest in peace. I know that he's his close friend."

"Yes, best friends."

"I heard him tell his brother that he wasn't going to work tomorrow. Ricardo should go to work with his father and brother. Work keeps the mind from wandering and breaking."

"You are wise, Mama. He should go to work. You insist. He listens to you. I'm, we, are tired. The house upstairs has been full of people coming and going the past couple of days. I could use a good night's sleep."

"You go home. Take care of Ricardo and your friend Virginia." Angela gave her a warm motherly hug and went to find her son to convince him to go to work the next day.

Joe said he would drive in the morning, guessing that Richard might stay at work the full day if he didn't have his truck. Beverly went to work on Monday morning, too. Her shift ended at noon, so she would most likely be home about the time Ginny and her mother returned from the late morning appointment with Dr. Harris.

Ginny and Helen were in the back seat of the Foley's car. Duncan and Marjorie were silent during the short drive from the hospital. Duncan was as frustrated as his wife was frightened. Dr. Harris had an emergency and only met with them briefly and was vague about Chip's condition. He was undergoing numerous tests and they were told they could visit that evening during regular visiting hours. When they rounded the bend towards Eliot Street, Ginny sat up straight in the car and barely whispered, "Damn, the psycho." Helen thought it was the comprehension of the gravity of Chip's illness.

The Foleys dropped off Ginny and took Helen home. Duncan was going to return to work, and Marjorie wanted to speak with her pastor.

Once alone, Ginny fidgeted. She couldn't concentrate and she couldn't sit still. She desperately needed to talk with Beverly and Richard.

Richard had come home from work later than usual. The drive with Joe was painfully slow; he was eager to get an update and galloped up the secret stairs two at a time.

Ginny and Beverly met him at the top of the stairs. "Richard, the psycho. We should tell the doctors that he might be the cause." Richard stopped short and squeezed his eyes shut at the mention of a psycho. Beverly walked over to him and touched his arm.

Ginny, all wound up, continued speaking at a frantic pace. "He's been telling us one way or another for months that he's been followed by a psycho who might be the FBI. Come on, that's what pushed him over the edge."

"Slow down, hon."

Ginny stayed focused on Richard.

"Did you say anything about his fears to the doctor Thursday while waiting for the ambulance? We have to tell the doctors." Richard flinched at the word *we*. "Richard, we have to tell someone." Out-of-breath, she followed him as he walked across the kitchen and automatically opened the refrigerator for a beer; grateful that his girls had started stocking extra for him. He pulled out the drawer with the bottle opener, opened his beer, and took a swig as he leaned against the counter.

"No, all I said was that Chip was stressed and under pressure with school. I'm so confused. The psycho? Do you mean the man that he now claims followed him for the last year? I never, never saw anyone. And the FBI, come on. After our talk that night, you remember, months ago, and the recent sessions with Rey, I believed that he had hit his head and broken his jaw because he flirted with a guy in the men's room. He flirted all the time when we were out, but he was always just innocent and playful. Damn, damn, damn." Richard pounded his fists against his thighs.

The women felt his anguish and let him ramble.

"Why didn't I believe that he was being followed? I should know better. He is such an easy target. Merda, I don't know what to think." He paced back and forth, near-hysterical with nerves and guilt. "You know, the sessions with Rey were eye-opening for me. I thought he had convinced him that the FBI would not be following a student. Of course, Chip then insisted that he was just overworked at school and with volunteering at the church and the house and he had let his imagination run amok. Stupidly I believed him. I thought he was so much calmer. Then, boom! He blew up!" Drained, Richard slumped into a kitchen chair and ran his beer bottle across his forehead.

"Maybe he was being followed, or maybe he was imagining it, but either way we should tell his doctor, at least. We don't have to discuss his flirting. His breakdown must be more than stress. His reputation will remain safe with us." Beverly tried to be firm and caring at the same time.

"You mean OUR reputations will be safe. *The Plan* will live on," Richard said snidely. The pressure of living a double life was wearing on him. He finished the beer and opened the fridge for another one. "I'm so fuckin' tired of all this. I want my man back. Damn it."

"Come on, we have to agree. Do we stick with it and only discuss the blizzard accident or Red's fear of a psycho or the FBI? I can't believe I'm calling him the psycho. Or, do we admit to everything and ruin our reputations and the reputations of your families? Crap. What do we do? I'm sick of hiding and I'm tired of being afraid to be who I am and I'm worried about us losing Chip to madness." Beverly felt conflicted and overwrought.

"Darn it. One minute I believe him, the next I'm not sure, and the next everything is wildly out of control. Is all this just because two men love each other?" Ginny wondered aloud. Richard finished his beer, stuck his hands in his pants pockets, and closed his eyes.

"We know Dr. Harris has been treating Chip for his headaches and oversaw his care when he was recuperating from his broken jaw. He never told him about someone following him, I'm sure of it. This is important, the doctors have to hear about this, they don't need to hear about our living arrangements."

Confusion compounded by raw emotions filled the room. Richard and Beverly finally nodded in agreement. The idea of broadcasting to the world that they were homosexuals and living a lie as married couples was too much to consider. Their souls yearned to tell the truth, but their fears bound them to secrecy.

"Should I call the doctor's office now? It's almost five thirty. His secretary might be there."

"Do it now but don't mention the FBI," said Richard.

She picked up the doctor's card that was on the kitchen table along with the growing pile of paperwork from the hospital and dialed the number only to get the answering service.

The secretary called back first thing in the morning and said the doctor was booked solid and would stop by the house at the end of the day if he wasn't running too late.

They waited impatiently for the bell to ring. Richard came down and opened the door and motioned for the doctor to go upstairs. Ginny began. She re-told the story of the blizzard and Chip's experience at the college dorm. The storm that the doctor was all too aware of. He was on duty and spent Thursday night through Saturday at the hospital emergency room, which was inundated with patients from car accidents and frigid cold-related symptoms. He said, "I know all this, what are you trying to get at?"

Richard picked up where Ginny left off. "He spoke to me. You know, man-to-man, that his headaches weren't improving and he said someone had been following him for months. All the way back to last summer. He thought he saw this someone on campus and on our street. I mentioned this to the girls here. The three of us confronted him and that's when he told us about the person he calls the psycho. We were not sure he was real because the, um, accident twisted up his head and he was overworked from taking too many classes." Richard agonized about calling the probable attack an accident.

Beverly added, "We suggested that he call the police, but he refused. He didn't think it would do any good. He stopped talking about it after that night to any of us."

"We are wondering if his believing that he was being followed should be discussed with the hospital. We, I, I don't know if Chip ever said anything to you about it. Although he spoke to a friend who is a therapist for stress reducing ideas," said Ginny.

"I sincerely wished you had divulged this when he was first brought to the hospital. He never discussed this with me, only that he had occasional severe headaches and that the pain pills I prescribed eased the intensity of them. This is a long time for anyone to be stalked, it's what, a year. Very odd. Have you notified the college of a possible stalker?" The doctor shifted in his seat as the others kept their eyes downcast. "If he was being followed, it would have an impact on his state of mind. We're certain that his head injury, it was a *severe* concussion, affected him and it may or may not be related to his feeling stalked. The specialists will determine that. I know he was resolute to stay on track with law school; such a driven and overachieving young man. Of course, tests have been ordered."

He got up to leave, but hesitated, "By the way, my son-in-law is a Newton College police lieutenant, I think he would want to know if there was a possible stalker on campus. I can get you in touch with him if you want to pursue this."

The three searched each other, the doctor didn't quite understand the hesitancy.

As he put on his hat and coat he paused, "Mrs. Foley, Ginny, let's not kid ourselves, it appears your husband has a long road to recovery. What you told me about his thinking that he was being followed almost a year after his accident changes things if it's valid or even if it's a delusion."

Ginny sighed wearily at the thought of what Chip would go through at the hospital.

"I'm getting ahead of myself. Let me discuss what you told me with the psychiatric team. It's important, thank you. I'll set up a consultation with the team for you and we'll take it from there. I assume that you are going to visit him tonight. Don't say anything that will make him upset. Keep a positive tone. I'll have my secretary send you the details." Ginny walked the doctor downstairs to the door and thanked him for coming to the house and for his suggestions.

"Damnit, long road to recovery, what does that mean? Was he talking in circles? He didn't ask about Rey. Should we contact the college? That's fucking scary. I'm sorry, I shouldn't be swearing in front of you so much," apologized Richard. He thought of his mother and how she would knock him senseless if she heard him swear in front of women.

There was a heaviness in the air. No one was ready to accept the worst.

Chapter Twenty-five

Later in the week Ginny visited the Personnel Department at Westinghouse to inquire about a formal leave of absence. Everything about work was annoying her, the workload was suddenly overwhelming, and her mind constantly drifted to the situation at home. The personnel officer said he couldn't approve a long-term leave away from the office until she used her sick and vacation days, and after that she would have to reapply for an unpaid leave of absence or resign. Reluctantly, she requested the use of her sick and vacation time.

Briggs was beside himself; she had missed two of the previous four days already. He wanted to fire her. The quarterly reports were in progress and he hired only dependable girls, quiet, hard-working girls. Virginia Stevens Foley was too uppity and inconsistent for him and her father, damn it, Mr. Tough Guy supervisor, didn't intimidate him. At least that's what he told himself.

On the day of the consultation with the medical team, Ginny sipped a cola and wondered aloud, "What do you think we should do when he gets home from the hospital?"

"What do you mean?" Beverly was digging through the refrigerator, trying to clean out leftovers from the food friends and family had dropped off over the previous week, to see if any were worth saving. She lifted out a big bowl wrapped in tin foil, opened it, and sniffed. She didn't know who brought it, but she knew what to do with it. She dumped the smelly contents into the trash and put the bowl in the sink. When she looked in again, four dozen eggs stared back at her. They never had the chance to paint Easter eggs. She shut the refrigerator.

"About The Eliot. This house, this romantic dream. Maybe we shouldn't remain here. I know I'm good with finances, but managing this big house takes real work. Arranging for all the repairs, bills, taxes, and who knows what else Chip does. It won't be easy for him to cope with everything while he recuperates. He's never really explained how his trust fund operates. Does it change if he's out of school and in the hospital or needs a long time at home to recuperate? I doubt Richard knows. Chip said Richard didn't want to know anything about the trust fund."

Beverly was stopped short. She presumed Ginny fervently loved The Eliot and the privacy it afforded them. Chip was passionate about the house; she thought he would never want to leave. But, then again, maybe he would be afraid to live here.

"What are you saying? Do you want to sell the house? Have you said any of this to Richard?"

Ginny leaned back in the chair. "I don't know what I want. I want Chip home. I want our normal life with the four of us. I don't want to go back to work at Westinghouse. I'm babbling." She started to cry, "I just want you and for this craziness to be over. I loved my brother and he died. Now Chip is in the hospital, what if he dies? My mother struggles. I hate hospitals." She picked up her cola, had a small sip, and put it down with a thump, spilling most of it on the table. Beverly grabbed the dish towel and cleaned up the spill without skipping a beat.

She hadn't connected Ginny's loss of John Jr. to Chip's illness. She didn't for a minute expect Chip to die. She inhaled, wiped her hands, and said, "He's *not* going to die. We have to believe that. It may take a while, but he will get back to his old self. Hon, if staying here is too much for you, then we can move." Ginny tried to stop sniffling. "Think about it though." Beverly tilted her head. "This might not be the best time. Moving is a big undertaking and I don't imagine it would be good for Chip's recovery. And, remember, we committed to living here with the fellas. Richard and I are married. I know it's a farce but think of the rest of the world and our families" she paused, wiping her hands again on the dish towel, "That is why we bought this house. Can I suggest something?"

Ginny nodded and wiped away her tears.

"My father used to say rash decisions are like opening a shaken bottle of beer, you get a whole lot of messy." Ginny scrunched her nose bewildered. Beverly continued, "What I'm saying is, why don't we stay here for now, maybe until the end of the year? You can take your time with the house and about work. We don't know how long he will be in the hospital. And *The Plan*. Do we keep it or toss it out in the trash? I think we should at least stay here while the next six months unfold." She sat down and waited for a response; her mind filled with concern.

Ginny didn't want to think. She didn't want to make any decisions. She didn't like going to the hospital every day and she wasn't looking forward to meeting with the doctors. She liked it when her steady Beverly emerged and was in charge.

"I love you. Let's keep on going. You're so practical; rushing won't do us any good. I'm feeling sorry for myself, that's all. What time is it? I have to get ready. I'm relieved that my mother is coming. I wish you could come." She saw Beverly fumbling in her sweater pockets. "Go ahead, I know you gotta smoke."

"I'll be right back. I have a pack downstairs. Sorry, girlfriend, I just can't quit while this is going on." She kissed the top of Ginny's head, "I know, excuses, excuses, excuses."

Beverly searched the downstairs pantry for a spare carton. After opening a pack, she noticed the bag of extra Easter decorations and a bag filled with goodies next to it. It reminded her of the Easter baskets she had bought and put on the bed in the attic guest room. Now that Easter was long over, she should bring them down and throw them in the trash. The front door decorations had to come down, too.

She lit a cigarette, put a pack in her pocket, had a couple of puffs then snuffed it and headed to the front door before going upstairs.

"I bought you and the boys Easter baskets," she said as she placed them on their kitchen table. "And I found a bag of goodies that were probably bought by Red. There's one with little trucks in it, I imagine it was meant for Richard. I'll put that aside and give it to him after work. Do you want me to empty everything and put the candy in a bowl? Maybe we can donate it to the afterschool group that Chip tutors at the church. I'll do that and put the baskets away in the attic storage closet. God, I want him to recover. This is beyond anything."

Ginny nodded her head and aimlessly picked up a few jelly beans before grabbing her bag and the car keys. She couldn't resist. Beverly unwrapped a chocolate bunny bought by Chip. He had bought the higher quality chocolate, naturally, she mused.

***

Helen was mindlessly picking through the jelly beans that were on the counter in the Representative's office. She had just informed the receptionist that she had to leave early again to meet her daughter. She enjoyed her part-time position and was more than willing to put in extra hours to make up for the days she had missed and would miss because of her son-in-law's illness. She selected another red jelly bean and went back to her desk. Her mind wandered to her son-in-law and then to John Jr. "Bolt and bar the shutters," she murmured to herself.

The morning staff meeting covered general updates about the work of the Representative. Tasks were assigned to the small staff; and goals for the next month were highlighted and distributed. The director emphasized that if there were any calls about Cuba, they should be directed to him. Representative Walsh was standing in concert with President Kennedy and he didn't want any rumors to spread. Helen was aware that a guerilla named Castro had overthrown the Cuban government in 1959, but she wasn't aware how that impacted the United States. It was a Spanish speaking tiny island somewhere south of Florida. She had never met anyone who spoke Spanish and certainly no one from such a faraway country. She made a note to inquire about Cuba in private after the meeting because she didn't want to appear empty-headed in front of the others. She often fretted about being the least knowledgeable in the office. Stuffing envelopes and logging suggestions and concerns from constituents didn't afford her much detail about the inner workings of the office. She assumed she had to work her way up from the bottom and that it would take time.

Chapter Twenty-six

Doctor Harris introduced the two psychiatric specialists gathered at the conference table. To Ginny, they appeared older than her parents, very stern and intimidating in their white coats. She held her mother's hand as the conference began. An hour later, her head swam. Helen wisely requested a copy of the doctors' recommendations for treatment and the list of the prescribed medications for the upcoming weeks. The specialists left the overwhelmed women with Doctor Harris.

"Ladies, I know that was an exorbitant amount of information and medical terminology to take in at one time. This is the most highly skilled team Milton Hospital has to offer. They'll provide superb care. If everything goes as hoped, you may be able to bring him home in a month and transition slowly back to a normal routine."

The drive home was somber, Ginny's mind was swirling with terminology that rolled off the tongues of the doctors. Delusional disorder, psychosis, disorientation, ECT, depression and schizophrenia, and the drugs with complicated names, and the scariest words, lunatic asylum, and a month in the hospital. Helen stayed with her to help clarify some of the confusing details from the meeting. Ginny had never seen her mother so poised and willing to research every unknown piece of information. She had become a quiet, reserved person after her son died. Her renewed vitality and staunch support since Chip's breakdown were a welcome and unexpected blessing.

Over a late lunch of tuna fish sandwiches and potato chips, Ginny asked, "Mom, how did you ever survive being in the hospital? Were you as sick as Chip? Somehow those months after Johnny died are a blur to me. I'm sorry, for what I didn't do and should have done. Thank you for being here with me."

Helen sipped her tea and saw the guilt and strain on her daughter's face. "I'll always be here for you. Honestly, it was a nightmare for me and your father. Still is. I fight every day to keep going." Ginny's eyes widened. "No, don't be worried. Let's work together through this maze." Inside she was petrified for her daughter and her young husband.

"Do you want to tell me any more about this stalker than you told the doctors?"

"Not right now, Mom. I'm too worn out." She saw the concern on her mother's face but wasn't ready to say anything more than what had been said to the doctors. "I want Richard and Beverly to be involved. I know the doctors only acknowledge me, but they're our closest friends. I can't do this without them. And, and, Mr. Foley is downright nasty. He's always bossy and cruel." Her eyes pleaded as she held her mother's hand tightly.

"I understand more than you realize. Don't worry about Duncan, I'll handle him." Helen didn't want to pry, so she pulled out the paperwork from the folder on the table from the doctors.

"Let's go over this slowly, so that you can explain it to your, um, friends," she said awkwardly and began reading the first page.

Ginny felt a strange twinge inside. *Did her mother know about The Eliot living arrangements?* She closed her eyes and listened as her mother reviewed the paperwork.

As Beverly came up the front stairs after work, and gave a cursory knock, both Ginny and Helen were ready to drop, their minds couldn't take in another medical term.

She asked how the meeting went. They tried to put on smiling faces, but their tone when replying said it all. Helen got up from the table. "I should get going. I want to be there to make dinner for your dad when he gets home from work." She turned to her daughter and thought of the enormity of

Chip's crisis. She kissed her cheek. "Father Riley helped me, still does. Plus, I find routine keeps me going. Think about that for yourself. I'll just grab my purse and walk to the bus stop."

"Gosh, no, Mom. I'll drive you home."

"No, you've had a trying day. I don't mind the bus."

"No, Mom, come on. I'll drive you home."

"That's enough. Both of you get in my car and I'll drive you home Helen. Otherwise, you two will be going back and forth and Helen will never get home. Let's go. I'll meet you at the side driveway in a minute." Beverly went downstairs to get her keys and jacket from the hall closet and took a deep breath.

On the way back to The Eliot, Ginny said that she was going to insist that Chip be allowed to see Richard during visiting hours. It would do them good to be with each other and give her a break.

Chapter Twenty-seven

Richard was sitting in the small room at the back of the house that Chip used as his study room, his mind a whirlwind of frustration. He found himself going through Chip's heavy satchel and dividing the contents into piles: books, papers, notes, stuff. He saw a small calendar in which he had written in his classes and the meeting times. On Tuesday nights he had D study group and on Thursday mornings D study group. He wondered about the study group. Which class was it for and what did the letter D mean? He felt guilty for feeling jealous and for snooping through the satchel. Yet, he couldn't resist going through everything. Lastly, he glanced at the four books, whose titles might have been in a foreign language for all that he could figure out. He flipped through the densely written pages of one of them and caught his breath when he saw on the back inside cover a drawing of what appeared to be a monster and three hand-written questions.

1. Who is *THE PSYCHO*?
2. Is he real?
3. Will I survive?

"Holy God Almighty," Richard said out loud. "Fuck, mio tesoro, you must have been scared to death." He grabbed the book and the calendar and headed to the stairs.

Ginny and Beverly were doing the dishes when they heard Richard call out to them. They were drained from another evening at the hospital, talking with his parents, and keeping Richard calm in the visitors waiting room.

"What could he want so late?" Beverly sighed.

The drawing and writing in the book terrified the women. "That's it," said Ginny, fired up by the revelation. "I'm making the call to the college police first thing in the morning and set up an appointment with the cop Dr. Harris suggested. This is bigger than us. Shoot, where did I put the telephone number, honey? I'm bringing this book. Will you come with me?" Both reluctantly said they would join her. Beverly gave Richard a kiss on his cheek and finished the dishes.

Richard lingered; he was curious about study groups. He showed the calendar to Ginny and asked what D might mean.

"Dennis Jenkins. You remember, the professor who was our lawyer at the house signing. That was the only time I met him, but Chip did mention that he tutored him after his accident and he enrolled in one of his classes, I think. Jeepers, don't you two ever talk about school? He's so proud to be there and to be one of the top three in his class. Even after his accident."

"Dennis Jenkins, huh? Yeah, he talked about him once or twice; he teased me, saying he was a handsome devil. Hmm. No, I've been a complete jerk about school."

Beverly interjected, "Are you jealous? You don't think he was fooling around with him, do you? That's preposterous. You *can* be such a jerk." She was on the verge of laughing but stopped when she noticed that Richard was not jealous, but sad. "Come on, don't overthink it. He loves you. You know it. We'll meet with the college police, that's something positive that we can do for him."

Richard picked up the calendar and started to go downstairs. He stopped and came back and hugged both of his girls. "I don't know what I would do without you two. I've never told any woman that I loved her and now I can say I love two women. Good night, my girls."

After he put the things back in his satchel, he sat in the study and went over, again and again, Chip's fall from poised and playful to a brooding and troubled shell of a man. Something didn't sit right about Dennis Jenkins, either. He made up his mind to pay "the handsome devil" a visit. Why

211

did Chip keep him hidden? Richard didn't know him but already disliked him.

***

Walter O'Malley was a great cop, worked hard, and had given 100% during his first three years on the Milton Police Force. A car chase and crash, which resulted in a civilian injury, changed the direction of his career. A broken hip from the crash confined him to a desk and he lost the incentive to move forward. He resigned, moped about for a year, and eventually found work as a guard at Newton College. Over time he was promoted to sergeant, then lieutenant in charge of the patrols. He intended to give his best to the college and was determined to complete his bachelor's degree before he turned forty. One day he aspired to be the Newton College Chief of Police.

O'Malley was curious about the message from a Mrs. Ginny Foley. The message said his father-in-law recommended she call him. Doc Harris and he were close, and Doc was not one to give out his name lightly. He immediately called Mrs. Foley and set up an evening appointment.

Mrs. Foley arrived with two friends, nervous, obviously not Newton College students, and too young to be parents of a student. Introductions were made and it was clear that the Ruggieros were very close friends and there for support. Mrs. Foley was younger than the other two. She carried a folder and what looked like a law school textbook. O'Malley made a mental note to consider law school after he completed his undergraduate classes.

Ginny began. Her husband, a law school student, was in the hospital as a result of a health breakdown. The lieutenant wasn't following how he should be involved.

"Excuse me, what does this have to do with the Newton College police?"

"My husband was here during the March blizzard. He stayed overnight in one of the dorms and was found in the men's room unconscious. He had a severe concussion and a broken jaw."

O'Malley interrupted, "That was one hell of a storm, I was here for five days straight. Some kids had minor injuries, frostbite, sprained wrists, that sort of thing. The lights were out here, like everywhere else, so a fall in an unlit building would have been easy to do." Facetiously, he added, "Not that any of our younger students would have been drinking or partying, either."

"Lieutenant O'Malley, my husband wasn't drinking. We are trying to confirm whether it was an accident or if he was attacked and then later stalked by the same man." It was difficult for the three friends to admit out loud that he was most likely attacked.

That caught O'Malley's attention. "Were the police involved? Were there any incident forms filed? What makes you think he was attacked? Why did you take over a year to bring this to me?"

Ginny hesitated. "I had no idea about a stalker until recently. With my husband in the hospital, we wanted to backtrack and see if we missed anything that led to his, um, illness."

O'Malley began to feel uneasy.

"I brought this book that, ah, we, I just found. Also, I have his medical report from Saint Elizabeth's Hospital that states that he was injured on campus in the dormitory during the blizzard." She passed the lieutenant the book opened to the back cover.

Chills went down his spine. Without saying a word, he went to his tall filing cabinet and flipped through folders that were aligned by month and year.

"Yup, here's March 1960. Fairly thick, this one. Because of the blizzard, I guess." He sat at his desk and went through the folder, page by page. About halfway through he stopped short. "Here it is." He read the form out loud.

"Hmm. Hill Top dorm. A student fell in the bathroom during the night, in the dark. Hit his head and fell to the floor breaking his jaw. Found in the morning unconscious and brought to St. Es." He flipped the form over. "That's it, huh." In his head, he was asking hard questions. *Were any other students injured in that dorm that night? Were any non-students sheltering there during the blizzard? Anyone keep a count of who was in the building?*

The three friends sat quietly, waiting for him to say something.

O'Malley sat back in his chair, alarmed. No one kept track of who was in any of the buildings during the storm. Everyone was trying to survive. He didn't say anything and reviewed the rest of the forms in the folder. He pulled out one other and his eyes widened as he read the report. "This one was filled out a week after the storm. It appears that a student was going to report an incident, actually an unknown intruder, in that dorm the afternoon that the storm started, but delayed coming here until the weather cleared. Hell, oh, excuse me, ladies." He immediately regretted telling them about the other incident report. He was embarrassed by the apparent lack of a follow-up report by his department, but he didn't let it show. He was a good cop and did right by his students.

"Another student filed a report? Do you think this could be the same guy? That he wasn't making this up? That his injuries weren't the cause of his breakdown?" Richard was stirred up and on the edge of his seat.

"Whoa. Slow down. I have no idea at this point about any of this. I have to follow protocol and this department judiciously investigates any concerns brought by students." He sat back and looked at the three people who stared at him.

"My God," said Beverly, "there could be a man stalking students on this campus. Lieutenant, something has to be done."

"Okay, listen, thank you for bringing your husband's experience to my attention. This is a safe campus and I doubt that there has been a stalker running around undetected for a year." Keeping a straight face, he continued, "But I promise to follow up with what occurred during the blizzard." He turned to the young Mrs. Foley and tried to show compassion. "I'll contact you when and if I find out anything. Thank you for sharing your story."

"Please, call me anytime."

"Doc Harris is overseeing your husband's care, right? He's a first-rate doctor. Your husband is fortunate to have him."

O'Malley stood up, his full six-foot three-inch height and solid build, imposing in the starched uniform, signaling that the meeting was over. The three left the office unsatisfied.

"Do you think he'll investigate?" questioned Ginny. "Geez, another student saw somebody too, that's creepy."

"I hope he does. It's been a year since the accident. That's a long time for a stalker or a psycho or a dumb ass troublemaker, whatever we call him, to hang around and not get caught. I think we've done all we can with the lieutenant." Beverly took in the seemingly peaceful campus. "It is beautiful here."

"I guess, if he's close to his father-in-law, he might put some extra effort into it," said Ginny trying to be optimistic.

"One thing I'm sure of, he won't want his reputation screwed for allowing a maniac on campus. I bet that he'll quietly do some snooping," Richard growled. "Plus, his father-in-law is a fancy Irish doctor, who's taking care of a good Irish Catholic student." When the women looked at him oddly, he proceeded. "Sorry, but you seem to be in charge and take care of each other. Irish, I mean. My family wouldn't be so lucky." Neither Beverly nor Ginny knew how to respond. He glanced at his watch. "Forget it. It's getting late. Let's grab some food on the way home."

Chapter Twenty-eight

Chip had been in the hospital for over two weeks. He knew that because he asked the morning nurse half a dozen times. His mind was in a fog; maybe he didn't ask the nurse and he was imagining it. His head hurt. Would it ever stop? He sat up in the hospital bed, glanced out the window and noticed the early signs of buds growing on the trees outside. Must be spring, he thought. Am I on school break? He tried unsuccessfully to remember how he got to the hospital in the first place. Which hospital am I in and why are there bars on the window? He checked for bandages, nothing was broken, and there were no stitches anywhere. What had happened to him? Where was Richard? Why were doctors poking and probing him? And, so many questions. He was foggy and confused and drifted in and out of sleep. When he slept the psycho stayed away. Was he never awake and the psycho penetrated his dreams? He fell back onto his pillow, talking to himself. Restless, he tried to get out of bed but couldn't. Why wasn't he able to move except for sitting up? What was that shadow moving across the window? Had he been found? His agitation built, his head ached and someone was screaming. Several nurses came into his room. Something jabbed his arm. The voices around him were hushed. The screaming stopped and he slept.

***

Mrs. Foley was visiting her son while the others sat in the waiting room. Ginny asked her father to walk with her to the cafeteria. She wanted to privately ask his opinion about work. She wanted to resign. The meetings with the doctors convinced her that staying home would ease her stress. She could create a 'course of action' as the doctors called it with Richard and Beverly to ensure that Chip was happy and secure at home, once he was ready to be discharged. Gone were her thoughts about moving.

"Dad, do you think it would be okay if I quit my job at some point? There's too much pressure at home, and I simply can't face the women in the bookkeeping pool. I don't want to work for Mr. Briggs another minute and I only have a couple of days left of paid time off."

"Well, sweetheart, of course, it's worth considering. This is a huge burden on your young shoulders. That Briggs is an imbecile, by the way. I never liked him. A real weasel if you ask me."

She chuckled at the term *weasel*. She agreed but her good Catholic upbringing stopped her from saying it out loud to her dad.

"Don't say a word until your leave is over to make certain it is what you want to do, then go to the Personnel Office and file your resignation papers. I can meet you there if you want." He opened the door to the cafeteria for her, thinking he could use a stiff drink instead of coffee. "Do you mind my asking if your income is needed? Does the downstairs rent cover your house expenses? What about medical insurance? Hospitalization doesn't come cheap."

He ordered a coffee for himself and a cola. She smiled at how her dad always knew to order her a cola. "Maybe you should make an appointment with his trust fund lawyer, just in case. Do it before you put in your resignation papers even if it delays it a week or so. Want me to go with you to the lawyer's office?" He paid for the drinks and motioned to an empty table.

"I'm pretty sure I want to quit; but you're right about waiting. My head's been swimming. Mom's been a huge help. I want to talk to Beverly, too." She took a long sip of her drink. "She went through a lot when her father died. I think she can help me sort out my feelings." She searched the room, for what, she did not know. "I hadn't thought about the lawyer or insurance to pay for the hospital bills. Yes, please come with me. Thanks, Dad," aching to tell her father about her love for Beverly. She closed her eyes and sighed. John assumed she was hurting for Chip.

"No need to say thanks. Not much more we can do tonight. I'm glad your friends are here." He pushed back his chair and placed the barely touched coffee on the return tray. As they strolled out of the cafeteria, his tone softened. "Sweetheart, you going to be okay?"

"Yes, I'll be fine."

"Time marches on. You do what you must for yourselves when he comes home. Maybe leaving work is smart." He kissed her cheek and gave her a warm fatherly hug. "Call me if you want me to go to Personnel with you and when you set up the appointment with the lawyer. Love you, sweetheart. I think we'll head home now."

The Foleys had left the hospital after Margorie's short visit. Ginny surprised Richard by sneaking him into the room while the nurses were busy elsewhere. Chip was dozing, but she whispered to Richard to go up to the bed and talk with him. She'd be outside the door.

"Mio tesoro, I'm here. I'm here." Chip was roused by the sound of Richard's voice.

"Richard, what happened? Where am I? Hold me, baby, please."

Tears rolled silently down Richard's cheeks when Chip called him baby. His voice cracked as he said, "I love you. You're going to be okay. You're in the hospital. I'm always going to be right here."

Chip smiled and outstretched his arms for Richard. Richard leaned in, held him, and sobbed. "I'm so sorry; I should have believed you, should have known. Forgive me, please, forgive me."

"Richard, I love you. Sleep with me." Chip dozed, still unaware of all that had happened to him.

Richard held him until Ginny poked her head in and said they had to leave, visiting hours were over and the nurses were beginning their rounds. He collapsed into Beverly's arms in the waiting room. "What have I done? How did I let him fall apart?"

She hugged Richard. "It's not your fault. We will take care of him. All of us. Come on, it's time to go home."

Chapter Twenty-nine

Helen wasn't going into the office on Monday morning, supporting Ginny was draining. The bus ride first thing Monday mornings was crammed with people and she wasn't in the mood to be jostled. Fortunately, her schedule was flexible enough that she could call ahead and come in at noon. She had the stereo on playing big band music as she hand-mixed the batter for a batch of molasses cookies to bring to Marjorie and Duncan. A batch of chocolate chip cookies was already cooling to pack for the office. During the long, distressing weeks of praying with Marjorie for some sign of Chip progressing, she observed how her friend had slipped into a dark hole similar to the one she experienced when her son died. She identified with Marjorie's pain and knew that no amount of molasses cookies would make it magically go away, but the gesture would be appreciated. Perhaps Marjorie would eat one, and take in some sustenance; though eating was as difficult as breathing when your light has dimmed. Helen found herself licking the spoon as the pain in her own chest pounded.

The staff in the office were unusually busy when she arrived at noon. She unwrapped the cookies and put them on the counter to share. Dorothy, the perky receptionist, leaned over as she selected a cookie. In a hushed voice, she said, "Helen, have you heard, there's been an invasion in Cuba? No one knows what's going on, but it doesn't sound good."

"Are they trying to oust Fidel Castro? Is it the United States who invaded?" She searched around the office for signs of Bob. "Is Bob calling a meeting?"

"He's been holed up in his office since I got in. The phones have been ringing off the hook. Here's another call. Hold on, Helen." She picked up the phone and wrote down a message.

Helen removed her light jacket and put her purse with it next to her desk while Dorothy spoke on the telephone. "What should I do?" she asked when the receptionist hung up the phone.

"Stay alert. Be ready, but for what I have no idea."

Helen took one of her cookies, walked to her desk, and sat down. She prayed for President Kennedy. She didn't know what else to do.

The President and his advisors were huddled behind closed doors anticipating a victory in Cuba. But, from the start, the mission didn't go as anticipated. For three long days, the entire country held its breath. On April 17th, the invaders, mostly Cuban expatriates, surrendered. Relations between the United States, Cuba, and the Soviet Union were strained to the point of a potential war.

Many radio and television reports berated the young president as reckless and ill-prepared. Opponents loudly called the fiasco 'one of epic proportions' that could ruin the United States. The debates within both the Republican and Democratic parties raged for weeks. The little office in Milton spoke valiantly in solidarity with the President, as calls to the office mounted against him. Helen, worried about Chip's slow recovery, and struggling to offer constant comfort to her daughter, found herself shrinking within herself. She admired the president and felt the blows against him personally.

***

Reynaldo was in Miami, listening closely with other Cuban expatriates to the reports on the Cuban invasion. He had been actively supporting the evacuation of unaccompanied Cuban children to the United States. With the invasion quickly turning into a debacle, he feared that

Castro would permanently close the airport to all flights to the United States, stranding thousands who wished to flee the country.

Chapter Thirty

Professor Dennis Jenkins didn't fit neatly into any of the scenarios conjured up by Richard. He hadn't made an appointment with the professor, just impulsively showed up at his office door after sifting through Chip's satchel. He berated himself on the drive over to the college campus for his suspicions, but try as he might he couldn't let it rest. He had to confront the professor.

He introduced himself to Jenkins as Duncan Foley's friend. Chip had told Richard that he only used his given name on campus, so he would be taken seriously. Jenkins greeted Richard with a firm handshake; closed his office door and immediately asked about Duncan's condition. Richard was irked that Jenkins was aware of the illness and asked him how he knew. Jenkins sat back on his chair and took in the striking, well-toned young man with the slight Italian accent.

"He's one of my students. Someone in his study group called his wife and mentioned it to me. Of course, I'm concerned about him and all my students. Why are you here, Richard?"

Richard was suddenly unsure as to how to confront Jenkins with his suspicions. Finally, he blurted out, "Why were you spending so much time with him? And what do you know about his accident in the dorm and the fact that he thinks he's being followed by some maniac?"

Jenkins didn't want to divulge his attraction to his redheaded student to this guy, or anyone for that matter. He kept his private life private. Any dalliance with a student, especially a male student, would be grounds for immediate dismissal. He quickly surmised that Richard was Chip's secret lover, and a jealous one. Jenkins recalled how on several occasions Duncan had let something slip about his friend Richard. Yet, Duncan flirted with him and had given him a small gift for putting in the extra hours of tutoring.

Leaning forward, Jenkins said, "I know Duncan Foley the *student* well. He hired me as his attorney for the purchase of his house, I tutored him after his accident and oversaw his study group. Nice kid, very determined to succeed." Dennis tried to separate any feelings he might have and to come across as strictly an academic-minded professor. Using his most sensitive tone added, "A terrible accident during that god-awful blizzard. I nearly slid off the road on the way home myself." Richard continued to stare.

Jenkins paused, "What do you mean, he is being followed? He never said anything to me." A trickle of sweat went down his back. *Had Duncan seen him the couple of times he drove or strolled by his house, tempted to present himself as an interested friend?*

"He's quite sick, um, a breakdown. So, he never said anything about being followed?"

"Nope. Did he report the guy to the campus police? I'm sorry that he's sick. Is there anything that I can do?" He said with an *I truly am concerned* voice.

"No. None of us can do anything but pray that he recovers and returns to his old self. Oh, and, yes, his wife and my wife and I went to the campus police. Some cop named O'Malley said he would investigate. Kinda late, I think."

Jenkins stood up and shook his hand. Richard didn't notice the slight shaking of Jenkin's hand. "The lieutenant is an ace cop. Great guy. Thanks for coming and letting me know about Duncan," he said to deflect any jealousy that remained with Richard. "I do hope he recovers enough to return for his last year of school."

Richard reluctantly shook Jenkin's hand and left. His gut said that Jenkins was phony and definitely a fairy. As he walked back to his truck, he opted to stop in to see O'Malley. He was anxious, no desperate, to find out if the stalker was real or a figment of Chip's imagination.

Lieutenant O'Malley was wound up about talking to the student who filed the incident report. The student had left the state during the recent Easter break and didn't pick up the message in his mailbox at the dormitory until a week later, then forgot about it. O'Malley, perturbed by the lack of response, decided to track the student down himself in person and demand a meeting in his office.

Elmont Mitchell was an undergraduate, short and pudgy, which bordered on fat. He squirmed in his seat in front of the imposing lieutenant. His upper lip glistened with sweat.

"Mr. Mitchell, thank you for agreeing to meet with me. I'd like to ask you some questions about the incident report you filed after the blizzard last year."

"I'm sorry I forgot to return your call when I came back from break. I didn't do anything wrong. As a pre-law student, I know that documentation is important to a case. Paper trails, my professor called it. Why are you asking about it a year later? Has something happened?"

He ignored the questions. "Mr. Mitchell, can I call you Elmont?" he asked politely.

"Yes, um, call me Monty if you want, that's what my friends call me."

"Thanks, Monty. I've read the incident report but would like to hear in your own words what occurred that day. Start from the beginning and don't leave anything out, regardless if you think it is important or not. Got it?"

Elmont wiped his lip with his shirt sleeve. Swallowed hard. Sat up straight and started,

"I was in my dorm room most of the day studying. I was giving a presentation for a class and had a report to prepare. It's important to be prepared, you know." O'Malley nodded his head in agreement, showing that he was listening intently.

"About noon, I guess, I was hungry and walked down the back stairs to get to the snack room. My room is on the fourth floor and I could have taken the elevator, but sometimes the

226

stairs are quicker and I like to stay in shape." *You should take the stairs every day*, O'Malley thought to himself.

"There was this guy, huge guy, at least six feet coming up the stairs. This was about the third floor. He stopped short when he spotted me. He stared, in a creepy way, then bolted out the door to the third floor. Really creepy guy. I didn't move. *Holy Moly*, I thought. He was too old to be a student, but maybe a worker of some kind. I didn't think about it anymore because I was hungry and ready to eat so I could get back to my presentation prep. Until…can I have a glass of water?" He glanced at the lieutenant.

"Uh, sure, kid, there's a water bubbler in the hall. Here, use my mug. It's clean." He passed the student his Newton College green and white mug.

He hurried out the door. "Back in a sec."

Something about the kid seemed off, maybe he was just very awkward. O'Malley wondered if he was that strange when he was young.

He started as soon as he sat down. "Oh, yeah. I went back to my room after lunch and stayed there until the lights began flickering about, I don't know, five or so. Then I went downstairs to find out what was going on. I had noticed that it was snowing, but hadn't paid it much attention. I was practicing my presentation. Sorry, I said that already." He had a gulp of water before continuing.

"Anyway, I was on the ground floor with everyone when I felt someone staring at me. Have you ever felt a stranger staring? Hair raising. I turned around and there was the same big guy. He stared menacingly at me and then walked down the hall toward the staircase. None of my friends were with me, so I didn't say anything to anyone. In the back of my mind, I considered telling the residence rep, but then the lights went out. It had to have been at least a week later that I went to report it, this office actually, and filled out the incident form. I haven't thought of it since. Never saw the guy again. Did I do the right thing?" He looked openly for approval.

"Yes, you did, son. How old did you make him out to be, approximately? Can you describe him in detail? Have you talked about this 'creepy guy' with any of your friends?"

"No. With the blizzard everyone was scrambling to stay warm, eat, go out in the snow after being cooped up in the dorm, so the guy never came up. Oh, I'd say he was older. Younger than you. I don't know. No grey hair. Sorry."

"Don't worry about it. Do you think you can describe the guy to a police artist? I can set up an appointment here if you'd like." He knew he could pull in a favor from the Milton Police Office.

He hesitated. "I guess, I can try. Can I do it on Monday? I have classes the rest of this week."

"Certainly, Monty." O'Malley keeping it soft, added, "And you did well. Oh, and one more time. You said you never saw him again."

"Nope. Never saw him again, never want to be anywhere near him again." He noticeably shivered.

The lieutenant stood up and shook his hand. Relieved to be done, the student bolted out the door.

O'Malley tapped his pen on the desk. *It's a long shot, but maybe, just maybe, this kid can give enough of a description that I can determine if this asshole has been arrested somewhere, or worse if he is still lurking around here. I can't believe it took a year to hear about this. Christ, I hope he's locked up somewhere.*

"Hey, lieutenant, there's a guy out here, not a student, who insists on seeing you. Says his name is Ruggaro or something. Shall I tell him you're busy?"

"Na, send him in." He didn't expect Ruggiero to come by on his own. He sat behind his desk, dumped the water from his coffee cup into the window plant, and shook out the remaining drips.

"Mr. Ruggiero, Richard, right? What can I do for you? Have a seat."

"I was on campus with Professor Jenkins in the law school and thought I would stop by to find out if you have anything."

"Funny you should ask. The student from the dorm who filed the report just left. He confirmed that there was an unknown 'creepy guy', to use his words, in the dorm the first evening of the blizzard, but that he hasn't seen him on campus since."

Richard swallowed hard at the prospect of a stalker being confirmed.

"Now this doesn't mean the stranger attacked your friend. And the fact that he hasn't been noticed on campus since and that no one else has reported him could mean a couple of things. One, he was just seeking refuge during the storm. Two, that he had nothing to do with Mr. Foley's accident, or three, he was a criminal and is in jail. The student's going to work with a police artist to come up with a likeness of the guy next week. I'll let you know when it's completed. You, Mrs. Foley, and your wife can take a look at it. Perhaps Mr. Foley will be able to look at it, also."

Richard was speechless. The cop did investigate and the stalker was not only real but might be identifiable. "Thank you so much for pursuing this. I had my doubts, but you've come through."

"I'm a good cop and I always follow through. I'll be in touch next week."

Chapter Thirty-one

A significant change was proposed for Chip's treatment. The Milton psychiatric team determined that his chances for a full recovery would be increased at a highly-skilled facility.

He wasn't anywhere near ready to come home and the doctors clarified the logic behind transferring him to the specialized facility. Its team of psychiatrists was leading the field in innovative ways to address the mental health of patients. The facility was private and the cost of the care would be substantial, but completely worth it. The doctors cautioned that the facility would re-evaluate him and review the recommendations and the progress he had made at Milton Hospital before accepting him as a patient. If accepted, it would be wise to make the transfer as soon as possible. Until the decision was made and the facility accepted him, the current regimen, including high doses of Librium, would continue. The drug had recently been approved for the treatment of anxiety and it would help keep him calm. There were rare side effects, such as confusion, depression, and hallucinations but for the short term, it was the best option.

Helen had attended the meeting with Ginny, neither were expecting such drastic changes. Ginny was clearly distressed by the proposed change of hospital and doctors, one farther from home, additional drugs, and the potential financial cost as well as mollifying his intruding, acerbic father.

When they arrived back at the apartment, Helen suggested asking the Foleys to come over to hear the proposal and left a message with John's office to have him come over right after work.

"I think I hear Richard downstairs. When does Beverly come home from work?"

"What time is it? Four o'clock, yes, I'm sure that's him. Um, she comes home by four-thirty or five. Why?"

"The two of them should be here when you speak with Duncan and Marjorie. I know they're yours and Chip's family, too."

"We've become quite close." She was too worn out to say anymore.

Helen was equally drained. "I'm tired, do you mind if I take a quick nap?"

"Oh, Mom, I'm sorry for constantly dragging you to the hospital with me. You've helped me keep my sanity, otherwise, I'd be the one in the looney bin. Jeepers, I shouldn't have said that. Yes, a nap sounds perfect. You can sleep in our room or the room upstairs. When do you want me to wake you?"

"Thanks. I'm happy to be with you as much as I can. I'll just go to your room if you don't mind. Don't let me sleep past four-thirty."

Helen walked down the hall to the large bedroom. She hadn't been in the room in months and glanced at the photos on the two dressers. There was the wedding photo with both families, the wedding party, several photos of the four of them, and two striking photos of Ginny with Beverly. She picked up one of the photos of the two women and studied it closely. Kicking off her shoes she fell onto the bed, covered herself with a throw from the bottom of the bed, and fell fast asleep.

Ginny tried to collect her thoughts, scrambled as they were. She opened a cola and went downstairs to talk with Richard.

He was getting out of the shower when he heard Ginny call from the front hallway.

He dressed quickly in his worn dungarees and a clean T-shirt. "What? Did something happen? Is Chip okay?" Her strained facial expression immediately made him anxious.

"My mom's upstairs napping. We were in the hospital for an afternoon visit when the lead doctor, Dr. LaConte, asked if I could meet with the team and Dr. Harris. They were just completing a conference about him and took advantage of our visit by pulling us in to talk. Dr. Harris stayed afterward to guide me through the medical lingo. Thank heavens for him."

Richard went over to the fridge and pulled out a wrapped leftover sandwich and a beer. He only opened the beer. Guilt for not being able to visit Chip every day tore at his heart. "Get to the point."

"The doctors want to transfer him to a long-term hospital."

"He's not going to Mattapan State Hospital or any other nut house, damn it."

"Listen." She sat down on a kitchen chair and put her bottle on the table. Irritated, she ran her hand through her hair and exhaled as she sat down. "The doctors want to send him to a specialized hospital where he will have one-on-one care. The facility, I can't think of the name, is in Belmont. Some fancy doctor from Pennsylvania is there and making a difference. I, we, have to decide as soon as possible. And, no surprise, the cost will be a lot. Also, I'm informing the Foleys, with my parents both here tonight before we go to the hospital. I want you and Beverly upstairs with me, too."

"Merda, does he know about the move?" He gulped down the beer and ignored the sandwich. "You know I want the best care for him. What do you want to do? Why are his parents so involved? Never mind, I know my parents would do the same. Damn, I'm trying not to fall apart." He joined her at the table. "Ugh, I almost forgot. I stopped by the cop's office at the school this afternoon. First, I went to Dennis Jenkin's office." She raised her eyebrows at that. "Anyway, more about Jenkins later. The cop followed through and he found the student who saw the asshole in the dorm. He's going to make a police sketch for us to review. What time are we meeting upstairs? You're waiting for Beverly, aren't you? My mind is racing."

"Jesus, God, Almighty, the psycho is real." Ginny's stomach turned as she made the sign of the cross. "Police sketch? We have to talk about this." She stood up. "Darn it, it'll have to be later. I have to call Mom Foley now. My guess is about five-thirty or six. I'll let you know. Can you grab Bev if she comes here first after work and fill her in?" He nodded and picked up the sandwich.

"I have a million things to say from the meeting, but I need my mother to help decipher all the goobly-gook." She gave him a big hug and hurried up the stairs and straight to her parlor telephone. Richard put the sandwich back down and covered his face with his hands.

The Foleys and John Stevens sat and listened to what the doctors had proposed earlier in the day. Beverly and Richard stayed in the background, with Beverly holding Richard's hand tightly as he impatiently tapped his foot on the dining room floor. Duncan Foley got increasingly agitated as the details were explained. Marjorie Foley wanted the best for her son and was willing to accept the doctors' recommendations. John was struck by how capable and secure his wife had become during the past month, despite her weariness, when she was talking about Chip.

The cost of the care at the facility was the last thing to be discussed. Ginny, who still aimed to resign from Westinghouse, stated that she would make an appointment with the trust fund lawyer to learn if there was money to be used in case of severe illness. Duncan shifted slightly on the sofa next to his wife; he was frustrated by the fact that his son had been left money that he hadn't earned. He was a hard-working man and always took care of his only child, weak though he may be. He cleared his throat. "Is there any upfront money that is required to get into this place? How is his care at Milton being covered? I should and I want to contribute."

No one had thought to ask about the cost of the current care. Ginny, recalling her brief conversation with her father, stared blankly at Beverly and Richard and then felt her mother's hand touch her arm.

"Duncan, when Chip was admitted, Ginny signed the papers at the hospital that confirmed that she is responsible for his care. He's covered by Westinghouse insurance as long as she's working full-time, in addition to the small policy he has through school. The Belmont facility will undoubtedly cost more than the insurance allows. We're researching the general costs and options as well as the ambitious therapies."

"I want to go to my son," Marjorie interrupted politely. She smoothed out her skirt and spoke directly to her husband, "The doctors said he should be moved within a couple weeks. I trust the doctors and I trust Ginny and Helen. Ginny, you're being so very strong. And, Helen, my dear friend, thank you."

Ginny added as everyone started to get up, "No one's to say a word about it to Chip until and if the move happens. Please, no adding to his anxieties." The group acknowledged her request and coordinated their schedules for the next few hospital visits.

After the Foleys left, Richard went up to Helen and asked if he could talk with her for a minute. "I have a friend who's a psychologist, his name is Dr. Rey Martin, maybe he can assist you with finding out about the, um, what is it, the, um, new treatment." He wasn't sure how Helen would react, and he was nervous.

"That would be a blessing, Richard. Thank you. Have Ginny give you my home phone number and he can call me. I have some journals from the library and I'll be home Sunday afternoon if he wants to call me after church. Oh, and, Richard, you're a good friend." She signaled to John that she was ready to go home.

***

Helen entered the kitchen after church to the sounds of John playing his guitar in his studio. The sounds were soothing as she opened the refrigerator to bring out the roast and vegetables to start their afternoon dinner. As she put the items on the kitchen table, she noticed a note written by John. Doctor Reynaldo Eire Martin had called and asked that she return his call. Momentarily confused, she hesitated and then realized that this was the doctor friend of Richard's. She was curious about his middle name, Eire. Was he Irish? She immediately went to the hall and called him back. Dr. Martin was gracious and enthusiastic. He confirmed that he had read about the latest treatments and could come over that afternoon and share what he knew. Helen invited him to Sunday dinner and he gladly accepted.

Dr. Martin was not what Helen expected. He was slightly older than her, she guessed, and very soft-spoken with a hint of an accent that was not Irish. John thought he was a "little light on his feet" and patiently tried to make conversation during dinner. John was surprised to learn that he had come to the United States from Havana to study psychology at Princeton University as a young man and had played saxophone in a jazz band throughout his undergraduate years. John offered to show him his studio after dinner while Helen cleared the dining room of the dishes. The doctor picked up his dishes to bring to the kitchen for Helen, but she shooed him away.

Helen had Chip's entire folder ready. Though he asked that she call him Reynaldo or Rey, she insisted on being respectful and using his proper title, Dr. Martin. The two spent an hour reviewing the contents before shifting to the potential move to the Belmont facility and the innovative treatment program. When she remarked that the current hospital was using a drug named Librium, he paused. As a professional, he would not openly criticize the treatment prescribed by other doctors. He was wary of this drug and had read some of the early reports about its effects on patients. Aloud, he offered to find out the details for Helen, but said he believed the doctors at Milton were wise in exploring additional options for her son-in-law. He illustrated the differences between the two hospitals, and what colleagues told him about the Belmont facility and its use of psychotherapy. Lastly, he shared his thoughts on the recently published book *The Divided Self*, by Dr. R.D. Laing and how it might impact emerging work in the mental health field and benefit Chip. Helen was attentive and asked pointed questions. He sat back and while finishing a slice of Helen's devil's food cake, acknowledged how hard she was working to ensure optimum care for her son-in-law.

He watched Helen as she gathered the papers neatly into the folder and created a separate folder for additional information about the facility and the latest drugs. She commented that she wished she could do more to improve the quality of mental health services for others. "Surely, there are people who don't have a family to support them," she said rhetorically.

Rey thought that given the opportunity, she could be a force for the mental health community.

"Helen, did you know that in 1955 Congress passed what's known as the Mental Health Study Act?"

She stopped what she was doing and gave the doctor her full attention.

"This act led to the creation of the Joint Commission on Mental Illness and Mental Health. I have colleagues who are involved with the Commission and I know that they are preparing a New England Regional report to send to

Congress later this year with recommendations for significant and overdue changes. A group of us Boston area mental health professionals and community members are eager to change the way mental illness is treated and patients cared for in this country. We plan to prepare statements for the New England report. I think you would be a welcome and valuable addition to this group."

"Dr. Martin, I want to tell you something about me. I was hospitalized after my son died in an accident. I had a complete breakdown and I am prone to being depressed. I've been prescribed Dexamyl. I saw some very awful things in the hospital, and while I had good care and was hospitalized only for a short time, I know there is a tremendous amount of neglect. I've recently become involved with politics. I'm a staunch supporter of President Kennedy. I don't know if Richard told you, but I work part-time for Congressman Walsh." She smiled broadly, "Rumor has it that the President and I are distant cousins from Ireland. Seriously, I want to hear about the group. Perhaps I can be of value."

Dr. Martin left promising to invite Helen to the next group meeting. She thanked him profusely for wading through the thick folder of information and for the invitation to his group. She was uplifted.

Chapter Thirty-two

O'Malley spent Monday afternoon in his campus office. He was studying the sketch of the man that Elmont Mitchell had created with the police artist. The man didn't ring a bell, and hell, he could have been an innocent staff worker in the building. But he bristled at the idea of a sicko lurking around Newton College. His campus was safe and he was hell-bent on keeping it that way. A full-on security staff meeting would be called at the next shift and he would explain in no uncertain terms that his men should visually check out all outside contractors and inside maintenance staff for a resemblance to the man in the sketch. Phase One would be completed without anyone's knowledge. Phase Two would involve interviewing students and using the premise that the guy was missing and had worked there the year before. No one was to say he was a potential criminal. He would call Mrs. Foley and the Ruggieros in the evening and set up a time to show them the sketch and find out if it resonated. Satisfied, he put the sketch in his Foley folder and turned on the radio to listen to the Red Sox pre-game show.

There was no answer at Mrs. Foley's. Richard told the lieutenant that the women were at the hospital and that he would come immediately to his office. Richard flew to the campus.

"Here's the sketch." He pulled out a printed copy of an 8x11-inch pencil drawing and passed it to Richard.

He took one look at the picture and dropped it on the desk. O'Malley sat patiently. The picture hit a nerve.

"That's the man I pulled out of the car last November in front of the house. Long story. The guy acted like I was the crazy one and he was Mr. Innocent driving down the street. I let him go, and he got in his car and floored it. Merda. What does this mean?"

"I'd say that Mr. Foley might have been harassed and this is a person of interest. Are you sure it's him? Do you remember what kind of car he was driving? Did you get his license plate number?"

"He was driving an older car. Maybe ten years old, I don't know, maybe a Buick, I think. Black. I have no clue about the license plate. Do you think he attacked Chip here at the school? Jesus, do you think he's still here? Fuck, man, tell me something. Do something." Richard was worked up and losing his grip on his emotions.

O'Malley was calm and collected. "It's too soon to tell. I'm investigating one step at a time. My men are going to scour the campus and ask if anyone recognizes him. I'm going to personally interview students. I've already sent this sketch out to all the local police departments to see if I get a hit. If he is around, I *will* find him."

Richard thanked the lieutenant and said he would have Ginny and his wife call him so they could see the sketch. He left the campus despondent for having let Chip down and not believing him. He drove straight to his parent's house, craving the comfort of his family.

Richard left his parents for home at about 8 p.m. There was no sign of his girls upstairs. He put the food his mother had packed in the refrigerator and pulled out a beer and his bottle of whiskey. He had drunk too much at his parents and didn't care. The memory of the past month burned and the thought that the psycho was real and he had doubted Chip over and over tortured him. He downed a shot of whiskey, picked up his beer and bottle of whiskey, and trudged to the parlor. Drinking was easy and uncomplicated.

He was in a drunken stupor with the radio full blast when his girls found him.

"Hi, Gin-Gin, hi wifey Beverly," he slurred. "The bad guy did follow Chip. Me, I'm just the asshole who ignored him. It's my fault he's in the hospital." He clumsily stretched for a bottle of beer and dropped it back on the coffee table when he realized it was empty. His eyes were glazed over and he was near passing out.

The women sighed.

"Should we let him sleep or try to sober him up?"

Beverly shut off the radio. "Let's clean up in here and see what he does."

They picked up six empty bottles of beer, the upside-down chair, and the broken whiskey bottle that had been thrown against the wall.

"What a disaster. The poor guy's falling apart." Ginny sat down and started to cry. "I miss the old Chip. Why did I go along with his grand idea and then force it on you and Richard. I'm so sorry."

Richard stirred, "Mama sent some meatballs and lasagna and wedding soup. Ha, wedding soup. Fuck weddings." He tried to stand up, wobbled, and steadied himself against the side of the sofa. "I gotta go." He stumbled towards the bathroom.

"He's up. Let's get him some food and coffee." Beverly swept up the last of the glass and motioned towards the kitchen.

Eventually, Richard was sobered up enough to go through the conversation he had with the lieutenant.

Chapter Thirty-three

Chip was allowed to socialize with fellow patients in the game room during the afternoon. That was a recent change and somewhat unsettling. *What if the psycho snuck in and grabbed him? What if he couldn't run back to his room?* Most days when the nurse encouraged him to join others in the game room, he said he was too tired. Today the nurse insisted. He felt trapped, he missed Richard and his home, his Gin-Gin and her Beverly. His parents came to visit often, but his father intimidated him, always had, and his mother looked like she was about to cry all the time. Ginny was upbeat and caring and she brought Richard with her sometimes. He wished Richard could visit every day. *Why couldn't he go home? Why was his head foggy? When did the next school semester start? Had he finished his finals from the last semester? Who kept screaming during the night?*

"I want to go home," he yelled. He started banging on the game room door with the large window. He banged with both his fists as hard as he could, tears streamed down his face, and he started to scream in agony, the agony of not being told the truth. He kicked the nurse; he recoiled in the corner as several aides came to return him to his private room. They wrapped him in a wet sheet to calm him down until they could get him secured in his bed and medicated.

That evening as the daytime nurses were leaving, the psychiatric nurse supervisor spied Ginny arriving. She took her aside and told her about Chip's episode earlier in the day. She implied that he probably required higher-skilled professionals than what Milton could provide and she thought he deserved more individualized care.

"That's it," said Ginny firmly to Richard when he met her after parking the car.

"What? Who was that?" said a perplexed Richard as they walked towards the elevator.

"That was the psychiatric nurse supervisor. She was on the floor today and saw Chip have a meltdown. She, off the record, says he should have intensive one-on-one care. Richard, it's time to move him."

"Hell, yes! Let's get him moved as soon as possible. Can you talk to the doctors tonight?"

"No, I don't think so. Come in and we'll tell him that we are going to get him out of Milton. To hell with having his father's approval."

Chip was quite listless from the extra dose of medication when they entered his room. He struggled to sit up in bed and stay alert. His arms strained for Richard but they were tied to the bed. Richard choked back his tears and held his hand as he sat on the edge of his bed.

Ginny began softly. "My darling, we have an important decision to make. This isn't the place for you to recover, to shake off the stress and worries you have. Would you like to go to a nicer, safer, hospital?"

His blurry eyes went from one to the other. "Will it keep the shadows away? Can I go back to school next semester? I have to finish my law degree and stay on schedule. Richard, will you come with me? I need you."

Richard leaned over and kissed him lightly. "I'm with you every step of the way. The whole family is pulling for you. Ginny's mother and Rey researched the new place and the doctors there. I think you'll recuperate faster and get back to our Eliot. How 'bout it?"

Chip closed his eyes; coping with a serious conversation was draining. "What is wrong with me?" he said almost inaudibly. His eyes were still closed, the room shrinking.

"Chip, Chipper, wake up."

He opened his eyes, momentarily alert. "Yes, Gin-Gin."

Knowing that she and others had explained his breakdown many times since his admission to the hospital, she never-the-less spoke gently as if explaining the situation for the first time.

"You hit your head last March during the blizzard."

He interrupted, "I remember that."

"You've had terrible headaches, and became overworked at school, you were going non-stop. Then," she was wary about this part but the doctors told her to confirm what she could when trying to keep him calm. "Then, some big horrible guy badgered you."

Chip interrupted again. "He is in the shadows, he calls me a pervert, he wants to hurt me." He started shifting in his bed and squinted at the window.

Richard sensed his growing anxiety and put his arm around him, and kissed his head, "Mio tesoro, no one will ever get close enough to hurt you. I promise. I swear to God, that will never happen again."

Chip began to relax.

"It's time to get out of this place and to a safe hospital. Are you ready?"

He never knowingly let her down, and although he didn't quite grasp what he was agreeing to, he said, "Yes, but I am tired." He closed his eyes. There was no screaming during the night.

Chapter Thirty-four

Richard and Beverly spent Saturday morning together cleaning up his apartment and talking about small, inconsequential things. Ginny was convinced by her parents to spend the weekend with them. It was Helen's birthday and her father promised to drive Ginny to the hospital in the evening. With Ginny gone, Beverly went with Richard to Sunday dinner at his parents' house. She had come to love them and somehow her Romeo as well. Richard held her hand while there and she responded warmly to his touch. Yet, she wished with every bone in her body to get back to her life with Ginny.

Ginny was home alone on Monday afternoon when the hospital called to confirm that the transfer would take place the following week. She was on pins and needles waiting for the others to come home to discuss the transfer.

While waiting, she found herself on the small porch off the attic guest room. She had tried to paint but finding solace in her art escaped her. Exhaustion consumed her. She sat on the floor of the porch and leaned against the house which was warmed by the late spring sun. Her mind was a kaleidoscope of duties to perform, roles to play, desire to quench, and the consuming sadness from time lost, not just for herself but for her Eliot family. Her mother had said something about joining a group to support legislation for mental illness reform. *Was that part of her job?* The meeting with the trust fund lawyer had been a revelation. Her father attended the meeting but she had felt confident in asking questions about how the trust would cover medical and living expenses. She silently thanked her mother for bolstering her confidence since the ordeal had begun. She sighed and ran her hand through her hair, relieved that there was a secure amount of money available for medical care.

The monthly allotment remained during illnesses, which allowed Ginny to give her resignation to Mr. Briggs. "Thank goodness," she said aloud to a plump red cardinal who sat on the porch railing and flew away upon hearing her speak.

She watched as Richard pulled up at the side garage after work. He stopped at the small rose garden, made the sign of the cross, and slowly made his way to the back door. Ten minutes later, she watched Beverly drive up in her convertible with the top down and a cigarette in her mouth. She frowned at the thoughts of Beverly's failed attempts to quit. She didn't have the will to move until she heard Beverly calling her from their kitchen.

"Up here."

"Where?"

"On the porch." She listened to her climb the stairs and enter the room.

Beverly came onto the porch and was troubled by her appearance. "Hon, what are you doing out here?" She sat down beside her, hugged her, and kissed her cheek.

"Nothing. Thinking about Chip and his horrid illness." She placed her head on Beverly's shoulder. "How could it all go so wrong so fast? The hospital called. The transfer is all set."

"That's good news. I don't know. I don't know. Do you want to come in with me? Shall we call Richard up and have something to eat and talk about the transfer? Come on. We have to eat. You'll feel better." She stood and pulled Ginny up. "I love you, girlfriend."

"I love you, too, forever love."

Together they walked downstairs to the kitchen.

"You bought Simco's! I was wondering what you were carrying. I do love you. Call Richard up and let's dig in."

They had barely finished their hot dogs and French fries when the outside doorbell rang.

"I'll go," said Richard. Shortly afterward, the two women heard laughter and stomping up the front steps. Joe came in with his arms full of his mother's cooking.

"You know, Mama is always cooking, but you've eaten already. I guess I'll take these home and stash them for myself."

Beverly got up from the table and swatted him on the arm and feigning shock said, "Don't you dare, brat. You know how much we drool over your mother's cooking. Do you know what's in the bag?" She took the bag, while Ginny got him a beer.

Joe opened his bottle of beer, sat at the kitchen table, and asked about Chip.

"Oh, yeah, Mama wants to know if you two are coming to dinner on Sunday and to the graves with us afterward."

"Man, it's Memorial Day already. I have no sense of time these days."

Joe finished his beer and got up to leave. "Hey, I'm going to the game at Kelly Field, you wanna go?"

Richard sought his girls' approval. He knew an evening at a baseball game with his brother was just what he needed. Beverly laughed. "Go, you fool! How often do you get a chance to escape from your wife!"

With Richard gone, the women went for a stroll around the neighborhood.

"The fresh air feels good. It's so nice to have a quiet evening to ourselves. Thankfully, Paul's visiting Chip tonight. No talk of the hospital, okay?"

"Definitely. Let's stop at the corner store and buy an ice cream. The spring flowers are everywhere. I think I'll buy some at the nursery to plant around the front of the house. What do you think?"

"That would be pretty. I think I'll have a hot fudge sundae."

Chapter Thirty-five

O'Malley had his troops out scouring the campus for a week. No one resembled the person in the sketch. He was going to personally talk with students at the dorm, while his officers talked with other students around the campus. There weren't many students on the day he walked over to the dorm. The sun was shining and the semester was about over with the seniors already preparing for moving out and graduation. His showing of the sketch was getting him nowhere when he spotted a young student sitting reading outside the dorm next to a tall maple tree that was sprouting its spring leaves.

"Hey, kid. You got a minute?"

The student was startled and almost dropped his book. "Um, yeah, I guess? What do you want?"

The lieutenant sat down on the grass next to him. He was sweating and his hip ached from the walking he had been doing. The student unconsciously moved away from him.

O'Malley pulled the sketch out of his shirt pocket and opened it. "Is this guy familiar? Maybe you've seen him in the dorm or around campus?"

The jittery student held the paper tentatively and then glanced down at it. His hands started to shake. He flung the paper at the lieutenant and squeaked, "No. I'm, I'm late." He put his book in his bag and scrambled to his feet and stopped, "What'd this guy do?"

"I don't know for certain. I want to talk with him to clarify a couple of questions from last year."

"Good. I hope you find him." He ran off as if he had seen a ghost.

"I'll be damned." He called after him. "Hey, kid." But the student rounded the corner of the building and was gone. O'Malley got up gingerly, his hip howling at him for sitting on the grass. He asked another group of students that were sitting nearby if any of them recognized the student he was talking with. They laughed, "Old scaredy pants, you mean. Yeah, that's Timid Timmy Flowers. He always looks like he's about to pass out from fright. Pretty much sticks to himself."

"Weirdo," added one of the students.

"This his dorm? Was he here last year?"

"Yeah, we all were. What's up?"

O'Malley showed them the sketch. No one recognized the man.

The burliest student asked, "Who's the old guy anyway?"

O'Malley closely studied the group of students.

"You guys play football?" Their size gave them away.

"Yeah, first team, except for this bozo. He only plays baseball." The students gave each other a push and laughed loudly.

O'Malley walked slowly back to his building. He went into his office and closed the door. Irritated that he found a student who recognized the sketch, the thought of a criminal on his campus riled him. The other students didn't recognize the sketch, but then it dawned on him that they were big jocks. *Flowers and Mitchell are small wimpy guys. I'll bet ten bucks that this asshole preys on the weak. Flowers, I'm going to get you here in my office.* He called the residence director at the dorm, who had Timmy call him back. "Tomorrow, first thing tomorrow."

O'Malley had come in extra early for the appointment and was going over some of the sparse notes the campus police had gathered. "Mitchell and Flowers are legitimate leads. Where the fuck is he?" he said to himself. Flowers arrived a half-hour late.

There was a knock on his door. The receptionist opened the door slightly.

"Lieutenant, Timothy Flowers is here."

"Show him in. Mr. Flowers, hi. Thank you for coming this morning. Have a seat. This shouldn't take long."

Timmy shrugged and sat, clearly nervous.

"Let me cut to the chase as to why I wanted to speak with you. This is very important. I'm investigating a possible attack and this guy," he held up the sketch, "is my number one suspect. Do you know him?"

He squirmed in his seat. "Was there another attack on campus?"

"There has been no sign of an attack this year. You are safe here."

"Safe," he said sarcastically. He started to shake, controlled it, and briefly started to shake again.

"Son, how do you know this guy?" He questioned cautiously, not wanting to have the student shut down.

"I don't know him. He, he, oh damn, he." He closed his eyes and prayed to hold it together. "He attacked me. He attacked me."

"How did he attack you, son?"

Timmy began to shake. He looked at the lieutenant. He was afraid to say the words out loud.

"Timmy, it's okay. You can tell me."

"The asshole raped me in the dorm men's room last year during the blizzard." Timmy sobbed and hid his head in his arms on the desk. The release of the burden he had carried for over a year came rushing out between the sobs. "I didn't come on to him. I swear. I was in the john to, you know, take a leak when he grabbed me and shoved me against the wall. He yanked down my pants and growled in my car, *pervert*. He said he wasn't finished with me and I was too petrified to move. I swear he was too big and strong to fight against. When someone opened the door, he dropped me. I heard him take a swing at the guy who came in. I heard a crunch and a bang. I fixed my pants and ran out of the bathroom and up the stairs to my room. It was dark and cold in the entire building, but I hid in my room. I pushed the bureau against the door and cried all night. I swear to God, I never saw that guy before and haven't since. How could I tell anyone what he did to me?" Timmy choked back more sobs and wiped his face with his arm.

O'Malley struggled to maintain a calm voice. "Timmy, I'm sorry about what he did to you. But I have to ask, did he say anything else? What was he wearing? Did anything about him stand out? Had you seen him before?"

"No, I only had a glance of him and barely saw anything because it was dark. I had just a small candle and he knocked it over when he slammed me against the wall when the other guy came in. I'm one hundred percent certain that this" he pointed at the sketch on the desk "is the same guy. Do you think he would have murdered me?" Panic was written over his face. "I should have quit school. I wanted to but my parents made me come back. I didn't tell them what he did. How could I?"

"Look at me. You are safe here. This guy, it appears, has vanished. Do you want to file an incident report to have on record?"

"No. No. No. Can I leave now?"

"Yes. Here is my card. You can call me anytime."

Timmy glanced up at the imposing policeman and left the office as quickly as he could.

O'Malley stood up and peered out the window at the beautiful spring morning. He thought, surprised, *Mother of God, the asshole does exist and I bet my house he attacked and stalked Foley. Flowers never asked about the guy who came in and probably saved him from worse. Schmuck.* He sat, closed the folder, then exhaled "Fucking mess."

***

Helen had spent the evening with Dr. Martin at the Boston Regional Mental Health Committee meeting, which she referred to as MHC, at the Copley Square Central Library. She was invigorated. The doctor's intuition was correct, this group was the perfect fit for her. This was her third meeting and she was prepared to discuss the work of the group to support the Federal Commission on Mental Illness and Mental Health with her director. He would be able to confirm the interest of Representative Walsh, and if this was an issue of interest that she could move forward with as a Walsh staff member.

Ginny called not long after Helen had told John about her meeting. Chip was in the midst of a comprehensive thirty-day evaluation at the new facility and somehow his spirit was already lighter. Helen thought Ginny sounded tired, but not defeated. She explained to her daughter the work of the MHC, her involvement, and the renewed sense of purpose it gave her. She casually invited her to attend a meeting with her, hoping beyond hope that she would say yes.

She hemmed and hawed and finally said, "Mom, you've been here for me every step of the way. Yes, I'll go with you."

Helen was elated when she hung up the telephone. "This is a turning point," she said to John as he walked towards the parlor to catch Andy Griffith on the television.

"Huh, oh, yes, I'm pleased for you Hon, and Ginny, too."

Helen cheered to herself, the foul winds were abating, and the Dexamyl energized her and repelled the murky edges.

After Ginny hung up the phone with her mother, she went downstairs to speak with Richard. Beverly and he were discussing his parents' upcoming fortieth wedding anniversary party with Anna and Joe.

"Hi. How's Chip doing? I haven't seen you in ages. How are you doing, are you getting any rest?" asked Anna.

She glanced first at Richard, then put on a happy face. "He's improving. This hospital's treatment is working. Thanks. How's little Dom?"

"He's growing like a weed. Dom Sr. is home with him tonight. I think he's staying with him so he could watch the game on TV."

"Richard, can I bother you for a minute with something upstairs?"

He readily agreed and followed her upstairs to the parlor.

"My mom called; she's worked up about this mental health committee thing. She's somehow involved with Rey. Do you know anything about it?"

"Yeah, sure. He met with your mother a while ago, remember? He stopped by here last night for a drink and mentioned that he's been coaching her with the whole medical language and procedures thing so that she would be prepared to help you with the doctors."

"Hmm. She asked me to go to this committee with her. I think I will. I have to do something productive. Thank him for me, will you?"

"Do you think Chip's improving?"

As she was about to answer, Beverly called Richard from downstairs that he had a phone call from Lieutenant O'Malley. The two of them hurried downstairs to the parlor telephone while Anna and Joe resumed the party discussions at the kitchen table.

Richard paled as he hung up the phone. "The cop said he tried calling you. You must have been down here." He looked at her with pain in his eyes. "He's real. At least the fucker was in the bathroom in the dorm. He must have knocked him out that night. Damn. Why did this take so long?"

Beverly went into the kitchen to let Anna and Joe know that Richard was helping Ginny with Chip's illness.

"Maybe we should go. The party's all set. You two will be at dinner on Sunday?"

"Of course, I wouldn't miss it. And, I'll take care of the flowers for the party as promised."

Joe had walked out of the room to talk with Richard. "Hey, you okay?" He hugged his big brother. "Anna, I'll meet you at the car." He turned back to Richard. "You got this."

When the three were alone, the questions and self-accusations flew back and forth. Richard sat on the sofa with tears in his eyes.

"Go upstairs girls."

Ginny started to speak, then simply nodded and left him alone in his thoughts.

Across town at the Newton College campus, the night shift was in full swing for Lieutenant O'Malley, with the remaining undergraduate students partying in celebration of the end of another school year. He had been so busy that he hadn't noticed the message left on his desk by his sergeant until after 10 p.m. He had a premonition that the message meant a break in the Foley and Flowers cases. Morning would tell.

Chapter Thirty-six

Morning came quietly for Chip. Three weeks at Belmont and the shadows of the night were becoming less frightening. He lay in his bed and felt the sun on his face. His nurse came in with his morning pills and asked if he was ready to have breakfast in the common room. Breakfast outside of the private room was only allowed for patients who could tolerate the presence of others without incident. This was a privilege he was slowly beginning to appreciate. He asked permission to shower and shave first and put on the summer clothes his mother had brought him. The nurse watched him take his pills and said she would return in fifteen minutes to escort him to the breakfast room.

Chip found himself humming. He stopped shaving with his electric razor, the only type of razor allowed, and peered at the mirror. He didn't quite have a solid sense of himself, but humming must be a good thing. He would raise it to the doctor at his session today. As the medications were absorbed, it crushed his enthusiasm, and getting dressed in his shirt and trousers became rote.

The patients at the breakfast table resembled cardboard figures as they nodded in unison when he sat with his tray. He gave back the same insincere acknowledgment.

***

O'Malley finally got through mid-afternoon.

Ginny was laughing when she answered the phone. "I'm sorry, lieutenant, I just came in from having lunch with a friend who's home for the summer. Sorry, you don't care about that."

He said he had important information about her husband's stalker.

Ginny recalled the horrible looking man from the police sketch. Neither she nor Beverly had recognized him.

The man was caught by the Boston Police in early spring while breaking into a downtown nightclub. He had been on parole for a series of crimes and was subsequently immediately jailed. His name was Earl Porchuk. He had a rap sheet that dated back to his teen years, including assault and battery on a high school classmate, exposing himself in public, and defacing graves in a Jewish cemetery. He was now serving a twenty-year sentence at Walpole State Prison for violating his parole, breaking and entering, and assaulting a police officer. There was another trial coming up in which he was accused of attempted rape and murder of a young man from Framingham. When his apartment was searched, the police found a bulletin board covered with photos of young men, including Chip. Next to each photo were the words, PERVERT, PANSY, ATTACK, SUFFER, and DEATH written in red. The man was a life-long criminal, a predator, dangerous, and not remorseful.

"Because he'd been out on parole, his arrest and sentencing were kept quiet-- certain politicians didn't want any scrutiny of the parole board. Fuckers!" O'Malley added when Ginny questioned why no one had heard of this guy.

She was relieved and appalled at the same time. She asked about the picture of Chip. He said it appeared to be one taken from a bulletin board announcing club activities. She was curious about the other young men, but was afraid to ask.

O'Malley thanked her for meeting with him. He was going to try to convince the student who was attacked by Porchuk to come forward and file an official report with the police and perhaps additional charges would be brought against him and he would remain in jail for life. He recommended her husband do the same.

Richard and Beverly were equally stunned. Relief came first, then anger. Pain filled their hearts knowing that Chip was more than physically injured by Porchuk. His mind had snapped and he cowered from the shadow of the monster that was no longer there.

Ginny called Dr. Harris the next day and informed him of what Lieutenant O'Malley had uncovered. The doctor said she should immediately bring the information to the attention of the team at Belmont.

First, she had to inform Chip's parents. Helen and Beverly had both offered to go with her, but she was adamant that she had to speak to the Foleys alone. Drawing on all her strength, she nervously and carefully shared with Duncan and Marjorie the information about the attack. She was embarrassed to admit that she hadn't thought that he was being followed and deeply regretted being blind to his health issues.

Duncan erupted in anger while Marjorie cried for her son. Marjorie hugged Ginny and told her that they were equally culpable for not seeing what was happening to their son.

"What?" yelled Duncan.

Marjorie for the first time in her long marriage turned to Duncan and told him in no uncertain terms to be quiet. He stormed out of the house and went directly to the bar. Marjorie knew their marriage was over. She turned to her brave daughter-in-law again and said, "I'm sorry for Duncan's outburst. He's an angry, mean man."

Ginny expected no less from Duncan. She took a deep breath and sat next to Marjorie.

"Mom, I'm so very sorry. I'll keep doing everything I can to help Chip get better."

Marjorie held Ginny's hand. "I know you will, dear. And I will help."

Chapter Thirty-seven

The Joint Commission on Mental Illness and Mental Health was meeting with select groups from across the country as it prepared for the final push of data gathering for the report that would be sent to Congress. Rey invited Helen and Ginny to the mid-July New England presentation in Washington, D.C. They wouldn't have a speaking role, but their attendance as a former patient and the wife of a current patient would lend credence to the words of the regional speakers.

Helen's director encouraged her participation on her own time. She was not to say that she was attending in an official capacity but was asked to keep the office apprised. Although disappointed that she couldn't attend as her office delegate, she was eager to contribute at any level.

Helen and Ginny were genuinely aghast by the stories brought to the MHC by patients and their families in preparation for the July sessions. Although Chip was able to receive private care and had regular visits by family, many mental health patients were in large institutions, where they were left to languish for years on end without proper care. There were far too many understaffed and unregulated state and local facilities. Worse were the lunatic asylum procedures that conjured up practices that were not only barbaric and cruel, but also stifled any chance of recovery or hope by abandoned and ignored patients.

After several months of supporting Ginny and watching her confidence blossom, Helen had become inspired to be an advocate for those who had no one. The upcoming trip to Washington, D.C. was just the beginning. She lit a candle for John Jr. and told him she was ready to move on. She thanked him for being her biggest cheerleader.

***

Ginny started driving Chip's car regularly and visited him every other day, often with Marjorie. By the end of June, signs of his progress were evident, and strategies for discharging and treating him as an outpatient were discussed.

The lead doctor reviewed the team's proposed course of action. "As you know, our approach to treating Mr. Foley is based on the latest research. Mr. Foley, came to us severely ill. He had suffered a psychotic breakdown brought on by trauma and overall exhaustion. This was the early prognosis of the Milton Hospital team. Additionally, we tested him for schizophrenia, but he did not exhibit the signs. We confirmed that his psychosis was brought on by the combination of stress and the trauma of the accident, actually the attack, at school."

The doctor went on to methodically explain, "His disorientation and intense headaches were most likely due to his brain injury from the attack and the ongoing effects are not to be minimized. His anxiety over being stalked was grounded in truth, though only confirmed recently. Regrettably, the stalking lingered in his mind for months after it stopped. Additionally, Mr. Foley has a burning drive to succeed to the highest level as evidenced by his intensive studies and volunteer hours throughout his brain injury recovery. While he was properly prescribed medication for his ongoing headaches, unbeknownst to his regular physician, his anxieties over school and the stalker festered."

"So, here we are. Several medications along with talk therapy have been administered and monitored daily. It is our opinion that a small dose of Librium on a scheduled basis works effectively for Mr. Foley. He tolerates it more successfully than other anti-anxiety drugs," continued his therapist, Dr. Jurgeson. "Mr. Foley has expressed his goals, at times forcefully, but he now recognizes that recovery is a step-by-step process. Naturally, he wants to return home and finish his studies. We propose that he be discharged with supervised daily care, and a twice-weekly session with me, here or at my private office in Needham. Moreover, if all goes satisfactorily for the remainder of the summer, we suggest he attempt a modified school schedule in the fall, perhaps only one light course to start."

Chip was to return home Monday, July 17, 1961. It had been three months since his breakdown. Richard circled the date on the wall calendar in the kitchen. He could hardly contain his excitement and his trepidation. Ginny and Helen were in Washington, D.C. and would return on the eleventh. He and Beverly were alone in the house-- three days, just the two of them. It felt comforting and odd. He was ready to have his man by his side to start a fresh life together. As Richard cleaned their bedroom, Beverly was upstairs, preparing the guest room, her and Ginny's former bedroom, for evidence of a happily married couple. Beverly had surprised Ginny by moving their bedroom to the attic floor after she found her sitting and enjoying its small porch the evening she brought home Simco's. With a heavy sigh, she was resigned to the fact that The Eliot ruse was continuing. The guest room would be adjusted to appear as Ginny and Chip's bedroom once again. It would be not too Ginny and not too Chip in style. A smattering of wedding photos that included the four of them, a photo from their weekend in Provincetown, and Chip's favorite cologne on the dresser made the room complete. Richard brought up some of Chip's summer clothes and a small bookcase with his favorite books.

They sat on the bed together surveying their handiwork. "Are you ready for this?" asked Beverly.

"I'm ready and to be frank I'm scared. We can't go backward and I'm not sure how to go forward without being too protective and feeling guilty." *Fucking Plan he said to himself.*

"Are you talking with Dr. Martin, um, Rey? We all should. You know, we need to let some of the guilt go. Do you think we depend on your friend too much?"

"I don't know. Yes, he's been great, but talk is easy, we don't really know how Chip'll be, do we?"

"I guess we don't." Satisfied with the room, she suggested a break for lunch at the Villa Rosa.

"Sounds perfect. That's our place, isn't it?"

When the two entered the restaurant, they were caught off guard by Joe and a couple of his friends. The first thing Joe said was, "Don't tell Mama you saw me here." Richard laughed and said the same.

Beverly leaned over to give Joe a peck on the cheek and said, "You and Anna pulled off a wonderful anniversary party. What have you been up to since then?"

"Do you think you and this lug will make it to forty years like the folks?"

She laughed, "I hope to at least make it through lunch. Bye, brat, I'm starving."

Richard mumbled, "Sfigato," and punched his brother on his arm on the way by.

They chose a booth at the far end of the restaurant near a window.

"Do you think Joe suspects something is off with us?"

"Huh, I've no idea. I doubt it. You know, Mama asked me *again* about a baby." He exhaled and hailed the waitress.

Beverly lit a cigarette and groaned, "Crap."

Chapter Thirty-eight

Washington, D.C. in July was unbearably hot. Helen and Ginny had driven down with Rey and Dr. Ari Friedman, a founding member of the MHC. Their long drive was teeming with weighty conversations about the curse of mental illness and the recommendations they were going to present to the Commission. Dr. Friedman read his presentation aloud as they drove over the Tappan Zee Bridge in New York. When he finished the silence in the car was palpable. Tears rolled down Helen's cheeks. Rey cleared his throat and said to his friend and colleague, "Ari, you've brought Helen to tears. Now if you can do the same to the Commission members, our recommendations will be entirely incorporated into the final report."

Despite the heat, the two days in the capital were energizing. Driving by the White House and the Washington Monument was breathtaking. A tour was organized for the Capitol Building and during the tour, an aide of Representative Walsh sought out Helen. To her amazement, the Representative wanted to meet her and thank her for her efforts. While she only had five minutes with him, Representative Walsh's interest in mental illness and health was evident. He requested that she officially report her activities to the Milton office going forward. He would have his aide call Bob Crosby directly. Helen was in what she later described as second heaven.

While mother and daughter were taking Washington, D.C. by storm, Chip was having daily sessions with Dr. Jurgeson on transitioning to home. The storm inside his head had subsided, the minimum use of medication cleared his thoughts and lightened his spirit. Dr. Jurgeson had cautiously informed him of the capture, arrest, and prison term of his stalker/attacker for previous crimes. Though no longer afraid, the image of Porchuk fought to stay in his consciousness.

"Why does this guy keep finding a way to haunt me?"

The doctor replied as he always did, that it would take time and effort to erase the bad memories, and if not completely erased, handled so that he could manage to work through the anxiety they caused.

"I want to finish my degree. I must finish it. I am so far behind and that tears at me. Do you believe I will finish?"

"Yes, in time, and if you continue to pace yourself and not overtax your mind and body. Your recovery will slow you down, but with astute awareness and dedication to your health, you will keep yourself moving forward."

"I am ready to go home, doctor."

"That's what I recommend, but once you are discharged, remember we will continue to meet twice a week. Your wife, family, and close friends are going to support and assist you. They care for you and are ready for you to come home. Be mindful of their support, and let them help. Ten days from today. Let's work hard between now and then."

A confident smile stretched across the redhead's pale face. "I can do this." As he stood up to return to his room, he told the doctor, "My mother brought me the latest ads from Filenes and Jordans, I am going to select an entire summer wardrobe and she is going to buy it for me."

"That's terrific. I know you like to look sharp." The doctor came out from behind his desk, opened the door, and nodded to the aide who was to escort him. As he watched Chip walk with a bounce in his step down the hallway, he pondered, would he ever divulge in a session that he was a homosexual? As he closed his office door, the doctor pondered, *when will homosexuality be erased from the medical books as a mental disorder? It's the cause of so much pain and too often death.* Jurgeson was determined to pursue changes in the misguided beliefs perpetuated by the medical system.

***

Friends and family were reminded not to come by on Chip's first day at home. The doctors insisted he have time to acclimate, and too many people might be overwhelming for him. Marjorie said she would make his favorite chicken casserole and peanut butter brownies for dessert and bring them later in the week, without Duncan.

Richard told his father that he was taking the week off from work. His father started to question why when Joe interrupted,

"Geez, Pop, Ginny can't do this all by herself and Chip's his best friend. Besides Mama has already baked a week's worth of food for him to bring to them." Mr. Ruggiero didn't want to cross Angela and begrudgingly gave in. Joe winked at Richard and went back to work.

Beverly had adjusted her work schedule to three afternoons per week and was prepared to quit if her assistance was needed in the weeks ahead. She quietly thanked her deceased father once again for the small nest egg he had set aside for her.

A calendar was created to keep track of who would be home and when, medications, time administered, doctor appointments, and any questions that arose for the doctors. Chip would spend as much time as possible with Richard in their apartment the first week and spend time upstairs with the women whenever Richard wasn't home. Everything was organized; the three were concerned but prepared to make any adjustment necessary.

The first week was tense and awkward. Chip found it challenging to re-adjust to a relaxed routine, one not regulated by nurses and doctors. He asked permission before doing anything – everything from having a snack to going outside. It hurt Richard to have his Chipster so dependent and cautious.

Richard and his brothers had surprised Chip by building a six-foot-high solid fence around the backyard, with a gate that could be locked. The driveway extension had been finished while he was in the hospital and fast-growing bushes and plants on both sides of the fencing were in full bloom.

Chip had it in his mind that he must get his summer tan, so Richard sat with him in the backyard as he stretched on a blanket on the pristine grass in his blue striped swimsuit. The swimsuit exposed how thin he had gotten during the past four months, but Richard was still completely drawn to him. He wasn't sure how to approach the subject of making love. Should he make the first move or should he wait? He certainly wasn't going to ask his girls, that would be too embarrassing. He held Chip's hand, as Chip closed his eyes, and hummed an Elvis song. It was Saturday, almost a week since he came home, and for the first time, he felt at home and completely relaxed. Ginny and Beverly watched the two men lounging on the blanket in the backyard and holding hands. The day was unencumbered by illness and anxiety. The women wrapped their arms around each other and felt the tension of the week ease.

July slipped into August and slowly friends and family were invited to visit on the weekends. Several small cook-outs brought welcomed laughter to The Eliot.

Chip showed signs of normalcy, but was tired easily. Inside the house he kept his back to a wall at all times, still afraid of being approached from behind. When in the backyard, his eyes were constantly busy, making sure Richard, Ginny, and Beverly were nearby. His sunglasses hid his uneasiness, and the regimen of Librium before guests arrived reduced his stress.

The fall semester catalog of courses arrived in the mail shortly before Labor Day. The sight of the catalog gave Chip goosebumps, but he was intent on resuming his studies. He clutched the catalog as Ginny drove him to his Thursday appointment with Dr. Jurgeson.

"Gin-Gin, how about I drive home? I miss being behind the wheel of my car."

She wasn't quite sure how to reply. She wanted him to drive again and was happy to have him take the wheel. Hesitating, she said, "How about we ask Dr. Jurgeson? If he says yes, then the keys are all yours. Deal?"

He was tired of asking permission for what should be everyday occurrences. As he progressed and built-up assertiveness from within, the hold-over habit to ask permission had waned. "I guess, okay."

The session with Dr. Jurgeson went delightfully. The doctor understood the importance of returning to law school for his patient. He was edging towards resiliency and one class might be manageable. He argued, that two courses were a cinch and that he could handle the work. The doctor quietly approved of Chip's enthusiasm, but too much too soon would set him back. Together they went through the catalog and the time and dates of the courses. They settled on one elective that met on Wednesdays at mid-morning. He would not miss any doctor appointments and would not have to be out during rush hour or in darkness as the fall semester went to the end of December. Chip was elated. He would register immediately before the course filled up. He forgot about asking if he could start driving again.

Ginny was in the car reading a magazine when she saw Chip smiling and waving as he approached. The window was down and she waved. He called out, "I am going back to school. Bring it on!" He was walking on air as he headed straight to the driver's side. "Move over woman, I am taking the wheel."

She didn't want to sound like a mother hen and ask if he had permission. Instead, she said, "Great about school. About time you stopped laying around." Together they laughed as she slid across the seat to the passenger side. Chip sat behind the wheel radiating happiness.

"I want to stop to see my mother on the way home. Tell her about school. Do you want to come or should I drop you off at your parents? I will be maybe an hour."

"Yeah, my folks'. My mom should be home, but don't leave until I check. Actually, come in and say a quick hello. Okay?"

"Yup. Have I told you how impressed I am with you and your mom? My women activists. And working with old man Reynaldo, no less." He kissed her cheek, adjusted the seat and the mirror, started the car, and revved the engine, the same way Richard did.

"Ah, excuse me."

"Just teasing. I promise to drive carefully."

The drive to Readville was relaxing. The sun was shining and the radio played the top hits. It was like old times, two teens on the loose.

Helen was home and thrilled to see Chip. She gave him a long hug and congratulated him while he gushed about going back to school.

She and Ginny spent an hour fine-tuning their latest report for the MHC, then stopped for blueberry muffins that Helen had baked that morning.

"Dear, take some of these home for the four of you. Dad and I can't eat them all. Let me wrap them up. What time is Chip picking you up?"

Ginny noticed the time and was surprised at how fast it had gone. "Gee, he should have been here by now. Maybe I should call."

"He might be having lunch with Marjorie. Why don't you give him a few minutes?" They talked about Chip's progress, the care he continued to receive from Dr. Jurgeson, and his excitement about going back to law school. "When did he start driving again?"

"Today. I'm going to call Mom Foley. Now I'm getting worried."

Helen was wrapping the muffins in wax paper when she came back into the room.

"Mom, he never arrived at his mother's house. She only got home about ten minutes ago. What do I do? What if he was in an accident? What should I do?"

"Let's not panic. Maybe he went for a drive when she wasn't home and lost track of the time. Did he leave her a note? It's only one o'clock, maybe he was hungry and stopped for something to eat. Maybe he went home."

"No, no note. I tried to make light of it, and she said she would be home all afternoon; if he swung by, she would have him call me here. Hmm. Bev might be home. Let me call her." She rushed back to the phone and dialed her apartment. No answer. She dialed the downstairs apartment. No answer.

"No answer. I'm worried."

"Do you want to call the police?"

"Gosh, no. He doesn't like the police and I don't want to scare him if they try to pull him over. I think I'll call Margaret Mary; she hasn't moved back to Wellesley yet. Maybe she can pick me up and we can drive around the neighborhood. Perhaps he stopped somewhere as you said. If he comes here, tell him I left with Margaret Mary and to go home."

She and Margaret Mary drove around the neighborhood and as far as Simco's in Mattapan with no luck. By 2:30 p.m. she was in a panic. Margaret Mary drove her to The Eliot. She hoped he was there and if not, that Beverly was home. Chip wasn't there but Beverly was, so Margaret Mary left, promising to drive around the neighborhood again. She said she would call later to make sure he had been found.

Ginny immediately called her mom and Mom Foley. Neither had heard from him. Both offered to call their husbands, but Ginny thought it was too soon to pull them out of work for what could be a false alarm.

Beverly suggested calling Paul while she found her wallet and keys to drive with Ginny around town. Just as they were leaving, Richard pulled into the driveway. Ginny rushed down the back porch stairs as he was letting himself in.

"He's missing," she cried out.

"What? Who's missing? No! Chip's missing? What do you mean he's missing?" He ran inside the house and called Chip. He glowered at Ginny who had followed him, "What the hell is going on?"

Beverly entered the room and saw the fear in Richard's eyes. Trying to maintain calm and stave off sheer panic, she interjected, "Red is more, um, late than missing, but..." She explained what happened as Richard stood frozen.

"I called some of our friends and they are out searching for him. What should we do?" Ginny said as she ran her hand through her hair.

He sunk into the kitchen chair and covered his eyes. "I'm going to go look for him. Maybe he went to some of our favorite spots. You call the hospital and the police and check if there have been any accidents. Merda, this can't be happening. I'll find a pay phone and call upstairs in an hour and check in."

Beverly added, "You stay here. I'll take my car and drive around, too. I'll come home in an hour. We'll find him. I'm guessing he's galivanting and forgot about the time. I'm sure he's fine."

Richard bolted out the back door without another word.

"Please find him, Bev, please."

Beverly hugged her and promised that he would show up soon.

Meanwhile, Chip was sitting in his car overlooking the freshwater of Houghton's Pond. He had no idea what time it was and that his family and friends were frantically searching for him. When his mother wasn't home, he decided to take a ride and buy a milkshake and grilled cheese sandwich from Howard Johnson's and take a spin by the pond. The water soothed him. Once at the pond, he popped one of the pills that he kept in his wallet and relaxed with his lunch. He was free.

Dozing slightly, he heard his name being called. "Mmm, Richard, nap time, come join me," he found himself whispering. Then he heard loudly, "Chip, Chip, wake up."

Startled, he sat upright and tried to focus on the man standing next to the car. "Richard, hi. Where am I?" Nervously, he scanned the parking lot. Then recognized the pond. "Hi, how did you know that I was here?"

Richard went to the other side of the car and slid into the passenger seat. He spoke softly. "This is *our* quiet place. You were going to visit your mother and you never arrived. And you were supposed to pick up Ginny at her mother's house. Do you remember?"

"Oh, damn. Now I do. I am sorry. Am I in trouble?"

"No, you're not in trouble. We've just been worried about you." He leaned over and kissed him then sat back and watched a small flock of ducks fly by and land in the water. "It is peaceful here. He kissed Chip's cheek. "You ready to go home? Are you okay to drive?"

"Yes, of course, I can drive. I will follow you and your ugly truck." He feigned disgust and turned on the ignition. As Richard went around the car towards his truck Chip called to him, "Hey, put on MEX, we can listen together."

Richard stopped and walked back to the car. He leaned in and kissed Chip. "I love you, mio tesoro."

Beverly came in the back door while calling out to Ginny and hoping that Chip had been located. She was on the phone with Paul, who had driven by the library and the record store with no luck. An hour later, there was still no sign of the men. The women tried to stay positive and assumed that the men were together at one of their favorite hangouts with no pay phone handy.

Well after 5 p.m., the doorbell rang. They went downstairs together and were greeted by a young man with a very large bouquet of flowers standing at the door.

"Good evening, ladies, does a Gin-Gin live at this house?"

"Yes. That's me."

He handed her the flowers and left. The two went upstairs and read the note.

"Sorry, Gin-Gin. I lost track of time. Richard and I will be home soon. Your darling."

"Huh. The flowers are beautiful, but he's not getting off that easy."

"Son of a bitch," was all Beverly could say.

The men arrived home within the hour. They held hands once inside the confines of their fenced-in backyard. Richard spied their girls standing on the first-floor back porch.

"Oh, oh. Trouble ahead." Chip waved to their girls and smiled roguishly.

Chapter Thirty-nine

The following month was a blur of routine activities. The late summer faded into autumn, and the days and weeks of progress for Chip were measured in fits and starts. Watchful eyes were trained on him; his former self strained to assert itself only to ebb and falter. He struggled with the one class, but one of his former study group classmates volunteered to meet with him after every class to review notes. Chip made a point of avoiding Dennis Jenkins. His intuition said to stay away. He wasn't aware that Dennis Jenkins had also made a point of steering clear of his former student at all costs.

Chip insisted that the three others not feel guilty about 'you know who.' They each apologized separately and together. He implored them to look forward and not backward, as Dr. Jurgeson had said to him. He agreed that their talking with Reynaldo was a good idea. He had helped him, but Chip admitted that he wasn't always honest with Richard's friend.

Before they knew it, the bright autumn leaves had fallen off the trees and Thanksgiving was fast approaching. A sense of normalcy at The Eliot once again glimmered on the horizon. The four discussed the invitations to dine with their families, but preferred to celebrate the holiday together. The day would be festive with the Macy's Parade on TV in the morning and football in the afternoon. Relaxation was to be the order of the day.

Joe stopped by for an impromptu visit on Thanksgiving weekend. Richard and Chip had gone out for a drive. Ginny and Susan were treating the newly engaged Margaret Mary to lunch and some early holiday shopping in Boston. He was relieved to find Beverly home alone. She was in the backyard trimming the rose bushes one last time before deep winter set in.

He asked her to go for a walk with him. Intrigued, she put her tools and work gloves in the garage, washed her hands, donned her better jacket, picked up her pack of cigarettes, and met him in the backyard.

"I'm worried about you," he began. "My folks are worried, too, about how much time you and Richard spend helping Chip and Ginny, well, mostly about babies." He stammered, and wouldn't look into her eyes. "Do you know what you two are going to do? You know, I notice that you're always upstairs and Chip downstairs when I come by unannounced."

Beverly lit a cigarette and blew out a long puff of smoke. "What are you saying?" He seemed nervous, a quality he never showed before. Goosebumps appeared on the back of her neck. *What was he about to divulge? Was she ready for him to acknowledge the ruse of The Eliot?* She didn't know how she would respond. She took another long drag on her cigarette.

He stopped, put his hands in his jacket pocket, and blushed. "I think Ricardo is in love with Chip and you cover for him. I love my brother, love him. I'd never say a word about this to anyone, never to my parents. Am I close or am I way out of line?"

She dragged on her cigarette and stared straight into his eyes. "Yes. Yes. This is a pathetic ruse so that they can live together and Ginny and I can be together, too. Do you think us mad?" She waited for what seemed like an eternity for him to respond. The goosebumps stayed on full alert.

He kicked a stone on the sidewalk as he started to walk again. "No, I guess not. It's weird, not normal." He wrinkled his brow. "I always thought something was going on, I just couldn't figure it out. And, and you all got married. How does that work?" He was torn between knowing the truth and caring for his brother.

"You know, I truly love your family and Richard is my Romeo. Did you know I call him that?"

He shook his head and attempted a smile.

"But my heart belongs to Ginny. Do you want me to stay away from you and your family? I don't have any answers." She realized at that moment how much she loved the Ruggiero family. "You know, right now, we're still focused on Chip's recovery and that has been exhausting."

Joe was shocked to think of Beverly disappearing from his family. "Heavens no. They love you. My mother misses the two of you at Sunday dinners. Um, sorry, how's Chip doing?"

"Overall, he's getting stronger, certainly not his old self, but there are signs of improvement. He's distraught, confused, and struggling some days, but I can see the determination to conquer the torment in his eyes. He's talking about finishing law school again. A positive sign."

"That's good. Hey, it's getting late. I have to get home. I'll never rat on my brother. His secret is my secret. Believe it or not, I have a date tonight. That's why I have to run. Let's walk back. I'll tell my mother that you'll come by soon for Sunday dinner."

"Yes. Are you ready to have this conversation with him?"

He adamantly said, no.

"Do it soon. I won't say a word until you do. You have to tell him yourself that you love and accept him. He hates deceiving everyone. And, Joe, any girl would be lucky to have you." She locked her arm around his and rested her head briefly on his shoulder as they walked back.

1962

"All great changes are preceded by chaos." Deepak Chopra

Chapter Forty

Ginny and Helen maintained their involvement with the MHC. Ginny was riveted by the work and thrilled with the time spent with her mother. She was back to driving Chip to his doctor appointments. He refused to drive alone since the day he forgot to pick her up. He insisted that they trade in the Chevy and purchase a more sedate car.

By mid-December, Chip was preparing for the final for his one class and studying at home only until dinner time. He agreed to register for just one class in January and reluctantly accepted that one class a semester for now was his limit if he wanted to stay healthy.

The first snow covered the lawn and the girls placed red and green candles in all the windows. It was the weekend before Christmas, and everyone was in good spirits. Chip told Richard he had a quick errand and that he would be back in a flash. Although anxious whenever Chip went out alone, Richard didn't question him. His mind was lost in the memory of their carefree life during the first Christmas at The Eliot and how problems had followed them since. With Chip mostly recovered, the weight of deception towards his family emerged again, ripping a hole in his heart. *The Plan*. The ever-present damned *Plan*. Richard was finding it almost unbearable to reconcile his feelings for Chip with the lies to his family. He married Beverly never considering the expectation of his parents for them to have children. His faith condemned him. The layers were crushing his spirit and undermining his commitment to *The Plan*. How could he break Chip's heart just as he was recuperating from his own demons? Richard cursed the day he agreed to *The Plan*.

Adrift in his self-imposed torment, Richard was fixing a late morning snack when he noticed Chip from the kitchen window, opening the backyard gate and struggling to carry a number of large packages. He slipped but didn't fall and juggled the packages.

He raced outside. "I got this, buddy," he added with a grin. "Where did you get all these? Did you drive?"

"I had them hidden in the garage. Merry Christmas!"

Richard's love increased two-fold that afternoon. He pushed his doubts aside. Something inside him came alive as they lit their tree after supper and sang Christmas carols. Their girls heard the singing from their apartment and quietly applauded.

The foursome celebrated New Year's Eve in the downstairs apartment. The decorated Christmas tree was colorfully lit in the parlor window overlooking Eliot Street. The couples danced to their favorite songs and wore party hats with 1962 stamped on them. At 11 p.m., with a fresh glass of whiskey and slightly drunk, Richard, dressed in his dungarees and button-down white shirt with his latest red Christmas tie, announced a New Year's resolution. "I've been thinking about this for weeks. I want to change *The Plan*. I have had enough of deception. No displaying some of Beverly's things downstairs and Chip's things upstairs. No more keeping the back staircase secret. No more secrets about our lives. I don't give a fuck about the outside world. God forgive me, I have to do this to survive. Damn it. I am going to start the New Year with a clean slate."

The other three were shocked. Could it be, that he wanted to tempt fate and expose their lives? Now? How drunk was he?

"Ah, what are you saying?" asked Chip calmly.

"I'm exhausted. My insides are in knots. I don't know how to live according to *The Plan* anymore and feel good about myself. I want us to be free."

"Holy crap! Where is this coming from?" said Beverly, straining to speak calmly. "Listen to me. We have gone through hell to be together. Why now, after all we have gone through?" Perhaps, she wondered, she should mention her conversation with Joe.

Ginny was watching Richard in stunned silence. She started to quietly cry and grabbed tightly to Beverly's hand as he spoke.

"I'm beyond exhausted; and I have to come clean. I need all of you with me, I need to share my pain with you, and then I know we, I, can survive. We're a family here at The Eliot, but..." He paused, then added, "Am I making any sense? Maybe it's the booze talking."

Chip stood up and walked over to him. "I'm stunned and afraid. My heart is beating like crazy. Feel my chest. Richard, my love, I cherish and love you. Remember, we are building our dream *here*." Chip took a deep breath and continued, "We have all been under unimaginable stress the past year, but we have each other. Girls, help." Tears were streaming down Richard's face.

Tenderly, Beverly escorted Richard to the sofa. Chip sat next to him and held his hand. She spoke with all the gentleness she could muster while screaming inside.

"What do you mean by coming clean? Look at what Chip has gone through the past year, and is still going through. This is a lot to throw at us out of nowhere. This is dangerous talk. Think about it." She mumbled, "I'm getting another drink. Anyone want anything?"

Ginny snapped. "Richie, you God damned son of a bitch, you are not going to *fuck* this up. *Damn it*." She wiped away the tears that trickled down her cheeks as her vision of a peaceful life seemed to be shattering. Again.

Her cursing caught everyone's attention. Beverly stopped before going to the kitchen for her drink and hugged her and whispered, "I hear you."

"Okay, yes, maybe we need to revise *The Plan*," said Chip somberly. "But blurting it out like this is shocking. I agree with Gin-Gin. What the hell?"

Richard hugged Chip and in his deep soothing voice said, "Mio Tesoro, I've had too much to drink. Sorry. I will go as slow as you and the girls say. I, I, just had to say it out loud. I am burning up inside. I need help."

"Maybe you could go with me to my therapist? What do you say? Will you? I trust Dr. Jurgeson."

Richard looked from Chip to Ginny to Beverly, who had just come back into the room with a double shot of scotch and a freshly lit cigarette in her mouth.

"What?"

"Chip suggested that the two of them talk to Dr. Jurgeson together."

She sipped her scotch, tilted her head, let out a puff of smoke, and spoke slowly. "Richard, haven't you spoken about this to Dr. Martin? I trust him. He knows all of our situations. You two have had sessions with him before. Maybe start with him. Chip what do you think about that?"

"Um."

Richard interrupted. "I should have thought of that before I opened my big mouth. I'll talk with him. Until now, we've only talked about, well, Chip. Merda, why didn't I talk with him before scaring all of you? Chip, would you like me to ask him for advice?"

"I guess so. I have an appointment with Dr. Jurgeson next week. Think about coming with me, too."

"I will and I'll call Rey tomorrow," said Richard. He berated himself for stirring up such a hornet's nest. He had to find a solution to his turmoil. He said a prayer to calm himself. His thoughts were interrupted by Beverly.

"I'm sorry, what did you say?"

"I promised not to say anything, but here goes. Joe came by Thanksgiving weekend and asked me flat out if you two were in love. I told him everything." He started to speak. "Hold on. He said he doesn't understand but at the same time loves you and will always stand by you. He said he just didn't know how to talk with you about it. What if you start by having a conversation with your brother? Perhaps after all of us get some advice from Dr. Martin."

"You met with Joe?" Ginny was puzzled that Beverly hadn't said anything to her, but she was more concerned about Richard's declaration. "Richard, you should have told us ages ago that you were such a mess. I can't believe you never spoke about this with Rey." said a calmer Ginny as she ran her hand through her hair.

Their emotions were drained. Joe's knowing about them was a crack in the façade. The three did understand where Richard's frustration was coming from, though, and one by one they relaxed.

Chip spoke first, "We have weathered so much the last few years, and we are still together. I love all of you and want to spend the rest of my life with you. I believe we can have a life separate and together. A new year is about to start and, hell, we will get through this."

There was quiet for a moment in the room, then the wall clock struck midnight. The new year had begun.

***

Rey and Jeff were away for the holiday. When Richard finally contacted him, Rey was taken completely off-guard, but promptly arranged to come over. He warned Richard that the path he was about to embark on would be replete with complications, some of which could be severe and possibly deadly.

Rey paused before he hung up the phone, "I never expected you to be the one to jump off the proverbial cliff into the unknown."

Richard responded through his fear, "I'm jumping toward the light. See you tomorrow."

Rey spent two evenings with the foursome. The conversations were difficult; tears were shed and fears were revealed. Richard was the only one aching to tell his family. Rey reinforced the importance of letting the process unfold for themselves as individuals, as couples, and as a foursome. He didn't want them to harbor any expectations that telling family, and at some point, other friends would be a simple one-and-done conversation.

For emphasis, he added, "Admitting to yourself that you were attracted to men most likely didn't happen overnight, Rich. You've spent your lifetime understanding, accepting, and creating yourself. Remember, it may take as long for your family to acknowledge and accept you and the person you love; if they do at all. That's a very real possibility. Lastly, Chip is still in recovery mode. Nothing should be done to disrupt his progress. Nothing."

His advice hit home. As much as Richard yearned to live in a perfect world where he would be welcomed with open arms, he was again reminded of why he ran from the police, feigned marriage, and what hate had done to Chip.

Rey suggested he approach his brother, and that talking with him might ease some of his stress. Richard apologized through tears for scaring them. He would not say anything to anyone until they all were ready. If it was never, he would find a way to stay true to his promise. He profusely thanked his friend for his advice and friendship; and said, yes, he wanted his professional help.

It was resolved that Richard would invite Joe over to the house soon, and fully disclose himself to his younger brother. The date would be determined by Richard. When the time came, the other three would wait upstairs and be available for support.

"I'm a nervous wreck," confessed Ginny, "but if we're to have any peace here, I have to trust you. Beverly told me she trusts Joe completely to respect our wishes to live quietly. Can I really trust you?"

"I swear to God on my knees, I won't do anything to ruin our lives here. I promise. I promise."

"Gin-Gin, our Eliot dream will continue. We will get through this bump in the road," said Chip.

"Richard, as I said when Dr. Martin was here, no more holding back by any of us. We have to be willing to share our worries. No more being brave and fighting alone against the monsters. Promise? Everyone, promise? I do," said Beverly as she reached for Ginny's hand.

Chapter Forty-one

While Richard and Beverly had dinner at the Ruggieros, Chip and Ginny spent Sunday afternoon together listening to their favorite records from years past. They hugged and danced and shared their concerns about the future.

"Do you think we'll withstand all these pressures? Honestly, do you?"

"I have to believe we will, otherwise, I do not think my mind could survive another year of this hell. Richard will find a way through his own hell. He will never do anything to hurt me or us. I think the future is ours to grab. In fact, in the spring of next year, I *will* graduate from law school. Imagine that, one more year to go."

He pulled back and looked straight into her eyes. "But I have also decided to go to the college police about Porchuk to start the process of filing a criminal complaint. I, I, um, think it will help me move on."

She wasn't sure how to respond. She wanted to forget the misery and pain they had suffered.

"Well, first I have to talk it over with Richard. He told me how helpful the cop at the college was, so I think he will be okay with me filing with him. Then, I have to go to the Milton police. It is going to be a long, scary process. You are with me, right?"

"Wow, that's one scary big can of worms you're going to open. It petrifies me to think you could suffer more stress. I don't know. Yes, I'll stand with you, with wobbly knees, maybe, but yes."

The two were quiet for a few minutes. The last 45 dropped down onto the record player, *The Great Pretender* by The Platters. The title was not lost on them.

"One more dance, darling?"

"Duncan Foley, I love you. Do you think we'll ever tell our parents? I can't believe that my parents would disown me. My mother danced around the topic while you were in the hospital. Hmm. I had forgotten about that."

"I do not know. My father would disown me or worse, certainly. So glad my mother is divorcing him. Well, my mom would still love me, I hope. Someday."

"You know, I kinda like being married to you. Weird, isn't it?" She leaned her head against his.

"You are a strange girl, Virginia Stevens Foley, but you will always be my girl. I have loved you since you sat with me and touched my hair in the schoolyard," he said as they slowly danced one more turn around the parlor. "You want to take a drive to Simco's for some dogs and fries?"

"Only if you're treating and I can have a large chocolate frappe."

"You got it. In fact, I will drive. Meet you by the car in five minutes."

Ginny was beaming as she raced down the stairs. Chip offered to drive more and more often now. She wore the old leather jacket over her heavy sweatshirt and dungarees.

"Ah, my girl. You look great. Let's go."

***

It had been well over a month since Richard's disruption of the household. He had not yet spoken with Joe, but he had met with Rey faithfully twice a week.

Chip was apprehensive. He paced all morning. He trusted Dr. Jurgeson, but, and it was an anxiety-filled *but*, would he accept him and want to continue as his doctor? Richard's disclosure had him more anxious than he expected. He had to speak honestly with Dr. Jurgeson about why he had been distracted and tense all month. The drive to the doctor's office was filled with nervous conversation. Richard drove Chip's car, with Chip sitting up front and their girls sitting nervously in the back.

Dr. Jurgeson was concerned when he saw the four arrive in the waiting room. His secretary came into his private office and said that they all wanted to come in with Chip for this appointment. Dr. Jurgeson said to send in Chip first, alone.

After inquiring about how he was doing and before he could ask about the others coming in, Chip announced that he couldn't say another word unless his family was with him. The doctor agreed, went to the doorway, and motioned for the others to join them.

It didn't take long for the doctor to comprehend what was about to be revealed. He listened to each of them. When he noticed that the hour-long session was about over, he excused himself and informed his secretary that he would be working through lunch. The doctor's gentle demeanor, coupled with his extending the session, bolstered the foursome and they relaxed and opened up more than they ever had with anyone outside of their small circle of friends.

At the end of the two hours, Dr. Jurgeson requested a few minutes privately with Chip. He hesitated, but when Richard nodded, he stayed seated.

"Do you think you are prepared to tell anyone else about our discussion?"

Chip glanced at the closed door as if to see Richard on the other side. He closed his eyes and automatically searched for the medication in his pocket. He had left the medication at home. The realization that he hesitated and yearned for his pills stopped him.

"No, doctor, not yet. Is that wrong?"

"There are no hard and fast rules for disclosure. If you are not ready, then so be it. Maybe you will never want to disclose this part of yourself. It's your choice. Richard will understand. They each made the point that your well-being is critical to them. Do you believe them?"

"Yes, with my heart and soul."

"So, take your time. We will work through this. Let's schedule an extra appointment for this week, so we can discuss this further."

Chapter Forty-two

"Ricardo, you chose this," Joe said with warmth and candor. "Well, I don't know if you had a choice. I don't understand it, but I don't think you're a sicko, and I don't think that you should be hated or attacked because of your choice. I love you, you're my big brother."

"I don't understand it, but I've known that I was different since I was young. I prayed to God every day to give me a sign, then I prayed for Him to forgive me, and now I pray to Him to accept me. I need my family. I need your acceptance."

"I'm not going anywhere. Nothing's changed. But what are you going to do about Beverly? She's your wife."

"We've become close, as friends. I genuinely like her, love her. Our lives here are complicated and like Rey, Dr. Martin, that is, my friend and shrink said, 'We are intrinsically entwined', me, Chip, and the girls. Chip decided to talk about this with his Belmont doctor. We may never tell another soul. Any decision will be made by the four of us in total agreement. Beverly and I stay married. Chip and Ginny stay married."

"Jesus, are you ready to never say a word?"

"That's why I am meeting with the shrink now. I never thought I would be seeing a shrink, but man this stuff has messed up my head. Can you live with my secret?"

"It's your life. As I said, I love you. Your secret's safe with me. Where are the others?"

"Upstairs."

"Call them down, will you."

"Hold on. In fact, why don't you come with me upstairs? I want to show you something." Richard led his brother up the secret backstairs to the girl's parlor. The three heard the two brothers walking up and held their breath.

287

Joe followed Richard into the parlor and went over to Chip and held his hand out to him. "Chip, I don't know what you see in this loser of a brother, but God love you for doing so. Welcome to the family." He turned to Beverly. "You are one incredible woman. Man, I could use a beer."

Ginny got up. "I'll get some." She returned with a six-pack of beer and a cola for herself.

"Ginny, can I say something? I, I was a good friend of Johnny's, and he loved his baby sister. I think if he was here, he would be very proud of you."

"Thanks. That means the world to me." Her eyes filled with tears.

"That is one hell of a back staircase. Beverly, this lug head told me you helped him renovate it. If you ever want to get into the construction business, give me a call. I'll gladly be your partner."

"Sfigato, hands-off, she's all mine," said Richard.

"Hey, both of you, she's all mine," said Ginny.

"Excuse me, all of you. I make my own decisions," laughed Beverly.

"Bev, you can run away with me, anytime," added Chip.

***

Richard and Ginny went with Chip to meet Lieutenant O'Malley. Chip was a little shaky when he asked if O'Malley would set up a meeting with the student from the bathroom.

"I can't tell you his name until I talk with him, but, sure, I'll give it my best shot. The police will want to talk with you, too. They want to throw as much of the book at this asshole Porchuk as possible."

The three shook hands with O'Malley and afterward walked around the campus to shake off their nerves. Chip said he wanted to go to the dorm. Richard and Ginny balked but he insisted and changed directions straight towards the dorm. He asked Ginny to wait outside while he showed Richard the bathroom. He needed to see if he was strong enough to handle the memory of that night. At the entranceway, he took a deep breath, grabbed Richard's arm for a few seconds, and with determination walked in. The main floor was quiet with only a couple of students milling about.

"This way."

"Okay, buddy. Let's do this."

The empty bathroom was well lit and they could smell a fresh coat of paint. Chip stood there, closed his eyes, and remembered. He grabbed his jaw instinctively as he relived the first punch. Then nothing. The agony was gone.

"Fuck you, Porchuk. Let's go. I am done with this."

Richard had been silently praying that Chip was strong enough to withstand being there. He hugged Chip before moving towards the door. "That's right. Fuck Porchuk. We have a life to live."

They dropped Ginny off at The Eliot so they could some spend alone time at Houghton's Pond.

Alone time, thought Ginny as she walked into the house. Beverly wouldn't be home for at least an hour from work, giving her time to plan an impromptu romantic evening. She ran back down the stairs and headed to the corner store to buy some cheese and champagne, and a small box of Beverly's favorite dark chocolates. Delighted with the results of her purchases, she set the tone for romance in their bedroom-- soft music, candles, and a spritz of perfume on the pillows. She changed into her special silk pajamas just before Beverly came through the door.

It took Beverly but a moment to realize that the night was theirs. Her eyes filled with passion upon seeing Ginny waiting for her on the bed. They kissed hungrily as she allowed Ginny to quickly undress her. Their breath was ragged and their hands sought each other. Once on the bed, Beverly stopped, looked at Ginny underneath her, and smiled. "I love you. I love you so, so much."

Ginny pulled her head toward her and kissed her lips as she said, "Show me."

***

Helen and John sat on their sofa listening to the radio. John leaned over and kissed Helen's cheek.

"What was that for?" asked Helen.

"I'm proud of you," he said.

"For what?"

"You've accomplished so much this year." Helen smiled modestly. John continued, "Your job for Representative Walsh, guiding Ginny through Chip's ordeal, volunteering for the Mental Health Committee, and traveling to Washington D.C. You are amazing."

"Oh, thank you. Deep down I believe John Jr was watching over me and moving me forward. He's my guardian angel." Helen rested her head on John's shoulder.

"Your right. He's your angel."

The two sat quietly, remembering their son.

Afterword

Life at The Eliot was not to return to "normal" but to evolve. For six months, Richard worked hard during his sessions with Rey. He learned to moderate his temper and speak carefully, from his heart. He held on to Chip tightly, committed to living a life together and growing their already powerful love. Announcing himself to the world became less urgent. He knew he could count on his Eliot family no matter what.

Chip's frailty and headaches persisted, but he managed to finish law school and pass the bar exam in the summer of 1963. His appointments with Dr. Jurgeson were critical during the investigation, subsequent trial and conviction of Earl Porchuk for assaulting and stalking him.

"One day," Chip said to Richard at his graduation, "I will become an instrumental force behind the changes in society that are long overdue. Yes, Duncan Foley Jr. will have respect and influence nationwide."

"Yes," he leaned in and whispered, "Mio tesoro, I have no doubt and I'll be right by your side. Come on, our girls are waiting."

***

A new generation was emerging and times were changing. Attorney Duncan Foley Jr. was hired by the Boston branch of the American Civil Liberties Union and gained a reputation as a fierce proponent of the underserved. He traveled to the South to support voting rights and the repeal of Jim Crow laws and practices. Chip's dogged dedication defending those neglected and kept down by society influenced the other three. They each committed themselves to playing a more active role in creating a just society.

Beverly kept her Romeo close and enjoyed a more relaxed occasional Sunday dinner with the Ruggiero Family. She kept her forever love, Ginny, closer. Financial independence for women was always on her mind and with Ginny's blessing, and the funds from her father, she opened a bookkeeping business with a small staff of capable women.

On Saturday mornings she lovingly watched Ginny from their bed as she sketched or painted across the hallway in her studio. Beverly was thrilled that she had taken up painting again. Her new work was vibrant and alive.

Richard saved enough money to help his father expand the contracting business. As the business prospered, he was intent on backing up Chip's civil rights work with action of his own. He became a foreman and immediately hired two Negro apprentices from a Boston trade high school.

Joe married a 'nice Italian girl' during the autumn of 1963, pleasing Angela to no end. A High Mass preceded the wedding in Most Precious Blood Church and a large reception was held in the church hall. There was an overabundance of food, music, and dancing. Richard was his brother's best man. Chip, Ginny, and Beverly blended in with the guests and reveled in the celebration.

Ginny continued supporting her mother's efforts with the MHC and traveled once again to Washington, D.C. This time to witness the signing of the 1963 Community Mental Health Act by President Kennedy. Spurred on by their volunteer work, both were no longer content to be relegated to the role of a housewife or an underpaid office worker. Helen resigned from Representative Walsh's Office to become the assistant director of the expanded MHC. She kept a small photo of John Jr. on her desk, next to the wedding photo of Chip and Ginny with their friends, for inspiration.

Ginny set her sights on joining the fast-growing sex discrimination movement while continuing her volunteer work with MHC. Her paintings reflected the changing tone of the country and caught the eye of several galleries in Provincetown.

Life at The Eliot, delicate as it was, blossomed.

Acknowledgements

After taking a writing class with Grub Street in Boston, I was spurred on to re-explore a very short draft of the story that I had started more than fourteen years ago. Once I completed the story, Nancy Agabian, an independent editor associated with Grub Street, skillfully edited what turned out to be the first of many drafts. Nancy also recommended that I participate in the Grub Street Muse and Marketplace Conference. Thank you, Nancy, for all of your recommendations and supportive comments.

Thank you to my friends and family who took the time to read the many iterations of this book and to offer genuine feedback. Pat, Mary, Beth, Eric, Eileen, Maureen - I truly appreciated your input.

Most importantly, I thank my wife, Sydney, for encouraging me throughout all the revisions. She read the story over and over again and helped me smooth out the rough edges. Thank you from the bottom of my heart, you are my forever love. (The word is that she wants a continuation of the story as the characters live through the tumultuous 1960s.)

Made in the USA
Middletown, DE
17 February 2025

71017929R00176